FOUR BOOK COLLECTION

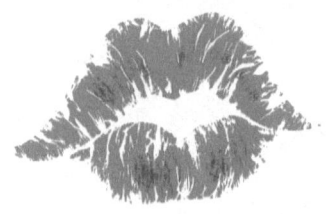

EVERNIGHT PUBLISHING ®

www.evernightpublishing.com

Copyright© 2016

Evernight Publishing

Editor: Karyn White

Cover Artist: Jay Aheer

ISBN: 978-1-77339-131-1

ALL RIGHTS RESERVED

FOUR BOOK COLLECTION

DEDICATION

To my wonderful family, thanks for letting Mummy
spend half her time in front of her laptop.
A huge thank you to Diana Stager Thomas for all her help
in getting this book just right.
I also want to thank Karyn White and Evernight
Publishing. Thank you.

FOUR BOOK COLLECTION

DILLON

Scandals, 1

Hazel Gower

Copyright © 2016

Chapter One

Ashlyn

I stood behind the VIP girls crowding the backstage entrance, waiting for the boy band and their dancers to finish.

The screaming, squealing and cheers got louder around me, and I saw the dancers come from the stage. My friend Sarah came straight to me and hugged me tight.

"I'm so happy you're here." The fans screaming for an encore made it difficult to hear. "We are going to have so much fun." Before I could reply, a lady with a clipboard and an earpiece headset handed her a water and a towel. Sarah gulped down the whole bottle, then handed it back before wiping the sweat from her face. Sarah winked at me. "Wait here. We do a two song encore and then I'll come right back."

I nodded. "Sure! See you soon. You look amazing." She did. I couldn't remember Sarah ever looking that vibrant. She smiled, turned, and ran back out onto the stage.

Squeezing through the bunch of girls to get myself closer, I watched my friend as she danced. She was a natural.

I stood close to the stage entry watching the band and dancers, barely able to hear the music over the fangirls screaming. Law, the only blond in the group, was currently singing. Alec, the one who seemed to work out a bit too much and looked like a body builder instead of a guy in a boy band, sang backup with the help of Zeck. I thought Zeck was gorgeous, with his long hair and a face that was meant for fame. Dillon, the fourth member, was pumping up the crowd, clapping his hands and throwing streamers and balloons to them. He then went to the backup dancers and danced with them. For some reason I couldn't take my eyes off him. He could move. He had perfect rhythm, and as I stared at him I wondered what it would be like to move my body against his. I started swaying to the music, and tingles shimmied through me the more my thoughts strayed to our bodies dancing together.

Dillon turned from the dancer and focused on the crowd. I almost stopped breathing when I heard him sing. It was deep, manly, and *so good*. Sure I'd heard the band's songs before on the radio, but I had no idea who sang which part. Holy panting wetting hotness, when Dillon sang he became the hottest member of the group. I imagined him singing only to me in a private session later in the hotel rooms, and I almost melted on the spot just thinking of that fantasy. A pounding started ringing in my ears, and it took me a moment to realize it was my heartbeat picking up, and I was jumping up and down. Oh no, I'd turned into a fangirl! Backing away before I started screaming too, I went and found a spot away from some of the chaos. If one performance had me reacting this way, by the end of my vacation I was doomed to be a boy-band-chasing groupie.

****

Two days later

"Let's go to the after-party tonight, Ashlyn. It won't be big. Just the band and dancers." Sarah and I had gone two nights without going to any band functions. After she finished a show, we'd go back to our room, talk, order room service, and go to bed early so we could get up and get some sightseeing in before Sarah had to be back for rehearsals.

"Are you sure I'm invited to go?"

Sarah nodded. "Yep. I told everyone you were with me, and they're looking forward to meeting you."

"Oh okay then, let's go." My stomach was a mass of butterflies. I hoped my strange reaction to Dillon was just a one-off thing. Whatever did happen, I promised myself I would have fun. I'd spent two days worrying when I should have just let go. This was a vacation. A time to enjoy being young and free.

When we arrived at the penthouse it wasn't what I expected. It was lavish, sure, but it looked more like a high end home. The lounge room we came into was decked out in neutral brown and cream tones. There were two cream sofas and two matching recliners.

Three of the five dancers sat on the ground, and two sat on the sofas with the four members of Right Time. It didn't look like a party, more like a get-together of close friends.

"Hi. Sorry we're late. This here is my bestie, Ashlyn." Sarah squeezed my shoulders, and I glanced at her to see a huge smile spread across her face.

Everyone turned and introduced themselves. Listening to the introductions gave me my first chance to get a good close up look at the boy band. Law was sitting on the sofa closest to where Sarah and I stood. His blond hair was gelled back in a short cut, and his big blue eyes looked up at me with warmth. Alec sat next to Law. He was solid, even bigger up close, with a military style haircut and serious brown eyes peering out from his boyish features. Zeck was in the recliner on the opposite side of Law and Alec, his thick brown hair swirling in glossy waves about his shoulders. He was *hot*. I mean, I thought he was gorgeous when I'd seen him on TV and photos, but this close he was even better. The last of the boy group, the one I'd saved to look at until last because I was scared of what he'd made me feel the last time I saw him, was the furthest from where I stood.

Dillon. Amateurish tatts covered his arms, and I had to wonder why someone so wealthy couldn't have sprung for better ink. His hair was longer in the front and short at the back. It wasn't black nor was it brown.

"Hey, Ashlyn. I like the name." Dillon sent a chin lift my way. Damn, the deep raspiness of his voice was making me melt. I could listen to him all night. He looked back up to my face, and I was captured by intense green eyes. My heartbeat sped up until I could only hear it thumping in my ears. My body started to tingle, and I had to admit that the whole package of Dillon did something to me. He might not be my usual type, but he sure was making me hot and bothered right now.

Sarah tugged my arm, breaking me out of my staring match with Dillon. I glanced at her, and she pointed to Law and Alec, who had moved so we could sit between them. Thank God. I didn't want to be any closer to Dillon, and the only other space I could see was by him. As I sat, I felt his gaze following me, and something didn't feel right. Or maybe it was that his gaze on me felt all too right. My skin prickled, and my belly tightened in awareness. I'd never had this strong reaction to a guy before.

"So Ashlyn, Sarah tells us you're our guest for the next week," Zeck said.

Grateful for the distraction, I turned toward him. "Um, yeah. I'm on three weeks' vacation."

"Three weeks? Sarah said you were only with us for a little over a week." This was said by one of the dancers, whose name I couldn't remember because I'd been focused on Dillon when Sarah introduced her.

"I'm only staying with the tour for a week. Once we get to America I'm going to do some exploring on my own." My first taste of freedom. My two overprotective brothers made going on any adventure, or basically having a life, hard. Thank God my parents were more trusting.

"Where?" Dillon's thick Yorkshire accent made the one word sound harsh. I looked at Dillon. His eyes were laser focused on me, and his lips were in a firm line. He did not look happy.

What the hell had I done? Had I said something? "What do you mean where?"

"Where you gonna explore, lov'?"

If my parents hadn't been English themselves and I hadn't grown up with their accents, I would have had to concentrate to understand him. I bit my lip and looked at the others around me. Half of them were now talking in their own conversation obviously not interested in me, but Zeck and Dillon were waiting for me to answer and even though he seemed to be in a bad mood, I was eager to listen to Dillon talk more.

"I'm going to explore the south. Visit Miami, New Orleans, and go to Key West."

They both nodded. "It's nice there." Zeck grinned. "Key West is a favorite."

"You shouldn't be going by yourself." I must have still been feeling jet lagged because I was sure there was a growl to Dillon's voice.

His attitude was starting to piss me off. He

sounded just like my brothers. "I'm a big girl. I'll be fine on my own." I smiled at Zeck and shot a tight smile Dillon's way, but it slipped when Dillon stood up and glared at me.

Dillon looked me up and down, and my damn body heated. "It's not very smart going off traveling by yourself. Are you even conscious of your safety?

What a wanker. He may have had my body aching to touch him, but he didn't know me. I really shouldn't care what he thought, but for some reason his rudeness got to me. "Not that it's any of your business, but I've made sure all the places I'm staying at have good reputations. I'm also checking in with my family daily so they know where I am and that I'm safe." *Ha, there.* I felt like I wanted to stick my tongue out at him, but knew that might be a little immature.

Dillon's gaze narrowed. I crossed my arms over my chest and stared him down, feeling victorious when he grunted, turned and walked away without saying another word. *Argh, what a wanker.* I plonked back down in the seat, looked over to Zeck and saw a flash of momentary shock as he watched his friend leave.

Zeck shook his head. "Sorry he's on his rags."

The serious tone and straight face Zeck said this with had me laughing so hard, I held my stomach. I could tell this week was going to be interesting.

****

Dillon
Two nights later

I couldn't stop staring at her again. Ashlyn. My dick was so hard over her it was painful. There was something about her. She was pretty, but nothing like any of the models. I'd dated before. I glanced down at her ample cleavage. Those skinny girls I'd been with sure as hell didn't have tits like Ashlyn. But since first seeing her two nights ago not only had I not been able to stop looking at her, I wasn't able to stop thinking of her. I liked that she wasn't afraid to put me in my place. No one did that with me anymore. She'd been hot the other night when I'd gotten her all worked up. A few times I thought I'd caught her staring at me, but tonight she wouldn't even turn my way. She sat at the end of the restaurant table, avoiding my gaze, and it was driving me nuts.

How could this woman not be interested? Everyone was interested me. I caught her brown eyed gaze, and her long lashes dropped. She stood to her five foot five height, straightened her dress and smoothed the fabric over her flat stomach. I watched her breasts jiggle as she fixed herself up. What would those beauties look like in the flesh? Gazing up, I saw her already thin lips thin even more as she looked over at me and then left the table.

I needed to talk to her. I needed to do something. These feelings were driving me crazy. Maybe if I fucked her, I could get her out of my system. Not bothering to excuse myself, I followed Ashlyn out into the back of the restaurant courtyard. She was standing near an outdoor table looking up at the night sky.

Slowly I came up beside her. "Does it have the answers?"

Ashlyn jumped and bumped against the table, almost falling onto it. I grabbed her without even thinking and gathered her against me, securing her so she wouldn't fall.

"You scared me." I caught the hitch in her voice as she stared up at me.

"Sorry." I wasn't, because right now her body was pressed against mine and God, did it feel good. It felt right. Reaching up I caressed her cheek. "There is something between us," I whispered. I could feel her chest rise and fall quicker. "Tell me you feel it?"

"I … I, yes. Yes, I feel it." Her fingers tightened on my arms, and she leaned into me.

I had her. Now to close the deal. "Let's go back and fuck it out?"

"What!"

Palming her arse, I squeezed. "Let's go work this chemistry between us out in a bed. Or even here on the table is fine with me." I raised my eyebrows up and down.

"Wanker!" She whacked my chest and stomped on my foot.

Startled, I let go of her. "Fuck." *What the hell?* Had I read this wrong?

"You're a dick. I can't believe you almost had me, but then you opened your stupid mouth." She turned to leave, and because I'm obviously an idiot, I grabbed her.

"No, wait. That's not what I meant." She tugged her arm free and kicked me. Bloody hell, this wasn't how it was supposed to go. My body was hot, and I couldn't believe how turned on I was from the little contact I'd had with her. I had to get her to give me a chance. She walked away, and I called after her. "Please. Please just give me a chance. I can't stop thinking about you, and it's driving me nuts. Please."

I couldn't remember the last time I'd had to beg, but it seemed to be working. Ashlyn stopped, turned, and narrowed her gaze for a moment or two and just stared at me. I hoped she found whatever she was looking for because I swore my dick could hammer a fucking nail, it was so damn hard.

She sighed. "Talking. That's it."

I nodded because I seriously didn't trust my voice right then. Moving to her, I reached for her hand. She hesitated before letting me thread my fingers through hers. Together we walked to the back of the restaurant and left the way we came in. Three black SUVs sat waiting, and we got into the one closest to the exit. I told the driver to drive to our Edinburgh hotel.

The car was silent. Ashlyn gazed out the window like she was searching for something. Even though neither of us said anything, the air sizzled between us. I looked down to see our hands still joined and squeezed her delicate fingers, liking the warmth against my own. She squeezed back, and my body tingled with an awareness that I'd never felt for a woman, and I'd been with a lot of women. I was young and in the world's most popular boy band, and I used that to my advantage. This feeling with Ashlyn though, it was different from the lust or plain want I'd felt with other women. "You feel it, don't you?"

Ashlyn turned from the window to face me. "I feel something."

I nodded. From the moment I saw her that night at the penthouse with Sarah, I was drawn to her. I had a burning need for her and an instant need to protect. When she'd said she was going off to explore on her own, my mind had gone to everything that could go wrong. I'd become angry that she was putting herself in danger. The way I was acting wasn't me. I was the first person to admit I was a selfish prick. I was a twenty-four year old superstar with the world at my feet. I didn't like what I was feeling.

Running my fingers through my hair, I squeezed her hand with my other. "Look, I know I sounded like a dick when I said come back to my room and fuck, but truthfully I don't know what else to do. I mean, don't get mad, but this thing between us needs exploring and well, you're not here for long and I mean us, well … fuck. I'm just going to say this, and then when we get out of the car you can do what you want. I don't do relationships. Not only do I not have time, but I don't want one. I mean you and me wouldn't work anyway. You live in Australia, and when I'm not on tour I live in London." I knew I sounded like a grade A jerk, but I needed things set out straight from the start.

The car stopped, and I was sure she was going to let go of my hand and run for her life. Ashlyn surprised me though. She kept a hold of my hand as we got out of the car and snuck back into the hotel. You could hear the fans screaming for the band out the front.

Ashlyn stayed quiet as we were guided through the hotel and taken to the top floor. Once we were in the suite and the door was closed, she let go of my hand. "I don't do this, ever. This is a vacation, though, and I promised myself I would have fun and let go. There is a spark between us. We are both consenting adults and know where we stand." She nodded. "I'm in. Let's have fun."

That was all I needed. I knew our first coupling would be quick and rushed, but I didn't care because we wouldn't be doing it only once. I reckoned by at least the third time we'd last longer than fifteen or twenty minutes.

Stalking towards her I gathered her to me and locked her mouth to mine. The spark exploded between us as I stroked her tongue with mine. I picked her up and stumbled down towards the rooms. When we reached my bedroom, I let her down, unzipped her dress and pulled it up and off, tossing it to the floor. I wrapped my arms around her and undid her bra, setting those big beautiful babies free. They were better than I imagined. Ashlyn yanked at my shirt, and I helped her lift it off. Her fingers went to the buttons of my jeans, and she undid them and slipped them down. Ashlyn eased her panties off, and I groaned when I saw she was bare except for a dirty blonde landing strip. Kicking my shoes off, I pressed myself to her, loving the feel of her naked body against me. As we kissed, tongues tangling together, I was eager to taste every inch of her. Pushing her against the wall I began working my way downward with kisses, but I had no patience. I sank down onto my knees and buried my face into her pussy. Ashlyn screamed as my mouth ravished her, licking and lapping at her nether lips. Her screams spurred me onward, and I drove my tongue into her. She gripped my hair and tugged me toward her.

Resting one of Ashlyn's legs over my shoulders I buried my face deeper, sucking at her slick core. Her moans were like sparks of need that shot straight to my already straining dick. Lapping at her clit, I felt her legs start to quiver. I eased away wanting her to come around my dick. She gripped my hair pulling me back. "No. Finish me. Please." I shook my head. "Please. Please, I'm so close."

I liked the sound of her begging, but I was adamant the first time she came it would be around my cock. Picking her up, I walked to the bed and sat her on the edge. Leaning to the side, I opened the top bedside drawer and pulled out one of the many condoms I had in there. Tearing the wrapper open, I let it fall to the ground as I took the condom and slid it on. Coming back to Ashlyn, I captured her mouth, kissing her with the desperation I now felt for her. Then without saying a word, I lined my dick up to her entrance and pushed in, burying my cock balls deep. Ashlyn wrapped her legs around me. Breaking from her mouth, I kissed my way down her neck and sucked on her skin. She arched up moaning, and her pussy walls pulsed. Closing my eyes I took a deep breath in as a wave of pleasure washed over me. She felt so goddamn good. She was slick and tight. Sliding out, I paused and stared down into her passion filled eyes before I drove my dick home, propelling deep with steady thrusts. I knew the constant pace drove her crazy.

"Dillon. Oh Dillon. Yes, yes!" she howled, arching and digging the heels of her feet into my butt cheeks to drive me deeper.

As she arched up, I held her close with one hand and caressed the tips of her pointed nipples with the other. Spreading my legs for better balance, I started pounding into her in a mindless frenzy. I was so close, but I would not come until she went. I knew she was close, too, because her core was tightening and it was getting harder and harder to move out.

Pausing, I stopped with my cock wrapped in her heat. "I'm going to move. I want you to ride me. Show me you want me just as much as I want you." I eased out of her, wincing at the feeling off loss. Climbing to the middle of the bed, I sat and crooked my finger at her.

The sight of Ashlyn crawling across the bed to me almost had me shooting my load right there. What the hell had I been thinking before? She was stunning. She was better than any damn model. Her tits swayed, and I groaned at the sight.

Ashlyn painstaking slowly settled over me. I watched with gritted teeth and clenched my fists as she wrapped her fingers around my cock and guided it back home. *Holy fuck.* I could swear she was tighter than just the moment before.

"Mmm, that feels so good," she moaned as she sank down. Once seated, she wiggled, and her eyes flared. Grabbing her hips, I slowly rose her up and placed her down. She was soaked, her core gripping me tight, never wanting me to retreat. The pull of her muscles as they wrapped around me was pure heaven. I stared down and watched my dick disappear into her pussy each time.

It was so hot.

Ashlyn rode me slowly at first until her walls quivered and her speed picked up. I was so close to coming, but I knew I couldn't have my own release until Ashlyn had had hers. Leaning against the headboard, I drove up meeting her thrust for thrust. Circling her waist, I brought her down so our sweat coated bodies rubbed together. Squeezing her arse I followed the curves of her cheeks down and around our joined bodies to find her clit. Strumming it, I drove up, held still and pressed down putting pressure on her nub. Then I let go and repeated the process again. Pushing up deep into her, holding myself still and pressing down on her clit, I circled it before sliding my dick out and thrusting in again and again, until her body shook with the need for release.

"Holy shit," she yelled.

Ashlyn's core spasmed around me and held my dick in a viselike grip. "Fuck. Oh fuck." I swore I was seeing fucking stars. I pumped into her, barely moving because of her pussy's tight hold and let myself go, roaring my release.

Wrung out, I closed my eyes and wrapped my arms around Ashlyn. Sex had never felt like that before. Damn. It was going to be a good week.

Chapter Two

Ashlyn
Four days later

I spent my days exploring Europe with Sarah, and my nights sneaking around with Dillon having wild, crazy sex. The more I was with Dillon the more I found I liked about him. His voice got better every time I heard him. He was easygoing and funny. And the sex was amazing. Tomorrow night we were all getting on a private plane and flying to America, and I felt sick at the thought of leaving him.

"Spend the day with me tomorrow?" Dillon asked as the pads of his fingers caressed the swell of my breasts.

I knew I should say no. I needed to not get any more attached than sex. I was leaving once we got to America. The problem, though, was our chemistry wasn't simmering out the more we were together. All I had to do was think of Dillon and I got hot and tingly with need.

To avoid the question, I spent time tracing his odd tattoos as I explored his body. "Where'd you get these tatts? Most of them look like a kid drew on you."

"My little brother used me to practice."

"What?" I sat up and studied his face to see if he was joking. He winked, but he wasn't laughing.

"My brother is a tattoo artist. I let him use my body for practice. He's gotten better." He rubbed his chest. "I needed something to intrigue the ladies." He raised his eyebrows up and down and puckered his lips and sent two kisses my way.

Falling back on the bed with laughter I rolled over onto him straddling his chest. "I love how you make me laugh."

"It's a skill." His smirk was so sexy. "The only

woman I want to make happy is you."

Running my hands over his chest I knew I was getting attached. Leaving him when we got to America would be the best thing for both of us because this thing between us didn't feel at all like friends with benefits.

"Are you hoping if you distract me like this I'll forget about what I asked?"

Crap! He caught me. "I'm going to York Minster with Sarah tomorrow, and I also want to see York Castle before I go."

His dark green eyes twinkled and his lips curled up in a cheeky grin. "You do know, I was born and lived most of my life in York. I know all the best places. I'll be your guide tomorrow." At the thought of spending the day with him my heart soared, and I couldn't help the smile that spread over my face. But Dillon wasn't a normal guy. He couldn't go anywhere without a bodyguard close by. Paparazzi followed all the guys in the group. Then there were the fans that mobbed them.

Sitting up I crossed my arms over my breasts. "As much as I would love that, I don't think you could do it, what with the screaming fans that follow you, the bodyguards and the paparazzi. Plus, I'm leaving once we get to America. Let's not make this any harder." My heart sank at my own words realizing that they were true.

Dillon didn't say anything for the longest of moments. He just sat there staring at me with intense green eyes. The more he stared, the more my heart squeezed. I fought with myself not to tell him yes. Not to tell him I'd do anything he wanted. Needing to be strong, I closed my eyes and reminded myself what he said when we started this. That he didn't want a relationship. That we would just be sex. That we lived in different parts of the world and he didn't have time for me. I reminded myself that this was just fun. I was on vacation being young and free.

I needed to leave and put distance between us. Easing out of the bed, I went looking for my clothes. I needed to leave before I changed my mind. To distance myself before I became what he didn't want, one of those girls begging him to give their relationship a real chance. I needed to stay strong. The sex might be amazing, but that was all we had. All we could ever have.

I found my underwear and leaned down to put them on not even getting a foot in a hole when I was yanked against his body. "Stay. Just for tonight. Message Sarah and tell her you'll see her tomorrow." I shook my head and clenched my fists trying to keep myself from caving. Dillon's teeth nipped the tip of my ear. "Please," he whispered, then pressed a kiss to the spot just below my ear. I shivered and knew right then I wouldn't, couldn't, say no.

Turning in his embrace I looked up at him. "I'll spend our last night together."

He lifted me up and carried me back to bed. Leaving was going to be so hard.

****

Dillon

I resisted the urge to play with the blond wig. The glasses were huge and a bit overboard I thought, with the preppy clothes, beige shorts with a blue and white striped button down shirt and to top the outfit off beige leather shoes. If I was being myself I would never be seen dead in these clothes, which made them perfect for a disguise.

I stood with Zeck by the SUV I knew was going to take Sarah and Ashlyn exploring in. Disguised in a get up similar to my own, he was here to keep Sarah occupied, so I could whisk Ashlyn away. "You know, I'm kind of digging this blond on me. These shoes are way comfy, too." Zeck jumped up and down in the shoes and then wiggled his nose. "Not a fan of the glasses, they're irritating me nose."

Only Zeck would enjoy having to dress up like this so he could go out and not be recognized. I looked around for the girls, spotting them heading towards the car. Smiling, I wondered if the girls would recognize us. I wondered if Ashlyn would know me. Winking at Zeck, I decided to see how far I could get before she realized it was me. Going straight to Ashlyn I wrapped my arms around her and pulled her to me. In my best posh accent I said, "It's so good to see you again. My friend and I have been waiting for you." My fingers explored Ashlyn's body, and she batted them away before I reached her breasts.

Ashlyn stepped away from me and placed her hands on her hips. "Who the hell are you?"

Trying not to laugh at her outraged look, I pulled her against me and without giving her a chance to react I placed my lips over hers. She gasped, and I slipped my tongue into her mouth. At first she fought me, hitting me and pushing against me to get away. After a moment though, she relaxed in my embrace and clutched me to her. The glasses got in the way, but I ignored them and basked in kissing Ashlyn.

Slowly I pulled away and she stared up into my eyes and whispered, "Dillon?" Chuckling, I nodded. She hit my chest. "You wanker. If it wasn't for your taste or cologne, I would never have guessed."

"That's the idea. Now no one will know me. So I'm spending the day with you." I reached for her hand and threaded my fingers through hers. "Zeck is coming, too." I lowered my voice. "He's here to keep Sarah occupied so I can be with you." I watched as her eyes lit up and a huge smile spread over her beautiful face. Damn, she got more gorgeous the more time I spent with her. I swore making her smile had become my new favorite thing.

"I can't believe you did this." Her gaze darted over to Zeck. "You both look amazing. Totally different. The glasses are a nice touch."

Fuck. I'd hoped she would think they were too much so I could take them off. "They're the most annoying part." She squeezed my hand, and I enjoyed the feeling. It was nice to do something so simple and have it feel good. Have it feel right. That was the thing with Ashlyn, everything with her felt right. Would spending the day with her feel as perfect as being with her at night? I was going to find out before I lost the chance.

****

Ashlyn

I sat in the comfortable leather seats on the plane trying not to think about my amazing day with Dillon. He had gone on a tour of York Minster and taken a million photos for me, even posing with me in some. Then he'd gone on another tour, one of York Castle, following me around like the tourist I was. It was what he did after the York Castle tour that had me telling myself not to crack, not to start falling for him. He'd hired a boat to take me around York on the river.

Then, before we left for the plane, we had dinner in this cute little restaurant that overlooked the river. He told me about his family. He had a younger brother, the tattoo artist, who drove him nuts. His parents were still together and they were still very much in love. He'd known Zeck the longest in the group. They were friends in school and later met Law. Alec was the last added to their band.

Dillon listened while I told him about myself, being the youngest in the family with two older brothers who were very overprotective. That I was a speech therapist and loved working with young children. We talked so much we had the others call and tell us we were late and holding up the plane. I couldn't remember a date—day out—with a guy ever going so smoothly.

"So what's going on with you and Dillon?" Sarah's question snapped me out of my thoughts.

I shrugged. "Nothing."

"Bullshit." Sarah rolled her eyes. "Not only was I there today to see you two, but he hasn't taken his eyes off you since we got on the plane. I know you've been sleeping elsewhere at night. Is he who you've been with?"

"It's nothing. Just fun."

"Uh-huh, the look he's giving you now and the kiss he gave you this morning, those aren't ones of two people just having fun."

"Mmm, it can't be any more. He doesn't want more. I'm staying one more night and then leaving to go off exploring. It won't work."

Sarah sighed. "If you say so. But I can tell you now that I think he's changed his mind. A guy who has his best mate dress up so he can spend time with a girl doesn't sound like someone who isn't interested in a relationship." She patted my knee. "I know you, Ashlyn. You could make it work if you wanted to."

I nodded, not wanting to voice anything. I needed to think. I needed to figure out what I was willing to do. Would I be willing to give Dillon a chance if he wanted it? I didn't have to think long because I knew my answer would be a big fat yes.

****

Dillon
New Orleans

Ashlyn was going to leave, and I knew I couldn't let that happen. I'd spent the flight thinking about what I

25

wanted and had barely slept last night. Was I ready for a relationship? Could I make something out of the chemistry Ashlyn and I had? Was I willing to put the effort into what it would take to have a relationship with Ashlyn? I hadn't had a serious relationship since I'd become famous.

Pacing back and forth in the suite I shared with Zeck, I glanced at the clock for the millionth time. It was early morning, and in a couple of hours Ashlyn would be saying her goodbyes and moving to a different hotel and starting her vacation alone.

"Just do it. Stop overthinking it. I swear I can hear you bloody pacing and thinking from the other room. I can't sleep with you being all moody and unsure. " Zeck patted me on the back, then grabbed my phone from the charger and handed it to me. "I have known you for a long time, and I've never seen you like this over a woman. Call her. Organize what you two want to do, and do it now because I need my beauty sleep, bro." He slapped me on the butt as he left, and I didn't bother responding because I was busy on my phone.

Chapter Three

Ashlyn

A bellhop had come and gotten my luggage. Sarah and I had just arrived down in the lobby of The Ritz-Carlton in New Orleans, where we stayed last night. It was a luxury hotel and way out of my budget just to stay on my own.

Going to the reception, I went up and handed back my key for the room I'd had with Sarah. "Miss Dobbs, your things have been moved to room 1002, one of our Vieux Carre Suites."

"I'm sorry, did you just say my things have been moved to another room?"

The man nodded. "Yes. Mr. Blake had them moved."

"He what?"

The guy took a step back at my yell.

Sarah pulled on my arm, and I turned to her. "Ashlyn, get the key and go see him. Please." She wouldn't meet my eyes.

"What have you done, Sarah?"

"I just helped. Please get the card and go up to the room."

Snatching my arm out of her hold, I glared at her before turning back to the guy at reception. "Sorry about yelling. Can I please have the key?"

He handed over the key card. Without saying anything to Sarah I marched to the elevator, punched the button to go up, and one of the elevators opened. I got on, scanned my card and pressed floor ten.

Furious, I couldn't wait to talk to Dillon. How dare he move my things without talking to me, and what the hell had Sarah done? The elevator pinged, and I walked out of it and to room 1002.

My keycard unlocked the room, and I entered. The suite was nice with lavish furnishings, but I wasn't getting attached. I was leaving and going exploring on my own. I found Dillon sitting on a sofa waiting in the lounge room. He stood up as soon as I stormed in.

"What the hell, Dillon? Why did you move my luggage here? I have to leave and check into my own hotel."

He didn't seem fazed by my yelling. He even smiled as he got up and came to me, gathering me against him. "No, you don't. Your reservation at the other hotel has been cancelled. Sarah and I got half your money back, but couldn't get it all as it was late notice."

I wanted to throttle him, but I settled for a hit to his chest. "You idiot. Why did you do that?"

"I don't want you to go. I want you to spend your vacation with me. I want us to make this relationship work."

I pushed at his chest and took a step back. "What? What relationship?"

"Our chemistry together has only been getting stronger. I've never had this with another woman. We have a connection, and it's not just sexual. I know you feel the same."

"You want me to spend my vacation with you?"

"Yes. I want you with me."

I couldn't deny what he was saying, and I wanted more time with him, but could I give up what I had organized for my vacation and follow him around? Even if I did, he had no right to organize my life without talking to me first. Before I could blast him for changing my plans without asking, he gathered me back to him and set his lips against mine. Damn, his kisses were my kryptonite, and my words failed as I lost myself to his kiss. My body melted against him.

Dillon slid his fingers under the straps of my tank and slid them down my arms. His hands moved around my back and undid my bra, freeing my breasts. His lips left mine, and he trailed kisses over my heating skin, pausing to lick the tips of my now-pointed nipples. His touch was amazing, and the more I was with him, the more my body craved him and his touch. Moaning as he left my breasts, his lips feathered over me as they made their way up my neck, stopping to nuzzle and nip at my tingling skin. His lips came to rest over mine, taking them in a kiss that made my decision easy. It was passionate, deep, possessive, caring, and told me that I would be crazy not to give him a real chance. His fingers came up to thread into my hair, and he ran them through to the ends, before trailing down my back, sending sparks of pure chemistry. He rested them on my arse, squeezing the globes together and pushing me tighter against him. I could feel his hard cock rubbing against me, and I knew at this rate we'd never talk.

Tearing my mouth from his, I panted for breath. Before we went any further I wanted him to know my decision. I wanted him to know that after that kiss, I would follow him anywhere. Dillon brushed feather light kisses down my neck, and sparks flashed over my body. "Dillon. Oh Dillon, we need … to ah … stop. You need to stop, just for a moment. I want to talk. To tell you y-y … yes."

"Thank fuck. I knew I would be an idiot if I let you go. Ashlyn, we have something, and the way you make me feel…" He rested his forehead on mine. "I've never been in love before. But with you, I think I could." He took my mouth to his and his fingers undid my shorts button and yanked them down. He didn't even bother taking off my cotton underwear. He just ripped them clear off.

Crap, how on Earth did he make that so sexy?

I stepped away and out of my shorts. Dillon pushed my tank down and off, too. Toeing off my shoes, I stood for a moment naked before him. His eyes darkened, and he licked his lips. Coming to me, he lifted me up, and I wrapped my legs around his waist. He walked us to the room and sat me on the edge of the bed. He took a step back, pulled his shirt up and off, he then yanked his jeans open and slid them down and kicked them off. I smiled when his cock sprang up proudly. He went commando. Spreading my legs, he came and settled between them, and I shivered with need when he kneeled and buried his face into my heat, nuzzling my pussy. Dillon used his mouth to spread my pussy lips and licked me from bottom to top, sucking on my nub. I was in pure heaven. Letting go, he moved down and stuck his tongue into my core as one of his hands came up and his fingers flicked my clit sending shards of heat straight through me.

As I arched into his face, he lapped at my pussy as his fingers spread my nether lips further apart and added another finger into my core to join his tongue. He pumped them in and out while his tongue lapped and delved in and came out to flick my clit.

"Mmm, God, that feels amazing," I panted. I hadn't had sex with many people, three including Dillon, but he was the best by far.

Dillon sank another finger into me and finger-fucked me while his tongue licked my pussy. I could feel that my orgasm was close, the pressure in my body wound tight, ready to uncoil. I clenched my thighs, close to exploding. Dillon groaned, and the vibration gave me the edge I needed to reach my peak. "Holy crap! Dillon, Dillon, Dillon," I chanted as I fell apart, my orgasm washing over me.

Dillon kissed his way up my body, pausing at my

breasts to suck one pebbled nipple into his warm, wet mouth, repeating his taste with the other breast. Slipping my arms around his back I clutched him to me as he fondled and sucked my breasts, building my need again. I was still basking in the blissed out feeling from my orgasm. My skin felt a million times more sensitive than I could ever remember.

Moving my hands up, I ran my fingers through his hair and yanked on it. I was ready to do some exploring of my own. "My turn. I want to play. My turn now."

Dillon gave me a sexy smirk, and his beautiful green eyes lightened. Letting go of his hair I caressed his cheek before tracing his lips. He nipped at the pad of my fingers and chuckled. "I like when you get bossy." He jumped up and dove onto the bed. I laughed when he crooked his finger. "Come and get me, lov'."

Crawling across the bed to him, I watched the passion build in his gaze as I settled over him, straddling his legs. "Ah yeah, I like this position." I smiled down at him.

"I'm liking this position, too. Now you have me where you want me, what are you gonna do? "

"Oh, I have some pretty good ideas." I eased back and gazed down the length of his body. It was lanky, with muscles. Exploring his body I touched every crevasse and bump, and I marveled at the texture of his smooth soft skin against the hardness of him.

My lips followed my fingers, and I tried not to miss any part of him. Settling between his thighs, I circled the proud member before me and ran my hands up and down his thick cock. It wasn't the longest cock I'd had, but it sure was the thickest and he knew how to use it. I'm not saying he wasn't a decent length, but his width drove me mad.

Gazing up at him, I saw lust flare in his eyes and knew he was enjoying me playing with him. Hovering over his length, I closed my eyes and sank my open mouth over him as I gripped the base. With my mouth open wide he filled me. Sucking on him, I circled my tongue around his tip and tried to remember to pump my hand.

"Fuck, Ashlyn, that's feels friggin' amazing," he groaned.

Opening my eyes I hummed, letting him know I liked his approval that I was doing well. I sucked him deep until I choked, coming up for air before getting back to it. Dillon's fingers ran through my hair a couple of times before gripping it tight and moving my head faster. I could feel his legs starting to quiver.

"Oh shit, lov', I'm gonna come." He yanked my hair to pull me off him, but I didn't budge. "No. I want to come in your pussy as it squeezes and pulses around me." Dillon let go of my hair, pulled me up and flipped me so he hovered over me. "You're so beautiful." His deep, raspy voice heightened my lust. I felt his cock run back and forth over my pussy lips spreading them. The head of his cock slid slowly into me. His gaze captured mine and held it as he sank in deep. "Nothing has ever felt as good as when I'm deep inside you. You feel better every damn time." His lips crashed down on mine, and he ravished me as he fucked me with deep strong strokes that drove me wild. "When I'm in you like this I never want to leave. When I'm like this I know I want to keep you forever."

I nodded because his words were not only having an added effect on my tingling body, but my heart, too. I couldn't say anything. I was too lost in the building passion. I pushed up meeting his thrusts seeking the pleasure I knew he could give me. Dillon balanced on an elbow and his other hand grabbed my leg and lifted it so he could drive himself even deeper.

"Fuck, nothing, no one has ever felt this fantastic. Tell me you're mine. Tell me from this point on I'll be the only one to ever feel this." He propelled forward, and I gasped as I swore he went deeper than ever before and it drove me crazy. He paused and waited for me to answer.

My body vibrated, and I ached for the high that was so close. I needed him to bloody move. Right then I'd have said anything to get him to move again. "Yours. Take me. Move. Please. I'm yours. Take me now. Only you. Please move."

A satisfied grunt left his chest. Dillon's gaze locked with mine as he pulled almost all out, until just the tip of his cock was at my entrance before he thrust forward. *Holy moly.* He felt freaking amazing. I'd never been so full, and the slight stretching feeling I felt from his thick cock only added to my pleasure.

Moaning, I clenched around him and hung on for dear life, digging my nails into his back as he pistoned into me. Pushing myself up, I met each thrust eager for more. I wrapped my other leg around him and he let go of my thigh and squeezed my butt cheeks.

My tightly coiled body was ready to unfurl. I was so close to falling over the edge and reaching the bliss that was almost within my reach. Dillon fucked into me faster, and I relished the strained look on his face knowing he was as close to coming as I was.

"I'm going to explode," I panted.

"I'm so close. Your pussy is so fucking tight, I'm fighting not to come." Dillon's voice came out breathless. He gathered me up, so my breasts rubbed on his chest and he pushed deep and balanced on his knees.

"Close," I gasped. "So close." His cock hit just the right spot every time, the magical place, over and over. I couldn't hold it back and let go screaming as the pressure and passion built so high, I not only fell over the edge, but shattered into a million pieces. Euphoria seeped into every pore.

"Oh shit. Fuck." Dillon roared as he drove into me one last time and stilled.

Exhausted, I couldn't move. I was too blissed out. Dillon gently laid me back on the bed and eased out of me and came to lie beside me. Closing my eyes, I basked in this blissful state, smiling when Dillon's arm came around me and he hugged me to him.

It may have been my imagination, or my beyond satisfied feeling, but I was sure I heard, "Yep, never letting you go. I'm not an idiot. I know when I have something perfect."

****

Dillon
The next day

I listened in as Zeck spoke to our tour manger, trying to get me out of some interviews so I could spend some time with Ashlyn. "Oh he's right poorly. We can do the interviews today without him. Let him stay 'ere and get better."

"Does Dillon need a doctor?" Phillip sounded panicked. A giggle slipped from Ashlyn, and I covered her mouth with my hand. I could feel her body shaking with laughter.

"Nah, if he's still sick tomorrow you can get one. I think he ate something that wasn't good. He's had the runs all night. I'd leave him be. You do not want to smell what I did last night. It was horrid. All green and he just couldn't move without it coming out."

The voices faded, and I knew Zeck was working his magic and moving Phillip along. When we couldn't hear them anymore, I took my hand off Ashlyn and she burst out laughing.

"Oh I love how in detail Zeck got. He is so gross."

Groaning at the picture he's painted of me to Phillip I guided Ashlyn towards the exit. "Come on, let's get out of here before they send a doctor. The way Zeck's going on they'd probably quarantine me."

Ashlyn burst into a fit of giggles. I smacked her butt, and she laughed harder. Rolling my eyes, I looked in the mirror making sure my wig was on right. I then added the glasses to the costume. Sometimes being a celebrity sucked.

"Let's go, or we'll miss the boat and have to wait three hours for the next session."

"I'm ready." Ashlyn put the spare key in her bag and her handbag over her shoulders. She turned and walked to the door. I watched her arse sway as I followed her.

The elevators were quick. We got on, and I took her hand in mine after she pressed the ground floor button. "So I have everything planned. We get to have the whole day together. Everyone is coming on the haunted tour, though. They all wanted to do it as soon as I told them about it."

"That's okay. I'm just glad we get to go on the Natchez Steamboat. You said you picked a tour on a horse and carriage, too?"

"Yes. We're doing that after the boat." The elevator opened, and we walked out. It was only a short walk to the Mississippi from the hotel.

It was nice walking along hand in hand. The disguise was working. Gathering her to me I stopped on the sidewalk and moved her against a shop wall. Cupping her face I stroked her cheek before leaning in to kiss her. Tracing the seam of her lips with the tip of my tongue I slipped it in, and her own met mine and they tangled together. She tasted so good, of what I would imagine sunshine to taste with a hint of mint. Reluctantly I pulled away, knowing we didn't have time for more if we were going to make it to the boat.

"What was that for?" Her voice was a breathless pant as she stared up at me.

I shrugged. "Nothing. Just because I can."

The smile Ashlyn gave me lit up her whole face. Her brown eyes became big pools of happiness. "You're kind of sweet, you know that? You're blowing all my preconceived notions of you out the door."

"Oh yeah? What did you think of me before?"

"Truthfully?" She tapped her finger on her chin, and a cheeky smirk covered her face. "A cocky arsehole. Who only thought of himself and was an attention seeking dick. I thought our sex life would be all about making you happy. I was very pleasantly surprised."

Chuckling, I kissed her forehead and threaded my fingers into hers moving her to anchor her to my side. We started walking slowly again. "Well, by all means don't sugarcoat how you felt or anything."

"Well, someone has to deflate that ego of yours, as otherwise doors will have to be widened for your head to fit through." She laughed, and it was one of my favorite things about her. It was a sweet musical sound like soft bells. I'd have done anything to hear that sound for the rest of my life. My heart pounded faster, and I knew in that moment I was a goner. How had she done this in such a short time?

"Let's hurry, before we miss the boat."

****

Ashlyn

I loved New Orleans.

Okay, so it might've been those really good

Mississippi River alcoholic drinks, or it could've been the amazing guy I was with, but whatever it was I had a ball. We sat at the front of the steamboat, ignoring the guy who was speaking about New Orleans history and talked, just the two of us.

"You have two older brothers?" Dillon held a beer, and we ate between asking questions.

"Yeah, I told you about them in York." He nodded, and I continued. "I'm the baby. I love my brothers, but thanks to them I was very sheltered. They don't know I was going to go off exploring on my own. My parents did. They're less overprotective then my brothers." It's true. My brothers had called me every morning, which was their night. I didn't even speak to my parents that much. My brothers needed lives, or girlfriends, so they'd stay out of my life.

"As you know I have a younger brother. No sisters, but I can imagine how I would be if I had one."

Groaning, I leaned back in my seat. "I hope you wouldn't be as bad as my brothers. If it wasn't for my parents covering for me and helping me to move out I don't think I would have ever gotten a boyfriend. Well, not that any stick around." Rolling my eyes, Dillon raised his eyebrow in question. "My older brothers are cops. Yes, both of them. Let's just say guys don't like it when your cop brothers have it out for them and be arseholes, booking them for any little violation."

"What do you mean?" Dillon's lips were tight, and his eyebrows furrowed.

"Mmm, let me think. Jason, my first boyfriend, lasted the longest, but he had a nice debt at the end for things, like going sixty-two in a sixty zone, his brake lights not bright enough, jaywalking, his tires not having enough air, which then made his vehicle a road hazard. Oh and a bunch of other little petty things. The other guy

I started dating left after they threatened him."

Dillon chuckled. I loved that deep smooth sound. "Well, it's good that I'm getting to know you and spend time without them close."

Finished with my food, I put it to the side and snuggled into his side. "Yeah, it is." I looked out at the beautiful surroundings of New Orleans and its old world charm. "So have you been to New Orleans before?"

"Yeah, but we didn't get to sightsee much. We just did quick stopovers. It's hard now to go out exploring without being recognized."

"Do you like it?"

"Like what?"

Easing away to study his face, I asked again. "Do you like being who you are now?"

He didn't look at me. He stared out at the river for a moment, his eyes looking like they were far away. "Yes," he said slowly. "I'm lucky to have a job I love and have come so far with it. Like with any job I suppose there are times were I wish I was wasn't doing what I was, but that's only for things like lack of privacy and always being on guard." Dillon turned to face me. "You know one of the many things I like about you is, you don't treat me different. You say a word that I very rarely hear anymore: no. With you I feel like I get to be just Dillon." He winked. "Enough about me, even though I'm awesome." I rolled my eyes, and he chuckled. "Tell me, why did you choose to become a speech therapist?"

"I love children. I love watching their faces when they're learning. I love how eager they are. I originally was going towards being a preschool kindergarten teacher. In my last year of school I did work placement in kindergarten. There were two children who were hard to understand. It wasn't that they weren't smart. It was just that they couldn't vocalize themselves properly. I spent my free time with them trying to help, and in the two weeks I was there the improvement from my help was huge. It also felt amazing to know what I had done for those two. They still had some work to do until you could fully understand, but I gave their parents numbers for a great speech therapy group. From then on I knew what I wanted to do." I smiled at him. "I'm really lucky to have been hired straight after I graduated from the same place I did my PRAC through University."

Dillon squeezed my hand. "Music teacher."

"What?"

"That's what I would have done if this all didn't work. Mr. Patterson was our high school teacher, and he really inspired us, always encouraging us to do our best and follow our dreams. I'd love to help kids the way he helped us. One of my favorite things to do is visit primary schools, or Zeck, Alec, Law and I go to the children's hospitals. We try to do that as much as we have time to. I donate a quarter of my earnings each year to a different children's organization. "

Oh God. My heart melted, and I fell head over heels for Dillon Blake.

Chapter Four

Dillon
Two days later

Phillip dealt with Ashlyn staying on the tour longer with me better than I thought. He wasn't an idiot though and knew I'd lied the other day about being sick.

"Do you want to tell me how there aren't photos of the two of you plastered all over the media?" Phillip had one hand on his hip as he glared at me.

I shrugged. "I've been wearing a disguise."

Phillip closed his eyes, and I watched as he counted to ten, then opened them. "Please tell me you at least had security around in case you were recognized?"

Instead of saying no, I opted for a smoother answer. "It's a really good disguise. It wasn't the first time I've used it, and I wasn't made then and that was in my hometown of Yorkshire."

Phillip went a bright shade of red, and I gazed at my friends and band-mates for help. They looked anywhere but at me while I was being told off by Phillip. "Dillon, you don't know how lucky you are. We aren't in England anymore. We are in the south where every man and their dog has a gun." He ran his fingers shakily through his thinning hair. "I'm going to ask you a question, and I need you to be one hundred percent honest." I nodded, because just then Phillip didn't look so good. "Is this just a fling, some fun together while this girl is here on tour, or is this a relationship? Do you plan to see her when you have time off?"

This was easy to answer, and our outing together in New Orleans just confirmed it. "Ashlyn and I are in a relationship. I will be flying to her when I have time off or flying her to see me. "

Phillip massaged his temples. "If this was any of

the others I wouldn't take this so seriously, but you haven't had a relationship."

"Hey, I resent that," Zeck whined.

Alec groaned. "Thanks for the faith, Phillip."

Phillip grunted. "Friends with benefits. Groupie love. One night stands. Yes, you've had all of those, Dillon, but a relationship? No." He huffed. "Okay, I need to meet her, and she needs media training. I need her to know how to handle the vultures when they find out about this. America is different from the UK. We have extra roadies and more groups that are joining the tour, and it will be harder to keep a lid on this."

"I'll talk to her and give you a call."

Phillip turned his gaze on the other members of the group. "Get to the arena on time. I want to introduce you to the new groups joining the tour." We all agreed to be there on time.

Phillip left the room, and I turned to go, too, but Law grabbed my arm. "Not so fast, lover boy." I stuck my middle finger up at him. "If you leave now are you going to make it to the concert on time? Covering for you talking to reporters and doing media days is one thing, but not making it to a show is another."

What the hell? Why would Law think I would bail on a concert? What the fuck was up with him? My bailing on the media day was the first time I'd ever done that. Snatching my arm from Law I glared at him. "Fuck you, Law. I have never been late or missed a concert. The media day was the first time I've ever even missed one of those." I looked at Zeck, who avoided my gaze and glanced at Alec to see him staring at me. I captured their attention. "I have covered at one time for all of you, and I've done it more than once. Think about that next time before you ask a stupid question like you just did."

Storming out of the room, I headed straight to the

41

gym knowing I needed to cool down.

****

Ashlyn

Instead of watching the concert, Phillip, Right Time's manager, took me off to the group's dressing room and gave me a crash course in media training. It scared the hell out of me. I didn't realize so much went into keeping the fans happy and the media under control. I had no idea there was so much I wasn't supposed to say. I definitely didn't think I was ready for any of the media circus Phillip had told me about.

I stayed in the dressing room until the concert was over, and then chaos broke out. People were running and shouting everywhere, and though I fought to catch a glimpse of Sarah or Dillon, there was too much confusion. One of the security people hustled me out toward the exit where I finally found Dillon and rushed into his arms. Before we could say anything, Phillip's voice came over a megaphone, and we saw him standing up on something near the door.

"We have an overwhelming number of people at all exits. The police are here to help with the influx of fans, but they didn't expect this many. They called in reinforcements, and I received confirmation moments ago they're ready for us to leave. The local police are going to give us a vehicle escort to the hotel. There will be no signing out the back to fans because we need to get out and into the vans as quickly as possible."

Everyone around agreed, and I clung to Dillon as the back door opened. The screaming and yelling was deafening, and through the peephole of the security I could see the back security fence barely holding up the fans against it.

Gripping tightly to Dillon I froze, terrified to move and leave the safety of the stadium. Dillon turned to me and tilted my chin up so we were eye to eye. "I promise I won't let anything happen to you. We're safe." He leaned down and gently brushed his lips over mine. Before I could respond he moved us, and I followed in a daze to the waiting vans.

I smiled when security tried to get Dillon in before me, but he was having none of that. He shot a look of pure anger at the bodyguards and helped me get in before him. We sat on a seat next to each other, and I didn't care about being seen when he leaned in and brushed his lips over mine.

****

Dillon
Two days later
Atlanta

Guilt assaulted me as I watched Sarah comfort Ashlyn as she changed all her settings on Facebook and went through deleting a bunch of people from her friends list, leaving her with only close friends and family. She canceled her Twitter account after reading some of Right Time's diehard fans rip into her.

We'd been on lockdown in our rooms since waking up two days earlier to see a media frenzy. Photos of the two of us were everywhere. A photo sequence of me making sure she got in the van before me and giving one of the bodyguards a bad look for putting me before her was the first photo. The other photos were what had the fans and media buzzing. They were of our quick kiss at the entrance where Ashlyn had frozen in terror seeing the crazy fans. It may have been just a brush of my lips over hers in a brief kiss, but from the looks on both our faces there was no denying that something was going on and we felt something more than friendship for each other.

There was a record number of paparazzi out the

front of the hotel, and Phillip had called at least ten times to tell me all the different shows and places begging for an interview, or a response to the photo and many of the rumors. Reports had come in from the UK that on the end part of the tour there that I was absent from many of the after parties, and that I wasn't documented to have been with any women. I hated the fact that people were monitoring my sex life and knew my usual habit was to party after a show and get with a woman, or women.

Phillip had told me this would happen as I didn't date, and people were putting two and two together about my absences in Europe. I was the first in the group Right Time to change my pattern and according to the media, have a relationship longer than a night or two. Half the fans were happy, but the other half were angry and heartbroken that I was now taken and by someone who wasn't famous. Rumors were flying left and right, and a lot of them stated that I was leaving the group to settle down, that I was marrying Ashlyn and we were moving to Australia. I had no idea how the rumors got so farfetched. Even if I went off the media and fans' timeline I'd only been dating Ashlyn for a couple of months and they already had me leaving the group and moving overseas. The reality was we hadn't even been dating a month or even half that.

My phone lit up, and Phillip's ringtone came on. Reaching for my mobile I swiped the screen across, answering it.

"I've been discussing the issue with the record company and other management and we think you need to make a media statement. As this is a first for you and the group, we feel it will be better than ignoring the situation."

I wasn't sure how I felt about the way Phillip and the record company were handling this. I knew I didn't like Phillip referring to my relationship with Ashlyn as an "issue", or that our relationship caused so much upheaval that Phillip needed to talk to the record company and other management for advice. I was happy to make a statement if it had even some people backing off.

"Sure, I'll make a statement. Maybe then we could get back to some kind of normalcy."

****

Ashlyn
Three days after the media statement

Dillon's media statement wasn't long or anything elaborate. He simply said, "I know there has been lots of speculation over the last few days. First, I'd like to address the rumor that I will be leaving the group. I am in Right Time for the long haul, and I have no intentions of leaving the group. Second, I'd like to tell you all that, yes, I'm in a relationship with Ashlyn Dobbs. I do realize that this is my first relationship since Right Time got signed, and I ask if we could please have some privacy so I can enjoy our time together. I'm excited about this tour and look forward to seeing many of you at our concerts. Thank you for your time." He'd left the media conference without answering any questions.

Last night's show had been in Florida. They'd performed at Disney's Magic Kingdom, and it had been epic. This time, I wasn't as scared by the swarm of fans. I knew Dillon wouldn't let anything happen to me. Now that our relationship was out we didn't hide our affection for each other. I kissed him before the show, and he came straight to me after and kissed me in front of the VIPs. One thing I liked about us being out in the open was I got to make-out with real Dillon, not disguise Dillon.

Last night had been an eye opener. Besides traveling to venues, I still hadn't left the hotels, so I had only dealt with diehard fans who were upset Dillon was now taken on media outlets. I was assigned my own bodyguard, and last night he'd definitely worked for his paycheck.

Pictures of Dillon and me from last night were already circling, and in the early hours of this morning I received a call from both my brothers, and to say they weren't happy was putting it mildly. They wanted me to come home so they could "protect me". Instead of getting eight or so hours sleep, I tried to calm them down. But they hadn't listened, spouting something about the crazy women—girls—who were attacking me on social media. In the end I'd had to hang up on them both. I'd spoken to my parents, too, and even they were a little upset, but their upset was more that I hadn't even mentioned Dillon. By breakfast time I was exhausted, sick of my family and turned off my phone.

Dillon offered to speak to my family, and I didn't even have to think about it. My brothers would rip him apart, even over the phone. My parents would be safer, but I wasn't ready for Dillon to talk to my family yet. Everything was happening so quickly. We hadn't even been together for a month.

Sarah and I had spent the day at Disney's Magic Kingdom getting our picture taken with as many characters as we could. Tomorrow we would be doing the rides. I was exhausted, but happy. I'd needed today with my best friend, to stop worrying about my family and my relationship with Dillon. I needed to just have fun.

"Did you have a good day?" Sitting up on the bed I looked over at Dillon at the desk. "It would have been nice to go. You were right though. I did have a lot of work things to catch up on. Zeck's been covering for me, so we could have time together." Dillon turned and looked up from the table where he was going over paperwork he'd been sent by his lawyer. The band had been offered different promo opportunities, and Dillon had put off reading over them as he'd been spending time with me.

Shrugging, I got off the bed and made my way over to him. "I had fun with Sarah. No one recognized me. Today Sarah and I did photo character day, so I'm sure you didn't miss anything that you would have wanted to spend your day doing." I know he had wanted to come with me this morning, but he had work to catch up on and I needed time away. I wanted to do things on my holiday just for me. *Argh.* I hated that I sounded so selfish.

His brows furrowed, and his lips thinned. "Why would you say that? I wouldn't have minded posing with Mickey with you." He pushed his chair back.

So he didn't have to get out of the chair I came and stood before him leaning against the table. "I just meant that I thought you'd be sick of posing for photos, and I did mostly Disney princesses. So I didn't think that would be your cup of tea."

He pulled me so I sat on his lap straddling him in the big chair. "I haven't posed for many photos with you. I wouldn't mind doing it so we had some more together. So no, I wouldn't have minded." His voice was rising, and his green eyes darkened. "The only fucking photos I have of us are the ones the fucking paparazzi took and those ones when I'm in a disguise." He was pissed. His body shook beneath me.

"I know." I felt guilty. He couldn't control the fans or paparazzi, and that was why we had to be careful. "Maybe we can get some photos tomorrow if you can organize with your manager special time for photos with Disney, but today you would have been recognized and hounded." I sighed. "I spent most of my time in line waiting to get my photo taken. Then Sarah and I would rush to get into another line."

"You're happy I wasn't there? What? So you didn't have to have people follow you around or a bodyguard? So you could be quick and not have me slowing you down? So you could have peace and get out of the hotel?" He was yelling, and I wiggled off of him getting angry myself.

"Argh, that's not what I friggin' said." I threw my hands in the air. "I just meant that now we're out, you can't wear your disguise to go out as they'll see me. Even though I think I wasn't recognized, I may have been and not realized it." Groaning, because I was getting flustered and confused, I stared at Dillon's face, and that was when I noticed his eyes flash not with anger, but sadness and annoyance. His lips were nearly non-existent in his frown. I gazed down and saw his shoulders droop. I'd never seen Dillon like this, his confidence and cockiness gone. I didn't like it.

"I'm sorry." I closed my eyes and took a deep breath in before opening my eyes and slowly letting my breath out. "You're right. I didn't want you with me today." I went back and straddled his lap. "I love spending time with you, but with everything that's been going on, I needed a normal day. A day with just me and my bestie." I reached up and stroked his cheek. "I needed a rest from all this." I let my hands fall and moved them around to encompass everything around us. "I'm not used to all this. You've had years to get used to being followed and attacked by the media and crazy people. This is all new to me."

"I'm an arse."

I nodded. He chuckled, and I giggled. Dillon's hand came to rest on my butt squeezing it before he hit it.

"Hey." My giggles turned into laughter. One thing I discovered I had with Dillon was we didn't stay mad for long or drag our arguments out, and we always had amazing make-up sex.

"You're supposed to say, nah, you're not an arse."

I was really going to miss this when I went back home to Australia.

Chapter Five

Dillon
Two days later
I knew Ashlyn was disappointed we could only spend one night in Key West. We didn't have time for more as she only had three more nights before she had to get on a plane home, and I needed to be in Miami for a show tomorrow night.

"Ask for leave. Stay on tour for longer. Stay with me. Please." I'd asked at least twenty or so times over the last couple of days.

Ashlyn had given the same answer. "I wish I could. This is my first year at my job. I'm lucky to have such a good position straight out of university. The only reason they gave me the time off is because it's school holidays and a lot of children go on holidays so they cut back appointments."

The tour wasn't arriving in Australia for another three and half months. It would be a month before I'd have a long enough break between shows to visit her. I had already booked my flight from Japan to Australia, but that break was only five nights, and then I had to be in Tokyo for a concert. My next long break wasn't until Australia.

Ashlyn's squeal beside me brought my attention back to her. Our driver slowed out the front of our hotel. I'd booked the Southernmost Beach Resort for our time in Key West. I'd stayed in the resort before and knew Ashlyn would love it. It was in the spot where everyone wanted to be on the island, the southernmost point.

"This is amazing. A million times better than the room I had booked." Ashlyn's happiness was contagious. She opened the SUV car door without waiting for the bodyguards. I followed. I didn't want to miss any of her enjoyment. Ashlyn grabbed my hand and dragged me through the reception area and to the desk. Ashlyn bounced with excitement.

Rick, one of our bodyguards, came over to us not looking very happy. The reception wasn't busy and I hadn't been recognized, but I knew the drill. I shouldn't have left the vehicle until I was told it was safe. I wasn't with the rest of the group. The guys had decided to give me and Ashlyn some time together and they were going to have fun in Miami. I hoped that people wouldn't notice me. Rick was staying back so he didn't draw attention, but was close if needed.

Ashlyn was so excited she skipped to our room barely waiting for me to follow. She entered the key card, opened the door and entered the room, then started screaming. "Oh. My. God. This is amazing!"

I walked faster to catch her and glanced behind me to see Rick close on my heels. I went into the suite and saw Ashlyn jumping up and down. She spotted me and ran at me, jumping on me and wrapping her legs around my waist. I stumbled back before I got my balance and held her to me. I chuckled as I gazed at her. Her cheeks were rosy, her eyes wide, and her face was bright with so much happiness it shone from her.

"Thank you." She kissed one cheek. "Thank you." She kissed my other cheek. "Thank you." Her lips came down onto mine, and I opened and deepened our kiss. She moaned and ground against me. When my fingers slid under her shirt she groaned and pulled her mouth from mine. "We don't have time for that now. Daylight is burning, and I have so much to do." She slid down my body, and I reluctantly let her.

Ashlyn turned bright red and I turned and saw why. Rick stood at the entrance of the room, and I watched his lips twitch trying not to smile. Ashlyn sighed, turned to her bag and got her phone out, then turned to Rick and pounced. "Take my phone. You have to take photos." She yanked on my arm, pulling me to her and out onto the deck. "Okay. Take a bunch, Rick."

I laughed at her enthusiasm and even saw Rick couldn't help smiling at Ashlyn. "You do realize that taking photos isn't my job?"

Ashlyn waved her hand. "Bodyguard. Photographer. It's all the same."

Rick shook his head and mumbled between chuckles, "No. No it isn't."

I hugged Ashlyn to me as she posed with me for photos.

****

Ashlyn

Key West was amazing. I didn't want to leave. The resort we were in was right in front of the most southern point. The sky was clear, and the weather was perfect for the beach. We'd arrived early, and after checking in, Dillon, Rick, Toby—another guard—and I went exploring. I'd had things I wanted to do this morning before I spent my afternoon on the beach of the most southern part of America.

Dillon hadn't been recognized, and I was on cloud nine. We walked around hand in hand and stopped to kiss and cuddle all the time. We enjoyed a tour of the Ernest Hemingway Home and Museum and wandered the shops. I now sat in a chair next to Dillon looking out at the ocean next to our resort.

"Thank you for this. Today was incredible." I sat up in the laid-back chair to look at Dillon.

Dillon sat up and grabbed me so I straddled him in the chair. "You don't have to thank me." He stroked my cheek, the tips of his fingers came down to trace my lips before going down my chin. "Seeing how happy this has made you and seeing it all through your eyes has made it all worth it." My stomach fluttered, and I shivered at the feel of my heart feeling like it was going to beat out of my chest. "You're so easy to be with." His lips came to meet mine, and I rested against him and savored his touch as he deepened the kiss. And that was when I knew.

I'd fallen in love.

****

Miami Airport

Tears slid down my cheek, and I didn't bother to brush them away. I didn't want to leave Dillon. I didn't want to go home. I wanted to continue my adventure of exploring America and spending time with the man I was in love with. My chest ached, and my stomach rolled.

Dillon's hand was entwined with mine, his grip tight. Bodyguards surrounded us as we made our way through the airport towards the security. The fans were crazy now the tour was well on its way. I gripped my big leather hobo handbag in my other hand. It held all my paperwork and electronics. Dillon had me upgraded to first-class and paid for my carryon to go with my big luggage. I'd told him I was happy with the economy plus that I'd paid for and he didn't need to spend his money, but he insisted and wouldn't listen. I was too unsettled and upset to argue.

The security checkpoint wasn't far before us, and we stopped in a corner with the bodyguards standing before Dillon and me. Snuggling against Dillon, I breathed him in. I buried my face into his chest. His fingers settled under my chin and he tilted my head up so I stared at him. "We'll Skype. I will see you in a little over three weeks."

Choking on a sob I nodded, unable to talk. Dillon rubbed my back before coming up to brush away my tears.

"Don't cry, lov'. This isn't goodbye, more like I'll see you later."

Hiccupping through a laugh I shook my head at his view of our situation. "I'll miss you."

"I know." He winked, and I embarrassed myself by snort laughing.

Oh God. Not only was I ugly crying, with puffy eyes, red nose and my body shaking with sobs, I was now snorting. Wiping my eyes, I took a deep breath in and slowly let it out trying to calm myself. "I'm sorry I'm a mess. You've just became this huge part of me. I don't want to leave you. Argh, I sound crazy." Stepping away from him I tried to gather myself so I didn't look as crazy. I knew I sounded like a clingy, infatuated girlfriend, not just a woman who'd spent almost three weeks getting to know a new boyfriend. I should've been horrified at my behavior, but I was too upset to care.

Dillon's arms circled around me gathering me back against him. "This isn't a one sided thing." He caressed my cheek, and I leaned into his touch. I was really going to miss this, just the simple touches like, his hand holding, or him brushing my cheek. "You're sane, because I'm just as crazy about you as you are about me. I mean I know why you like me so much. I am irresistible and one of the most eligible bachelors in the world." His hands came down, and he squeezed my arse. He raised his eyebrows up and down, and I burst out laughing. This was one of the reasons why I'd fallen for him. He always made me laugh even when I wasn't feeling very happy. He made fun of himself for me, and he always knew what I needed to hear.

Reaching up, I captured his mouth to my own and kissed him with all the love I felt. Wrapping my arms around his neck I pressed my body to his, and delved my tongue into his mouth and tangled it with his.

Rick cleared his throat and said in a clear soft voice, "Sorry to break you two up, but you've got about ten or so minutes before they start boarding your flight."

Reluctantly I pulled away from Dillon. I needed to leave now or I'd miss my flight and I didn't know if I'd rebook if I did. Checking my handbag was still on my shoulder I gripped it tight and took a couple of steps back, looking at the sad green eyes with hair falling over them and the slouching body of the man I loved. I held back a sob. He was not what I had expected on this vacation, or for a boyfriend, but he was mine. "I love you."

Dillon blinked and stepped towards me. "What did you say?" His voice was hoarse as he stared at me like he'd imagined what I'd said.

Crap. I'd said that out loud. I stepped back and opened my mouth to tell him again, but I couldn't. It was too soon to tell him that. We had a connection and I may have been in love with him, but I didn't want to tell him and scare him away. "I'll miss you," I mumbled. I blew him a kiss and turned, scurrying to get in the security check line. I hoped I didn't just blow it.

Chapter Six

Dillon
Two days later

I'd waited over forty-eight hours to talk to Ashlyn. With all the flights, she'd had eighteen hours on planes. I knew she'd go home and sleep. So I gave her enough time, but it was damn hard. I knew what I'd heard. Ashlyn had said she loved me. I should have said it back, but I'd been stunned. It had taken me a moment to realize she had said it, and I hadn't imagined it. I was in love with her. I knew it was quick to fall for someone in the short time we'd been together, but being with Ashlyn was easy. She was loving, loyal, caring, and easygoing. She was like a breath of fresh air when you'd been using recycled air for five or so years.

Leaning back on the resort bed, I sat the laptop on the pillows beside me. I'd messaged Ashlyn fifteen minutes ago to tell her I would be calling her. She had just gotten back to me. Setting up the chat I pressed call. Ashlyn answered, and her beautiful face came up on the screen. Her eyes had dark circles under them, her hair was in a messy bun, and her skin look almost translucent.

"Hi, lov'. I miss ya. How was your flight?"

"Good. The first cla—"

"He sounds like a snooty idiot. Tell him to fuck off and you want a real man. Give me a look at him." A guy's voice cut off Ashlyn's words, and seconds later a man in his early to mid-thirties pushed his way onto the screen.

Ashlyn hit the guy on the back of his head and pushed at his shoulders. "Go away, Tyler." This was one of her brothers. I'd heard her talk to them plenty of times and seen photos. They wrestled for the screen, but I could see Ashlyn's brother was careful not to hurt her. Ashlyn won after a nipple cripple and took back over the screen. "I'm sorry, Dillon, my brother is being a dickhead." She yelled the last word, and I heard laughter in the background.

I wrestled and fought with my own brother all the time, so I wasn't bothered. "Don't apologize. I have a brother. So I know what it gets like."

Ashlyn nodded and then smiled. That simple thing sent warmth flowing through me. I loved her smile. It always seemed to brighten any room. She sighed. "They're taking turns. Tyler and Torrance are staying with me." She closed her eyes. "They've taken friggin' holidays and moved into my townhouse. They're saving me from the media and crazy people." Ashlyn rolled her eyes.

"I'm sorry." I hadn't thought about the media and what they would do when she went home. I'd assumed they would leave her alone and think I'd moved on when she left. Fuck, I hated when I was wrong.

She waved her hand across the screen. "Dipshit one and two—"

"Hey, sis, I can hear you. My feelings are getting hurt," Ashlyn's brother shouted, interrupting her.

Ashlyn snorted and yelled over her shoulder. "Feelings, my arse. Stop listening and whining. You're worse than an old woman listening in."

"Am not. And men don't whine."

I laughed at their banter, and Ashlyn turned back to the screen. "Give me a second. I'm going to go and shut the door so it's harder for him to listen."

"Sure." I watched as she left the screen and came back a moment or two later.

"Okay, take two," she said. "Hi."

"Hi. It sounds like he missed you."

"Yeah." Ashlyn's eyes sparkled, and a cheeky

smirk spread over her face. "I think they've gained a bit of weight. They usually split their time between mine and my mother's food. Without my food they got takeout."

"You cook, too?"

"Yep. I had to learn when my two brothers ate everything in sight. There were never any leftovers for me or spare food." She shrugged. "So I made things."

Nodding, I listened to her and wondered if I should say anything to her. Was talking about what she'd said at the airport something you spoke of over Skype? Or did I wait until I saw her in the flesh? I wanted to say it back to her, but I knew I should say that to her when I could hold her and kiss her. Groaning, I watched as hair fell over her eyes and I ached to tuck the strand behind her ear.

I needed to talk about our love in the flesh. The next three weeks were going to be hell.

****

Ashlyn
Australia

We'd talked on Skype the last three and half weeks. He hadn't mentioned what I'd said at the airport, but I didn't know if when we were face to face I'd be as lucky. My love for him hadn't changed. It had only gotten stronger. I just thought it was too soon to voice my feelings. Especially to famous, could-have-any-girl-he-wanted Dillon.

I hadn't told my brothers Dillon was coming. My brothers seemed to be warming to him, well as much as my brothers warmed to anyone, but I didn't want to risk anything. I wanted to enjoy my days with Dillon, not be taken over with my family. I hadn't even told my parents. He was only in Australia for five nights. I intended to spend most of that in a bed or wrapped around him somewhere. Dillon was bringing my two favorite bodyguards, Rick and Toby. I was hoping Dillon wouldn't get recognized, but if he did Rick and Toby would be close by. Dillon was taking a private plane, and I was only moments away from meeting him at the country airport not far from my place. The rest of the band was even going to try to cover for him so we could enjoy our time together.

I'd picked up the big SUV Dillon had hired for his stay and drove it to the airport. I parked as close as I could get and then got out and walked into the small airport. Since arriving home to Australia no one really bothered me. I'd had the media contact me a couple of times asking for an interview to tell them details about the Right Time and my relationship with Dillon, but after a couple of weeks or so they gave up. My brothers helped get rid of them, too.

Going over to the arrival gate I glanced down at my phone again to check the time. He should've been coming out any minute. My stomach churned, and my palms were sweaty against each other. Wiping them on my clothes, I took a deep breath in and slowly let it out. It felt a lot longer than three and half weeks since I'd seen Dillon. My stomach felt queasy. It did that a lot lately, and I hoped that once I saw Dillon the queasiness would settle. I missed his touch, him holding me at night, or even just him caressing my cheek and tucking my hair behind my ear.

These last three weeks I'd been lonely. Before Dillon, I loved my life and didn't think I was missing anything. I'd had many thoughts lately of quitting my job and traveling with Dillon. Only a couple of things held me back. One—I didn't want to be a groupie. Two—I hadn't been with Dillon long just to give everything up, no matter how much I loved him. And lastly, I didn't have the money. I knew Dillon would pay, but I didn't want him to use his hard earned money. I wasn't with him for his money. I wasn't a gold-digger and didn't want to be called one.

Searching the gate I spotted him. He was hard to miss, in black skinny jeans, a white and black tank that showed his terribly done tats, black sunglasses, hair that wasn't black, but wasn't brown falling over his sunglasses and lastly two massive bodyguards standing by him, one behind and one slightly in front. Dillon was cocky, and he didn't care about the attention he was given.

My stomach didn't settle. It became full of butterflies. My heart felt like it started beating so fast I was surprised it didn't beat its way out of my chest. I wanted to run and jump on him so bad. I knew Rick, who stood a little in front of me, might stop me if I ran fast and he didn't see it was me. I'd seen Rick take down people many times while I'd been with Dillon, and I did not want to become one.

Slowly moving forward, I intertwined my fingers to stop my fist clenching with my nerves. I was scared. What if when he saw me in person again he didn't like what he saw? What if he saw me again and there was no spark, no chemistry for him?

I stopped directly before them. "Dillon, I've missed you." Rick stepped to the side, and I stepped closer, terrified.

Dillon slid his sunglasses up on his head and slowly took me in from head to toe and back again. Then a massive smile spread over his handsome face, and he closed the gap between us and wrapped his arms around me and hugged me tight. "Fuck, I've missed you so much. You're more beautiful each time I see you."

His lips crashed down on mine, and I closed my eyes savoring his taste and touch. I clutched him like he was my life line. I didn't care where we were, or if we had an audience. I wasn't giving up this kiss for anyone or anything. His tongue sought entry, and I opened, letting him re-explore.

I don't know how long we stood where we were making out, but when I needed air I reluctantly eased away. His hands came up to caress my cheek, and I leaned into his touch.

"I love you." His voice was clear, and there was no mistaking what he said.

A heavy weight lifted off my shoulders, and I beamed up at him. "I love you, too."

He winked at me. "I thought I'd tell you now. Well, since you seem to think airports are the place to say it."

I groaned and squeezed him against me. "You didn't say anything when we talked."

He brushed his lips over mine. "I thought this was something that needing talking about in person. Then I realized I'd tell you how I feel when I saw you next." He rested his forehead on mine. "I love you."

Sighing in contentment I squeezed him against me. "I love you, too. Come on let's get out of here so I can show you just how much."

He chuckled and smacked my arse. "Lead the way, lov'."

****

Dillon
At Ashlyn's house three nights later.

I didn't know if I was relived or upset that Ashlyn hadn't told her family I was here. I'd been at her house for three nights now and she still hadn't said anything to them. Our first two nights we'd spent in bed, but I at least thought today when her parents called she would mention she was with me. I didn't like the feeling that I was

61

getting. Was Ashlyn ashamed or embarrassed by me? Did she not think this would last? Didn't she believe in our love? Was that was why she wasn't saying anything or introducing me?

"Why didn't you tell them you were with me?"

She sighed and wrapped her arms around me. "You're only here for two more nights. I want you all to myself. I also don't want them butting in or scaring you off." She gazed up at me with a pleading pout and eyes that begged for me to let her have what she wanted. What she'd said made sense, but I didn't like it. I started to feel like her dirty secret. "Please let me just enjoy you. I promise the next time I'll introduce you."

I had two more nights, and as much as I wanted to argue my own point, I didn't want to fight. I wanted to enjoy my short time left with her. Reaching over beside me I circled her waist and pulled her to straddle me. "Fine. Next time I'm here I want to meet all the family."

Ashlyn moaned and clenched her thighs. "How about next time you can meet my parents?"

Sitting up higher on the bed I held her waist as I inched up. Trailing my hands up her body I rested them on her cheeks, caressing her smooth skin. Tilting her chin up with one finger, I traced her lips with my other hand committing every curve and surface to memory. "I want to meet your brothers, too. I know how important your family is to you and you love your brothers."

She pressed a kiss to my fingers and mumbled, "That's debatable."

Chuckling at her sulking look, I leaned up and feathered my lips over hers. "I'm not scared…" I kissed her. "…of your brothers." I brushed her lips. "I'm resilient. I can handle them. I promise." I licked her lips before seeking entry. She opened, and my tongue met hers and I kissed her with all the love and passion I felt. I could never get enough of Ashlyn.

Wanting to taste more, I rolled over so she lay on the bed naked before me. Settling between her legs I leaned down and I trailed kisses down her neck nibbling on her here and there, as I made my way to her pointed nipples, sucking on one and circling the tip with my tongue before moving to the other so it didn't feel neglected.

Ashlyn rose up giving me better access. Her hands came and rested on my head holding me against her. Her naked body was warm against mine. "Dillon … Dillon. Oh Dillon."

Easing down her body I licked, kissed, and nibbled her skin before I settled between her spread legs. Lifting her butt up, I buried my face into her heat, nuzzling her pussy and licking her as I spread her folds. I lapped her core and sucked her little bud, driving her mad. Her thighs tightened on my head, and she ground herself on my face. I loved pleasuring her. She made mewling noises that drove me insane, and the power I felt over making her lose control was the best high.

Ashlyn arched herself into my face, and I delved two fingers into her soaked pussy and pumped them in and out as I lapped at her clit.

"Mmm, feels so good," she panted.

Her fingers wrapped around the strands of my hair and pulled. The slight pain only heightened the burning passion that was building in me. I'm sure Ashlyn could make me come just from pleasuring her. I needed her to come because I was so fucking close to blowing my own load just from her sexy noises, and I wasn't even inside her. Adding another finger I picked up speed and sank my fingers deeper each time. I could feel she was close. Her legs were shaking around me and her grip on my hair was getting tighter. I knew she just needed something extra to fall over the edge, she was so wound up. Sucking her nub into my mouth I thrust my fingers into her as I lightly scraped my teeth around her clit.

Ashlyn screeched, "Oh God, Dillon, Dillon, Dillon." Her pussy clenched around my digits, and she yanked on my hair so hard I was sure she pulled chunks of it out. I didn't give a fuck about that though. I needed to be inside her. Sliding up her body I trailed kisses over her heated skin and came to rest at her breasts, sucking one pebbled nipple into my mouth before switching to the other breast. Ashlyn slipped her arms around my back clutching me to her as I fondled and sucked on her breasts. My cock ached, and I couldn't wait to sink into her tight warm heat and find my own release.

Ashlyn looked gorgeous as she stared at me. My cock lined up to her pussy ready for entry, but as I stared down at Ashlyn I wanted her on top. I wanted to watch her tits bounce as she rode my cock to another orgasm. Circling her waist, I lifted her and rolled so she was on top. Ashlyn giggled, and the happy sound had my heart pounding faster.

"I like this." She smiled down at me as her gaze roamed over me. Her hands came to rest on my shoulders gripping them tight before she ran her fingers over my chest. Shivers of heat coursed through me at her touch. My muscles clenched, building the tension.

Ashlyn eased down my body and brushed her lips over my skin not missing any part of me. She settled between my thighs and circled my dick with her hand and rubbed it up and down. Fuck, I was so close to coming without her playing with me. Ashlyn turned me on so damn much I didn't need foreplay for myself. She gazed up at me, and holy shit, I almost blew my load. She was so sexy, with her hooded brown eyes filled lust and her skin with the I-just-had-an-amazing-orgasm glow. I was a lucky guy.

Ashlyn hovered over my length, closed her eyes and sank her open mouth over me as her hand gripped the base. *Fuck, fuck, fuck.* I had never seen anything so hot. Her mouth was open wide, and I filled her, just barely fitting. She sucked on me almost pulling out of me the load I was barely holding back on. She circled her tongue around my head and pumped her hand.

"Fuck, Ashlyn, that's feels fucking amazing," I moaned. If she didn't stop I was going to blow my load, and I didn't want to come in her mouth. I wanted to sink into her pussy and come deep inside her. On a growl, I lifted her off my dick. "No. I'm coming inside you."

Holding her waist I moved her up so she straddled me and lined my cock up to her entrance. Taking a deep breath in and slowly letting it out, I dragged my dick back and forth over her pussy lips, spreading them before I thrust the head of my cock in. She smiled down at me and sank herself on my member. "I fucking love you, do you know?"

Her giggle had its usual effect. My heart sped up and I grinned. "I fucking love you, too." She leaned down and brushed her lips over mine.

My cock twitched inside her, and the tight coil of my muscles demanded she move. Holding onto her waist I lifted her. She eased from my mouth and rested her hands on my chest and rode me. I wanted to see her tits bounce. Grabbing her hands I held them. Ashlyn paused.

"I want to see these…" I let go of her hands and cupped her breasts. "Bounce, as you ride me."

Ashlyn's already flushed skin turned a darker shade of pink. She nibbled on her bottom lip and nodded. She lifted up and sank down slowly at first before she picked up her speed. Her pussy felt like what I imagine heaven would feel like all the time. *Amazing.* I watched her tits bounce, and as I stared at them, I was sure they looked bigger than the first time I was with her. They were fuller and looked damn heavy as they jiggled. I could stare at them all day. They were magnificent, large, round and with perfect dark pink nipples. I narrowed my gaze. I was sure they were pinker a couple of weeks ago. Rubbing my thumb over her nipples Ashlyn moaned and ground herself down as she came down on my dick this time.

I thrust up to meet her this time, and she gripped my arms to steady herself. "Cup your breasts and play with them." She did as I told her, and I glided my fingers down her chest and stomach and came to rest over her clit. Circling it, I groaned and she moaned her core pulsed around me. She was close to coming again, and I was straining to hold myself back from blowing my load before she did. Adding a little pressure to her clit I drove up as she sank down on my cock. "I'm so close," she panted.

Fuck yes. I knew what she needed. Sitting up I eased my hand around to grip her butt cheeks. Her hands came around to clutch my back and her nails dug into me each time my dick sank deep.

Driving up into her I leaned down to her neck and sucked on the skin just below her ear. Ashlyn let out an ear-piercing scream. Her core quivered around me before it squeezed the ever loving hell out of me pulling out the orgasm that I'd been holding in.

"Fuck, Ashlyn," I yelled. I felt my whole body shake as I shot my load deep within her.

I closed my eyes and eased my hold only to be yanked off of Ashlyn and thrown to the wall.

What. The. Fuck.

Ashlyn screamed. Gathering myself, I looked up ready to face who the hell had interrupted us and wondered where the fuck Rick and Toby were and was faced with two massive, beaten, blood covered, very pissed off brothers.

****

Ashlyn

Oh. My. God. Kill me now.

My brothers stood over a naked Dillon, who was crumbled against the wall. Tyler and Torrance looked like shit. They were covered in blood and their clothes were ripped, and I could already see bruises forming. What the hell happened to them?

Shaking my head, I groaned as I realized I was concerned for the idiots even after what they'd just done. Wrapping the sheet around my naked body I got up before they beat the crap out of Dillon. "What the hell, Torrance? Tyler? Get out."

They both turned to me, and Torrance stepped towards me. "We heard you screaming and thought you were being killed."

"Oh please God, I would do anything if I could disappear," I mumbled. I felt my cheeks heat. My brothers had heard me having sex and thought I was being bloody hurt.

Dillon, the dick, laughed. Torrance turned back to him and growled at the same time as Tyler. "Shut it, fucker."

Rolling my eyes I took a deep breath to calm my rising anger. How the hell had my brothers gotten into my house anyway? I got all the locks changed when I finally got them to leave me alone and move out a week ago.

"How the hell did you two get into the house? I had the locks changed." Fuck, how did they get past the two goddamn bodyguards down stairs? I held up my hand so they would wait and answer my next question first. "Wait. How the hell did you get past the two friggin'

67

bodyguards downstairs?"

Tyler turned sideways so I could see him better, and I watched the guilty look that came over him. Torrance was better at hiding his guilt, but he grunted. "I don't know about the guy I left to Tyler, but my guy will probably wake up with a really bad headache and will need keys to my handcuffs."

Tyler smirked. "Oh my guy's awake, but I bet he wishes he had the keys to my handcuffs. I don't think your legs and arms should be cuffed like that for long."

Closing my eyes I counted down from ten and scrubbed my hands over my face. I looked over to Dillon to see him struggling not to chuckle. He was standing now with his hands covering his dick.

"As you can see I am alive and well. So go downstairs and help poor Rick and Toby."

They both shook their heads, and I swore right then I'd make them pay. "No way, Ashlyn. We want to find out why the douche hasn't come and met us. Is he keeping you a secret? We need to teach him a lesson that he shouldn't treat you like that."

"Fucking hell," I screamed. I gazed at Dillon, and when he didn't say anything I sighed, knowing I was going to have tell my brothers. "Tyler, Torrance, Dillon isn't the one not wanting to meet you two. I have no idea why he'd want to meet you. Exhibit A." I circled around us. "It's me. I don't want him to meet you two. I like Dillon. No, I love him and I don't want you two idiots to scare him away."

I watched as both their gazes widened, and they stepped back, shocked at my words. I had never loved a man before. I'd never not introduced them to a guy I was seeing either. Dillon backed his way over to me making sure his hands covered himself. He reached his jeans on the bedside drawer and stepped into them quickly and did them up. Then he stood and came to stand next to me.

"I love you, too, my lov'."

Smiling at him I turned my gaze back on my still shocked brothers. "Dillon. Torrance and Tyler, my brothers." I pointed to each brother. "Torrance. Tyler. Dillon. Now you two have been introduced, so get your arses downstairs and help the friggin' bodyguards. Dillon and I will be down once we get showered and dressed."

"Separately," Torrance growled.

"Argh! Get out." I stomped my foot and clutched the sheet with one hand and pointed to the door with the other. I stared them down for a moment before they both slowly left the room. When they were both gone I fell back on the bed. "That was why I didn't want you to meet my family."

Dillon, the wanker, laughed.

****

Ashlyn
Two days later

The queasy feeling was constant and this morning the worst. I told myself it was worse this morning because Dillon was flying back today to meet up with the tour, but I was starting to think I wasn't even fooling myself anymore. I needed to go to the doctor. One more day and tomorrow I would book for a doctor's appointment.

Hugging Dillon tighter I wished I didn't have to let him go. His fingers were drawing soothing circles on my back. We'd been up for a while, starting our morning with hot goodbye sex.

"Come back with me."

"I can't. I have to work. I'm lucky to have my job. I know a bunch of people who graduated with me and still haven't got a job in the field we worked so hard for, for years to get a diploma and job in." I sat up and looked

69

down at him. "I wouldn't ask you to stay and quit because I know how much you love being in Right Time."

"You're right. I'm sorry. I'm going to miss you, and I won't get to see you in the flesh for months. That's way too long to go without touching you, tasting you…" He sat up next to me and leaned across and brushed his lips over mine. "To kiss you."

I melted against him. Damn him, he always said all the right things. "In a bit over a month there is a long weekend. I'm sure If I spoke to my boss she'd let me have an extra day or two off and I could come to you."

He cupped my face and kissed me so tenderly I almost said I'd quit my job and follow him anywhere. The more time I spent with Dillon the deeper I fell in love with him. This time when he left it was really going to hurt.

Chapter Seven

Ashlyn
Three weeks later
Since Dillon left I'd thrown myself into work. I had a doctor's appointment tomorrow. I was now pretty sure I knew what the doctor would tell me what was wrong with me. I was terrified. Scared of what I thought was true would mean for me. For Dillon's and my relationship. What it would do to my family and how my work would take it. I was barely eating anything. If I wasn't feeling sick, I was sick with worry.

The last two nights I'd been so exhausted from work and keeping busy I'd fallen into bed without waiting to Skype with Dillon. Tonight though I wasn't cooking and I was relaxing with my family so I intended to stay up.

Parking my car in the parking lot of my favorite restaurant, I was running late to meet my family for dinner. I hadn't even been home to change. I was working overtime so when I asked for time off next week my boss wouldn't hesitate. Grabbing my handbag I opened my car door and slowly stood, shut my door took a deep breath in and slowly let it out and then ran into the restaurant. I spotted my brothers and parents in their usual seat and rushed over to them waving at Tiffany, the maître d'.

I stopped in front of the spare seat, and that was when the whole world tilted. I reached for the chair and then as if in slow motion my body felt like a lead weight and everything went black.

****

Dillon
My phone woke me from sleep, and I answered still groggy. "'ello."

"Get your fucking arse to Australia yesterday.

71

Ashlyn is in the hospital." The voice of Tyler, Ashlyn's brother, growled down the line to me.

Bolting upright, any grogginess I felt left me in an instant. "What's wrong?"

"You mean your publicist hasn't told you? Look it up online, dickhead, and then get your arse down here." Without waiting for my reply or to even ask what the hell had happened he hung up.

Worried, I opened the browser on my phone and typed, Ashlyn Dobbs in hospital. A second later all the air went out of me as I read.

Ashlyn Dobbs, the girl who weeks ago was with one of the members of Right Time, was admitted to hospital earlier tonight after multiple reports of her fainting in a restaurant. Sources within the hospital confirm that she has been admitted to the Maternity ward for complications with her pregnancy. In addition, Right Time front-man Dillon Blake has been listed on the hospital forms as the father.

There was more, but I couldn't continue. Pregnant? We'd used condoms every time. Well except for that time in New Orleans. And when her brothers came in on us and... *Yeah, well... Wow.*

I went to Sarah's room and told her what had happened. She was on her phone within seconds, finding out what she could. While she did that I called the tour manager and the band. Once they reached my room where I was packing, I told them what was happening.

"For fuck's sake, Dillon! How could you let this happen?" Phillip had freaked and paced around my room. "We keep the condom supply stocked everywhere we go!"

"I know. We did use them, just not every time." I packed my shit in my bags, stuffing everything as quickly as I could.

"Obviously," Phillip said. "The publicists are trying to do some damage control. When you don't go flying right out to Australia the buzz will die down."

I whirled around. "I beg your pardon? I'm going."

"You have a show tonight. If you cancel you'll be proving these allegations and until you talk to Ashlyn herself, that's all they are. Are you sure the kid's ev—"

"I swear to God, Phillip, I will kick your arse if you finish that sentence. I'm going to Australia. I'm not going to perform when the woman I love and my child are in danger!"

Stunned silence met my declaration. I'd told Ashlyn I loved her, but besides my bodyguards, no one else had heard me say it. I loved Ashlyn, and she was more important to me than all the fame. I resumed packing while Zeck, Alec, and Law, rallied around me and said they could cover for me, that they'd figure out who could sing my parts while I was away.

I don't remember much after that. Sarah couldn't get much more information than I could, just that Ashlyn was in the hospital and they were keeping her. We couldn't get a commercial flight for a while, so I paid for a private plane.

I was at least thankful we weren't at home. Then I'd have been a twenty-three hour flight away. I was still a six hour flight away and those hours felt like triple that when I was worried about Ashlyn. By the time we landed I'd decided that Ashlyn was coming with me when I left Australia again. I was never leaving her behind again.

Only Rick could come with me. I wasn't worried though, I would be safe in the hospital, and I knew Ashlyn's brothers would be around if I had any trouble. Rick drove the SUV that was hired and we picked up at the airport.

So almost ten hours after the phone call we

approached the hospital entrance, which was surrounded by police and media. Rick suggested we call security and find an alternate way in, but right now I didn't care about fans or my image. All I cared about was getting to Ashlyn.

Inside I went straight to the information desk. "'ello. I'm looking for Ashlyn Dobbs. I was given this room number." I showed her the paper with the room number. I watched the exact moment the woman behind the desk recognized me. She let out a little squeal before composing herself and giving me the directions. At this point Rick and Sarah had caught up with me, and we made our way there. I saw her brothers first and then her parents, but I didn't stop to listen to them. I opened the door and walked right into the room. The room held two beds. I saw a woman asleep in one bed and the curtain drawn on the other side. Moving the curtains I pulled them back and froze at the sight before me.

Ashlyn lay in the hospital bed, a drip in one arm and looking not just tired, but exhausted. Her eyes held big black bags under them, and her skin looked so white it seemed almost translucent.

"What the hell happened, lov'?" I choked out. I wasn't a guy who cried, but seeing the woman I loved like this I was seriously close.

"Is this the father?" The voice had me looking up from Ashlyn to see two people, a man in his mid-fifties in a suit, and a nurse. The suit guy must be the doctor. It would explain why her parents and brother were waiting out of the room. The doctor held charts, and the nurse held a couple of devices.

I darted my gaze back to Ashlyn in time to see her nod her head, close her eyes and whisper, "Yes."

Well what do you know? The media was right for once. I'd knocked up Ashlyn. I probably should have been freaked out about this, but oddly enough I wasn't. I just wanted Ashlyn and my baby to be safe. "Listen, doctor, I don't know how you usually run a hospital, but somehow the media knows exactly what's happened and where she is. You have a leak. I'm telling you to speak to the head of whatever department deals with this stuff because my lawyers will be getting in contact with yours. If any more private information turns up I'll make sure you're looking for new jobs. Do I make myself clear?" I glanced at Ashlyn to see she was looking at me and not the doctor and nurse.

The doctor studied me for a while before he gave a sharp nod. "I'm sorry, Mr.—"

"Blake. Dillon Blake."

The nurse gasped and nodded. "I'll talk to the head of the department, Mr. Blake. I apologize," the doctor said.

"Great. Now could you please tell me what the hell happened?"

The doctor looked to Ashlyn, and I watched her nod to him. "Mr. Blake, I'm Dr. Hinton. Miss Dobbs came to us as she collapsed twelve hours ago from dehydration. She has hyperemesis gravidarum. It's severe nausea and vomiting, which results in weight loss. Dehydration is common, along with low blood sugar and fainting. A lot of women who have this are admitted for fluids and help with keeping on top of it. Usually this eases around week twenty. In some pregnancies it can be earlier, and some women have it the whole pregnancy. Miss Dobbs is about ten weeks so that gives you another ten, if this eases at twenty weeks. Let's hope she doesn't have it the whole pregnancy."

I nodded, because my head felt like it was about to explode. I looked at Ashlyn, and I knew I wasn't leaving her. I'd never been so scared in my whole life when I got the call she was in the hospital. Now I thought about it, if she was going to come to the hospital for anything, her being pregnant was good. It was something I could handle. *Ha. Weird.* The thought of Ashlyn pregnant didn't scare me.

Ashlyn was staring at me strangely like she was searching, or waiting for me to do something. I listened to the doctor say they were going to keep her another night to get her fluids up and see if they could find a nausea tablet that would work for her.

"Okay. I'll be here," I said when the doctor finished talking.

"Nice to meet you, Mr. Blake. I'll be back tomorrow around the same time and we can see how you're doing, Miss Dobbs. If you've improved I'll let you go home."

Ashlyn mumbled, "Thank you, Dr. Hinton."

Dr. Hinton smiled down at me and then turned to the nurse. "Rhonda here is going to listen to the baby on the fetal Doppler."

I stood and shook the doctor's hand before he left. When I turned back to Ashlyn the hospital gown was pulled up and I could see Ashlyn's black cotton panties. Rhonda the nurse was over her and squirted blue liquid on her stomach. Ashlyn didn't look pregnant. Her stomach was still flat. Now that I saw her stomach I could see she actually looked even thinner than she had the last I saw her.

Frowning, I gazed at her face. She wasn't looking at me. She was staring at Rhonda. I wanted to ask her why she hadn't told me. Why she hadn't gotten help. Why she'd lost weight when she was pregnant and should be gaining it. I knew the doctor said she had a condition, but... All my train of thought stopped as soon as I heard it. It was like a fast whooshing noise. I held my breath so

I could hear better and the beating became clear. *Wow.* That was my baby's heartbeat. Letting out my breath slowly, I listened to the most amazing sound I'd ever heard. Reaching over I intertwined my fingers with Ashlyn's.

"Thank you," I whispered. The tear-filled smile Ashlyn sent my way had me standing to kiss her tears away. "Don't cry. Listen to that little miracle we made." I must have said the wrong thing because she burst into tears. Panicking that she would make herself sicker, I darted my gaze over to Rhonda with a pleading look for help.

Rhonda smiled my way. "It can be very emotional hearing your baby for the first time. She's already on hormonal overload being pregnant."

"Oh." I had no idea what I was supposed to say or do. "Yeah." I looked at the Doppler thingie and wondered if I could get one so Ashlyn and I could hear the baby anytime we wanted. "Is there somewhere I can get one of those?" Squeezing Ashlyn's hand, I gazed at the Doppler thingie.

"Yes, you can buy a good fetal Doppler for about a hundred dollars or so."

"Great. I think that will be the first thing I buy."

Rhonda laughed and cleaned the blue gel off of Ashlyn. She went and checked Ashlyn's drip and then smiled down at Ashlyn. "I'll be back in a couple of hours to do your blood pressure and see if the anti-nausea drugs are working. Everything sounds good with baby."

"Thank you." Ashlyn gave Rhonda a stiff smile.

Rhonda nodded and smiled at me. "It's nice to meet you, Mr. Blake."

"Nice to meet you, too, Rhonda. Thank you for letting me hear my child."

"You're very welcome." Rhonda looked at

Ashlyn. "Do you want me to let your family in when I leave?"

"No," I said before Ashlyn could reply. "I'll let them in soon. I want to have a moment with Ashlyn."

Rhonda stared at Ashlyn until she got a nod from her. Then we both watched Rhonda as she gathered her things and left.

We were quiet and didn't say anything. I noticed that her gown hadn't been pulled down so I gently pulled it down before I broke the silence. "Ashlyn, do you have something to tell me?" I dragged my gaze from her belly and stared at her tear streaked face.

"I'm pregnant," she mumbled.

I felt it in my chest, and then it spread through me, a laugh so deep I felt like I'd fall off the chair. Was I not just in the room when the doctor was here? Did I not just hear my baby? "Why didn't you tell me?" I burst out between fits of laughter.

She eased up on the bed, and I watched as she crossed her arms over her chest and my gaze widened as I saw how big her tits had gotten. I thought they'd grown the last time I was with her, but they were huge now. Damn, I was a lucky man. "You're not going to even ask if it is yours or not?"

What the fuck? I stopped laughing. It hadn't even crossed my mind that the baby Ashlyn was carrying might not be mine. From the time I'd spent with her and what I knew of Ashlyn, she wasn't one to jump from man to man. The baby was mine, just like the mother. "I'm not even going to answer that stupid question. You silly woman." Getting off the chair I carefully moved myself onto the bed and hugged her. "I know this is all happening so fast, but you know I love you and I am actually kind of happy about the baby. Well not kind of. I am. When I got that phone call that you were in the hospital, I've never been so afraid in my life. All I could think of was I was never leaving you behind again. I love you so much and I know you think we're moving fast, but I'd marry you tomorrow if—"

"Yes," she interrupted me.

"What did you say?" What was she saying yes to? Did she just agree to marry me? My chest hurt, and I was sure it was because my heart was about to beat right out of me.

"I said yes."

"To what?" I held my breath in anticipation.

She closed her eyes and I watched her take a deep breath in and slowly let it out before she opened her eyes. "Yes. Yes, I'll marry you."

Chapter Eight

Ashlyn
Vanuatu

I groaned as I heaved myself up off the lounge chair on the beach in Vanuatu. I had to go help my husband from my brothers. *Whoa, that sounded weird to say.* Husband. Two days ago, I had married Dillon in a small ceremony on a little island resort in Vanuatu. I was twenty-two weeks pregnant. My hyperemesis gravidarum had eased, and I was cleared for travel.

Dillon had paid for my family and a couple of close friends to come, and his own family was here. All of his band-mates were here and even the dancers. I was nervous to meet his family, but his mother was so nice and I loved her almost instantly. She was so excited for the baby. I knew she would be an enormous help. Dillon's little brother was an even bigger flirt than Dillon.

I made my way over to the football match that was supposed to be tag, no tackles, but thanks to my brothers that rule was out. This was the third time I'd watched them tackle Dillon to the ground. I knew my brothers weren't really hurting him. They never would, but they did take their play wrestling a little too far. I was sure Dillon's bodyguards, who were on his team, were really in cahoots with my brothers. Although, when Dillon's brother joined in they were almost even with tackling each other. My parents were off on a tour with Dillon's parents today so they weren't here to help control my brothers. Dillon's band-mates weren't any help either. They thought how my brothers acted toward Dillon was hilarious.

"Get off my husband right this minute. If I have to grab you I will make sure Mum and Dad find out the stress you've put me through." One thing my doctor had said was to keep my stress levels low, so I was using that to my advantage. It was the only thing that got my brothers to leave Dillon alone. Well that and the threat of Mum and Dad.

Torrance and Tyler both grumbled, but they got off Dillon. I couldn't help the giggle that slipped free when I saw Dillon. His hair was sticking up on every end. His bare chest was red and his shorts were ripped and he looked dazed. Dillon staggered as he got up, and I watched him stand still until his balance came back.

Going to him I wrapped my arms around him and hugged him. He must really love me to put up with my brothers. My belly rubbed his bare chest.

"Mmm, I lov' you." His lips brushed my forehead. His hands came down and rubbed over my bump. I felt the flutter and a kick. The baby loved their daddy's voice.

"I love you, too," I said before I kissed him. He kissed me back until our baby gave another tumble kick.

At the movement of our baby Dillon kneeled in the sand and kissed my stomach. "Daddy lov's you, too, my Bean."

I groaned at the name he'd given our baby. On the first ultrasound I'd had only a couple of days after I got out of the hospital, Dillon saw the baby on the monitor and thought it looked like a bean. So now he called it Bean. Even in our last ultrasound at nineteen weeks he still didn't change it from Bean. We'd opted for a surprise instead of finding out the sex.

Gazing down into the eyes of the man I loved, I fell more in love. Dillon was nothing like what I ever expected. He was always more. Instead of going back on tour Dillon had stayed with me. Even when the record label called he didn't cave under pressure. I was surprised and grateful when his band members backed him up going as far to say they wouldn't sing together without Dillon. The tour was postponed. The fans were crazy and we'd had to double security, but Right Time promised extra shows when they reorganized the tour and to the people who'd had tickets, preference of the day they wanted of the two shows in each city.

Dillon got up, and he wrapped his arms around me. "You're amazing," he whispered against my ear as his hands rubbed my tummy.

Looking up at him I smiled. "No, you are. I love you so much. You surprised me. I never expected you. When I met you all those months ago I never thought I would have this with you. I never even expected this of you when we started our relationship. I didn't know this kind of chemistry existed. Every day I find something to make me love you more. You've risked your career for me."

He shrugged. "I'd do it again to have this."

I snuggled into him. He turned us so we gazed out into the beautiful ocean. "I know you would. If last year someone would have said I would be married to Dillon Blake and pregnant with his baby, I would have laughed in their face. For some crazy reason I thought you weren't my type."

He chuckled. "I'm everyone's type." I rolled my eyes and giggled. He replied by giving a dramatic sigh. "Is it sad that I can't see you but I know you just rolled your eyes?" He palmed my arse. "You're so bad for my ego."

This time I laughed. "Yes. And you need me to deflate your ego so I don't have to push your head through doors."

Dillon sighed again. His hands came around to rest on my belly. "Do you hear how your mother treats me, Bean? She's lucky I know she loves me and thinks

I'm the hottest man ever."

I did love him, and it was times like this I realized why. Because he made me laugh and beyond happy. He turned my world upside down, but even with crazy fans, bodyguards, and a demanding record label I wouldn't change our lives. I had a wonderful family and friends and a man that I loved more than anything.

Squeezing Dillon's waist I smiled up at him. "Let's go to our villa, and I'll show you just how hot I think you are." I winked and let him go, running the best I could towards our villa on the water. I didn't get far before Dillon scooped me up into his arms and carried me towards our villa. I knew in that moment that I didn't need anything else. Snuggling into him I felt safe, loved and blessed.

Epilogue

Dillon

"She's just been fed and changed, so she won't need anything to drink for at least another four hours." Ashlyn gazed down at our three month old baby girl, Grace, and then groaned. "Who am I kidding? Your daughter is a little piggy."

I smiled and looked at my daughter in my arms. She was a chubby thing, and could be my clone if she wasn't a girl. She was staring up at me with a milk-drunk, dazed look on her adorable face. She even had some milk leaking from the sides of her mouth. I brought the bib up and gently wiped each side. Then I looked back up at my wife, Ashlyn. Her hair was in a messy bun and falling out, her eyes had dark black circles under them, and her top had milk stains, two very noticeable ones, right over her breasts. She was wearing a pair of my boxer shorts and pink socks. I couldn't remember her ever looking so beautiful.

"Grr, don't look at me like that. That look is what got me looking like this." She waved her hand over at Grace and then down at herself.

I shrugged. "You look hot. I have ten minutes before I have to leave. What say I put her in her bed and we go—"

"Argh, don't you finish that, Dillon." Ashlyn huffed, turned, and went to the fridge. She got out a bottle and then a bottle cooler. "Here is some milk I expressed. I was saving it for tonight so we could go out after I come home from work, but sleeping more than three hours will be like heaven and way better. I know your daughter won't go three hours without being fed, but knowing your luck and what a daddy's girl she is I wouldn't put it past her to sleep four or five hours straight, just for you."

I didn't understand why she wouldn't take the help I'd offered a million times. She didn't want a nanny though, even for when she worked. The band members and their partners helped look after Grace, for a couple of hours while Ashlyn worked. I'd suggested a part time nanny, but Ashlyn didn't trust many people with Grace. I smirked as I peeked into the baby bag pretending to check I had everything so Ashlyn didn't see my grin. Technically Ashlyn did have a nanny. She just didn't know that was Issy's official job title. Ashlyn was so adamant on wanting to raise our daughter, and I would do anything for my woman, so I wasn't going to tell her. She already complained about how guilty she felt for leaving Grace for a couple of hours a week to work for the charity we'd created that helped children with speech difficulties. I awoke at night and got up to help, but Ashlyn just shooed me back to bed. "You work more than me. I don't want you looking tired and me getting the blame." I knew I should argue with her, especially since she worked hard, too, but she wanted to do it all, and I was happy to keep the peace. I did help in any way I could, even if that meant taking Grace some mornings so Ashlyn could sleep before she went to work.

My girls were my whole world. I would do anything to make them happy. I loved them more than anything and I couldn't believe how lucky I had gotten to be blessed with them.

****

The interviews for the day were about to start and the first interviewer, a tall leggy blonde, walked in and as soon as her gaze landed on me with Grace in my arms her eyes lit up like she'd just been given the biggest prize. "So cute," she cooed.

Zeck, who sat next to me, elbowed my side. I looked at him and saw him wink. "Why thanks. You're

85

not the first woman to say that."

The woman gave a fake laugh and then introduced herself as some music program presenter. She sat in the chair opposite us.

Grace's stroller was beside me, but she wasn't in it. She was asleep in her favorite spot, cradled in my arms. The band's media team hadn't batted an eyelid when I came into the room that the interviews were being held in today with Grace. She'd become a little crew mascot. They were surprised though when I said she was spending the whole morning with me, while Ashlyn caught up on some much needed sleep.

"Dillon, the rumors are running rampant about you leaving the group. They say you're going to become a full time dad." She looked down to Grace. "They're true?

I resisted the urge to roll my eyes. Since the world found out about the pregnancy there had been one rumor after the other. They got worse when I married Ashlyn. Since Grace had been born there'd been a new one each week.

The guys laughed. They knew I had no intention of leaving the group. I was happier than I'd ever been, and in the last month had even tried my hand at writing some of our songs.

"As much as I lov' my little saving Grace, I'll leave her mummy to be the primary career. So to set the rumors straight I am not now, or in the near future leaving the group. I lov' my wife. She is amazing and supports me in all I do. Grace is here today so my beautiful wife can catch up on some much deserved sleep. So as to another rumor I'm happy to set straight, I am happily married and more than adore my wife. I mean, look at the awesome gift she gave me. Isn't she just the most perfect baby you've ever seen?" I smile at the woman. "Ashlyn is not only an amazing mother, but the work she does with our charity, Learn to Communicate, makes her my hero, and I'm very blessed to call her my wife."

The interviewer sighed, and Zeck chuckled beside me and whispered, "Good one, bro. When the rest of the female population sees this interview, they'll fall even more in love with you and envy Ashlyn."

There was only one woman whose opinion mattered to me. I knew I was one lucky guy. I had a career only people dreamed of, great friends, an amazing family, and a super-hot wife who was beyond incredible and to top it off, I now had a gorgeous daughter. Yep. Luckiest guy in the world.

The End

www.hazelgower.com

FOUR BOOK COLLECTION

DEDICATION

As I wrote this story, Paris was attacked by terrorists. Innocent people attending the Eagles of Death Metal concert were murdered as they waited for the show to start. I'm dedicating this book to all those families who were affected by the horrific attacks on Friday the 13th, November 2015. #PrayersForParis

ZECK

Scandals, 2

Khloe Wren

Copyright © 2016

Chapter One

Zeck

Loud screams echoed behind me as I followed my band-mates down the hall to our backstage room. My blood still raced with the rush of performing and being able to interact with our fans. I let out a whoop. Our first show here in Paris was now over, and it had been awesome.

"Man, you crack me up every time. Never know what you're going to do."

I grinned at Law and did my stupid drunk dance through the doorway.

"What can I say? The crowd loves me!"

We all laughed and fell into chairs around the room. Except Dillon. He bee-lined for his girl. Like a magnet, my gaze followed him despite the fact I knew precisely what he was going to do. The way he caressed his palm over Ashlyn's swollen belly before leaning down to kiss her had my stomach twisting. I wasn't sure why. At twenty-three years old I was in my prime. I had no desire to settle down. Too much to see and do for that. But there was something about the intimacy, the bond they had that called to me.

"Zeck? Come with me for moment."

"Sure, Jas."

I rose to my feet, grateful for the distraction. I was struggling to hold onto my carefree facade in front of my friends tonight. Jasko, or Jas for short, was Right Time's head of security. He was Russian and as big as a fucking truck. His English was fortunately fairly good, but occasionally his accent would strengthen and make it hard to understand what he was trying to say. Knowing he wouldn't pull me away from the others without a good reason, I followed him intrigued over what he could want.

"What's up, big guy?"

Jas led me to a smaller room the band wasn't using, before closing the door.

"You look on edge tonight. I wanted to ask you some question."

I crossed my arms over my chest, nervous that he'd noticed my inner turmoil.

"I just have some excess energy to burn. We haven't been clowning around that much lately."

Not only was Dillon spending all his spare time with his new wife, but Alec was quieter and less energetic. I guessed that, like me, watching Dillon with Ashlyn stirred up Alec's inner desires. Law was no better, although I hadn't been able to work out why he was suddenly acting so serious most of the time. On top of all that, we'd been flying all over the damn place with this tour. Down time hadn't happened since our brief break for Dillon and Ashlyn's wedding.

The big man nodded, then rubbed his jaw.

"I know you like to laugh and joke, but underneath you are thoughtful. You observe around you, help anyone you can. You are caretaker, yes?"

I shrugged a shoulder as embarrassment heated

my cheeks. I liked to know everyone who I cared about was happy and safe. Was that a crime?

"I guess you could call me that. I know I'm lucky, that I have more than I deserve so I'm happy to share it around. I didn't think management had an issue with it."

While we'd been in Sydney, I'd ordered dozens of pizzas before driving around and giving them out to the homeless I found. Phillip, our manager, had said it was great publicity and humanized me. Whatever the hell that meant. I just wanted to help out. Feed a few hungry people. No big deal.

"You don't much like management controlling you, do you?"

"Jas, we've been touring all bloody year. You know all of us are over being told what to do and where to be."

I swallowed past a lump that had formed in my throat when I noticed the muscle along Jas's jaw begin to tick as if he was clenching and unclenching it.

"When you take lover, you like to control her, yes?"

My head snapped up, and anger flashed through me.

"Where are you going with this? I don't kiss and tell, you know that."

He grinned at me, a big stupid "gotcha" grin.

"Tonight we go to a special club. One I think you like."

I'd already been planning on heading out with the boys. I was hoping I could pick up a *chipie* for some relief.

"All of us, or just me and you?"

"Me and you. Other boys are not like you and me."

I had no idea what he was talking about so fell

93

back on humor like I always did.

"Well, so long as there's plenty of women there, I'm a happy man, Jas."

"I promise there will be women."

There was something about the glint in his eye that made me nervous.

"Ah, okay so when are we going and what should I wear?"

What I was wearing was damp with sweat from running around on stage, so I'd definitely need to change.

"I have it arranged. We go to hotel now, shower and change. Then we go."

****

"Where are we going again? And are the leather pants really necessary?"

As I asked Jas, I attempted once more to rearrange myself in the confines of the rear of the car. I'd checked in the mirror before we left and I knew they looked fucking spectacular, but damn they were restrictive on a man when it came to sitting down. I eyed the big man sitting beside me. Jasko looked completely comfortable in his own leathers. Like me, he wore a tight fitted black tank that did nothing to hide the massive amount of muscle the man was packing.

"Every man wears leather here. You get used to it soon."

The sleek town car pulled up smoothly in front of a bland looking stone building on the outskirts of downtown Paris. Jas got out and moved to my side of the car. With a nervous inhale, I ran my palms over my head, making sure my hair was still neatly pulled back in the elastic tie. I pulled off my glasses and cleaned them before resettling them in place. My skin tingled with unease. I hated having to disguise myself every time I went out. Tonight I'd taken it easy, with only the stupid fake glasses and my shoulder length hair tied up. The evening was warm and I couldn't be screwed mucking around with a wig that was only going to make me itch and uncomfortable all night. I hoped it was enough. The last thing I wanted was to get recognized at whatever this place was. I didn't feel like handling a mob of fans at the moment. Not with my mind reeling from what Jas had said. Was I really that transparent?

The door opened, and a rush of cold air flowed over me as I rose from the vehicle. Out of habit, I held my breath, waiting for the screams to start.

"Private club. No fans here. You regular tourist here."

I raised a brow at Jas. "Seriously? Not sure that's possible no matter how private the place is. But hey, I've got the toughest man in the city with me, so I'm all good no matter what happens."

Jas's shoulders straightened, and he smirked at me. I was pretty sure Jas knew I was just yanking his chain, but whatever. If it made him smile, it was all good. A horrible thought crept into my mind.

"This isn't some kind of joke is it? There *are* women in here?"

So help me if Jas had brought me to a gay club ... because if he had, he so had the wrong band member! While I have nothing against homosexuals, I wasn't one. And tonight I really could use some female company. Jas didn't answer me, but pushed open the door and ushered me through it. Heavy bass thumped through the walls of the small reception area. Jas strolled over to an expensive looking desk. The woman standing next to it froze my breath. She was a timid looking thing, dressed for sex in a purple corset and black leather mini skirt. I took a deep breath. This was definitely not a gay club.

Jas leaned in and spoke directly into the woman's

ear, and I smiled as the girl's eyes widened and her gaze zoomed in on me. She nodded at whatever Jas said, and before I knew it we were on our way down a flight of stairs to the basement.

Ducking through a dark red curtain, I found myself in another world. I stood still and blinked as my eyes adjusted to the dimly lit club. My spine straightened when they focused. There were women and a few men bound to benches and crosses, or kneeling at another's feet.

"Jas? How'd you know this place was here?"

"How you think?"

Before he could explain more a tall, curvy woman strolled straight up to him. I stood mesmerized as she gracefully fell to her knees in front of the Russian.

"Evening, Sir. How may I serve you?"

A grin curved my lips as excitement buzzed through my veins. Jas was a fucking Dom, and he'd brought me to a kink club. I wasn't so naive to have never heard of BDSM. After overhearing my sister wax poetic over some book she'd read, I'd secretly borrowed it from her to see what all the fuss was about. My curiosity was piqued, but I hadn't taken it further. I could just imagine what Phillip, our manager, would do if I was caught whipping some chick. It would make Dillon knocking up Ashlyn seem droll.

I chuckled when the woman preened and purred as Jas ran a hand over her head.

"Rise, *myshka*."

As the woman rose, I spoke to Jas.

"What did you just call her?"

"Little mouse. Endearment in Russian."

A soft smile formed on her face. Apparently, she liked the name.

"Follow me."

I had no idea if Jas was talking to me or his little mouse, but I didn't know what else to do so I followed him over to a couple of low couches surrounded by large floor cushions.

"Sit, Zeck. Observe for while."

He whispered into the woman's ear, and she trotted off toward the bar as I sat down.

"You've been here before haven't you?"

"Paris is not so far from England. Whenever in town I come. Jane is American, so she like Dom who speak English."

I had to laugh.

"But dude, you're Russian!"

With a low chuckle, he shrugged.

"She like Russian accent."

Jane returned with two beers and handed us one each. As I took my first mouthful, she lowered to her knees again and leaned against Jas's leg. Jas started up with the petting thing he'd done earlier, and Jane's body relaxed as she sighed. Pulling my focus away from her I glanced around the large space to see what else was going on. My attention caught on a beautiful, lush woman wearing only a lacy blue g-string over her curvy body being tied up. Her Dom was wrapping golden rope, which matched her hair color, around her nude body with precise movements and tying knots faster than a Boy Scout could. Her arms were behind her back and her large round breasts were thrust out as her Dom framed them with the rope. I moved my pelvis trying to give my dick more room. Damn, but that woman was hot. My mouth watered as I imagined what it would be like to suckle on her pretty pink nipples.

"Evening, gentlemen. Welcome back, Jas. I see you brought a guest tonight. Mind if I join you for a while?"

My mind cleared of lust, and I focused on the newcomer. I was a little stunned at the man's flawless English. He had only a slight accent. He was clearly French, but at a guess he'd spent at least a couple of years in the UK, or maybe the US.

"Of course. As we discussed, I brought Krys to come see if he like."

I smiled as Jas called me by my middle name. Another part of the disguise. The man let rip with a loud burst of laughter.

"I've missed your sense of humor, Jas. My club is filled with beautiful submissives being pleasured by their Doms. What's not to like, my friend?"

Smirking, I relaxed into my seat, instantly liking the club owner.

"It's a great looking club you have. What do I call you?"

I didn't want to break any Dom code or anything. I already liked the look of this place and really didn't want to get booted out the door.

"My name is Brian, but mostly I am called Monsieur here. So, you think this is something you'd like to learn more about?"

"Definitely. To be honest I'd gotten interested in BDSM a year or so ago but didn't want to risk the publicity of looking into it."

Brian nodded toward me.

"That I can understand. My club here is exclusive and private. Everything that happens beneath my roof is consensual, and there is also a no camera rule, which includes phones. Anyone caught breaking either of those rules is banned instantly."

My muscles relaxed in relief. This place sounded like heaven. It also explained why Jas had me leave my phone in the car earlier.

"No cameras sounds great. I might never leave."

I grinned over at the owner.

"If you would like to come back regularly, I'll need you to fill out some paperwork, but for tonight you're here as Jas's guest and I'm sure you'll behave yourself. Is there anything you've seen so far that has caught your eye?

I focused back on the scene I'd been watching earlier.

"I rather like the look of the rope stuff."

Brian chuckled. "That's called shibari, not rope stuff. What's your schedule like? Will you be able to make it in again before you leave town?"

I rubbed the back of my neck.

"So long as I can come in late, I'm good any night this week."

He gave me a nod of understanding, and I was grateful Jas had obviously explained to him who I was already.

"Tomorrow night then. Come back and I'll have a training session set up for you. I would offer you a place in our Dom training program, but you won't be staying that long. I'm sure Jas will be able to find you somewhere closer to home to train."

"Thanks, Brian. I certainly hope so. And I'm already looking forward to tomorrow night."

It was the truth. I was intrigued by everything that was going on around me, and that sweet little thing getting trussed up across the room still had my body hard and aching.

"Will the demonstration be on the same girl?"

Brian gave me a knowing smile.

"I shall request young Isobel join us for the session. I'm sure she'll agree. Little Issy loves being in the firm hold of ropes."

With satisfaction I leaned back in the seat and watched as little Issy got herself well and truly tied in knots across the room. Tomorrow night it would be knots I helped to tie that would bind her beautiful form. My dick kicked against the fly of my leathers. Yeah, shibari was definitely my kind of kink.

****

Issy

I slipped into the girls' change room and cringed. Monique was running her mouth again. I was going to miss a lot of things about France. Bitching little Monique was not one of them. It was thoughts of never having to see Monique again that would keep me from overstaying my visa.

After nearly a full year in Paris my nannying job was over, and I was left with a few precious weeks before I had to return home to Australia. I frowned at my locker. I knew the moment I got home I had some decisions to make. Shaking my head, I pushed it all aside. I wouldn't let worries over the future taint my night.

"I'm telling you, it was Zeck from Right Time. Monsieur Brian and Monsieur Jas were sitting with him last night. And Jane. Where is she? She was all over Monsieur Jas, as per usual."

Jane had been beyond excited last night. She adored Jas, especially his accent. I had to agree with her that when it deepened to his Dom drawl, it was pretty damn sexy.

I faced Monique. "That guy had glasses on. Zeck doesn't wear them."

I wasn't a huge fan, but I watched TV. I knew who Right Time was and that they were currently playing in Paris. Monique rolled her eyes at me as she zipped up her mini skirt, which barely covered her ass.

"Oh, of course he tried to disguise himself! But

I'd know that tattoo anywhere."

I thought back to the man Monique was talking about as I opened my locker and dumped my bag inside. A small sigh escaped my throat. He had been totally dreamy, with his dark hair pulled back into a sleek low ponytail. I hadn't thought the glasses looked right on his handsome face, but the leather pants sure as hell did. He'd worn a tight black tank that revealed his gloriously muscled biceps. Of course I noticed. I'd always had a thing for bulging biceps on a man. An intricate tattoo had curved around one arm and up under his shirt. A massive oriental dragon. *Just like the one Zeck from Right Time has.*

"Get over it, Monique. I doubt he'll be back, and even if he does, this is a private club. You can't go fangirling the man like some groupie at a concert."

I gripped the edge of my locker tightly to prevent clapping in applause as an older submissive dressed Monique down.

Monique responded predictably with a mouthful of creative French cursing I couldn't quite translate … not that I needed to. I focused on getting myself dressed for the evening. Monsieur Brian had called me this morning to ask if I'd be happy to be used to teach a new Dom shibari later tonight. Naturally, I said yes. Monsieur Brian was an expert with rope, and any submissive would do just about anything to be the one he tied up.

"How you doing tonight, Issy?"

I gasped and pressed a hand over my heart.

"You have to stop sneaking up on me like that, woman!"

I looked up at the beautiful Domme leaning beside her locker.

"Good thing we're not out on the floor, doll, or I'd have you over a bench for that."

I rolled my eyes and smirked at Raine.

"You love my cheekiness, admit it."

"Only because you make it look so adorable. The Australian accent helps, too. You still sure you don't swing my way?"

Heat bloomed over my cheeks. No matter how many times females hit on me, I always flushed.

"Sorry, still straight as an arrow."

"Ah, well, can't blame a girl for trying."

Smoothing out my mini dress I turned my back on Raine.

"Zip me up?"

Naturally, she ran her fingers up my spine first causing a soft sigh to escape. Her touch really was lovely. I'd been coming to the club for six months and had gone through their training program for new submissives. At the beginning I'd struggled with how comfortable everyone was being naked in front of each other. But over time, I'd discovered this lifestyle attracted all sorts. Not just young and thin, but all ages and shapes. It made me feel a lot better about showing my rounded curves occasionally. Which, with how much I loved shibari, was a good thing. It seemed like I was always flashing my boobs in the club. Good thing policy said I had to wear a g-string out on the floor. The private rooms were a different story. I frowned as I wondered if Monsieur Brian would want to give me aftercare in one of those rooms tonight. I loved being tied up, but I didn't have sex with every Dom that touched me. I was extremely picky with who I gave that privilege to.

"Such soft skin, doll. Monsieur Brian called you today, yes?"

My body started heating with arousal as the zipper slid up slowly.

"Yep, he's demonstrating on me tonight."

Raine's breath caressed my ear as she leaned in.

"Monique may be full of shit most of the time, but she's on the mark this time. Monsieur Brian is trussing you up for none other than Zeck from Right Time."

The whispered words landed in my stomach like a rock.

"Shit."

I let my head drop forward as my blood cooled. This was the last thing I needed. Monique would no doubt see me and make my life hell until I left the country.

"Dammit, I should have said no."

Raine gripped my shoulders and spun me around to face her.

"No, you should have said yes, just like you did. Every submissive here could have said no and Monique still wouldn't have been asked. She's only here because her big sister is dating Monsieur Brian's brother. We all tolerate her, but don't think we're all not keeping an eye on her. The first time she pushes things too far, she'll be out on her perky little ass."

I begged for Raine to understand with my gaze.

"She's going to give me hell every second I'm at the club after this. You know she will."

Raine tweaked my nose, and I wriggled it to ease the tingle she'd created.

"Have a little faith, doll. You, everyone likes. No one is going to let you get hassled. Now, I get to spend a couple of hours with you until Monsieur Brian's guest arrives."

I gave her one last pleading look, which only earned me a smirk. I squeaked when as I walked beside Raine, she spanked my ass. Laughing, she placed a hand on the nape of my neck and gently led me out into the main area of the club.

Two hours later, Raine led me over to Monsieur Brian's station. The closer I got, the faster my heart beat. My mouth went dry when it dawned on me that I was about to get stripped down to my knickers in front of a world famous singer. I began to tremble. I couldn't do this. Why on earth had I said yes?

"Relax, doll. You're safe. He's like any other man here. Focus on the rope," Raine whispered into my ear then kissed my cheek.

"Monsieur Brian, your submissive as you requested."

"Thank you, Madame Raine, and thank you for taking such good care of her tonight. Issy, you look ravishing as always."

As I'd been trained, the moment Madame Raine removed her hand, I smoothly glided to my knees to kneel in front of Monsieur Brian. *Focus.* I needed to simply keep my focus away from the superstar on my right. *Rope.* That's what tonight was about. The freedom and high I felt when I was enveloped by soft lengths of rope. With a deep breath, I smiled and allowed my shoulders to slump as the tension left me.

****

Zeck

She gracefully dropped to her knees, and my breath hitched. My skin had begun tingling with anticipation the moment I saw her moving across the floor toward me. She was bloody stunning. As I discreetly rearranged my erection with the heel of my palm, I wondered how long her hair would be if it wasn't pinned up like it was. My fingers twitched with the thought of how soft it would feel to bury my hand in the golden lengths.

"This is Issy. She's Australian, so we can easily do this session in English. With safewords, we use the traffic light system here. If Issy says red, you stop and free her as fast as possible. Yellow, you need to stop and discuss what the issue is before continuing and green means she's fine. Understand?"

I nodded, my mouth suddenly too dry to speak. I'd never had lust hit me this hard and the woman was still dressed!

"Rise and turn around, pet."

Crossing my arms over my chest, I frowned when she trembled. Was she afraid?

"Don't worry yourself. She's merely nervous. Everyone here at the club is here voluntarily, and as I said last night, everything is consensual. Issy? Where are we?"

"Green, Monsieur."

Brian turned her to face me, and I found myself staring into piercing green eyes. Recognition flared in her irises, and I knew she'd worked out who I was. I held my breath waiting for her to start screaming as disappointment swamped me. I'd had high hopes for this club. I'd thought I'd found somewhere I could be just another man.

"Good evening, Monsieur. It's a pleasure to be at your service tonight."

I cocked my head, struck silent for a moment. Had she not recognized me after all? And that voice. Her Australian accent had all my blood heading south, as she spoke in a husky sexy drawl I'd never get tired of hearing.

"Thank you, Issy. I'm so glad you said yes to tonight."

Her eyes widened, and her mouth dropped open. Brian started chuckling.

"Yes, pet. He asked specifically for you. You made quite the impression on him last night with your and Monsieur Pierre's shibari scene."

A peaceful look flowed over her face and her body loosened at the reminder. If the memory of a scene could do that, how would she react once she was trussed up tonight?

"Let's get started. Issy, present yourself."

"If you would please unzip my dress, Monsieur. I can't reach the zipper."

The big Dom nodded with a kind smile. "Of course, pet. It is a beautiful dress, but your skin looks so exquisite bound in rope, I don't want anything in the way. But I won't be doing it. Monsieur Krys? Would you move in behind Issy and help her undress, please?"

My lips quirked at Brian using my middle name. I wasn't used to it, so I'd have to make sure I paid attention for it tonight. My heart rate picked up as I moved faster than I ever had. Standing inches from her, I inhaled deeply, taking in her sweet floral scent. My fingers trembled as I gripped her small zipper tab. Slowly I slid it down, the sides of the pretty green dress split open revealing pale perfection. Lifting up my other hand I trailed my fingers down her spine. She didn't move, but I felt the shiver that ran through her and it had my heart racing. I clenched my jaw when I pushed the material over her fleshy hips. Emerald green lace flowed around her waist and disappeared between the lush smooth cheeks of her ass. I moved back as she stepped out of the material pooled around her ankles. I groaned and nearly swallowed my tongue when she bent over to collect the dress. Damn, but she had the finest ass I'd ever seen.

"Enjoying the view, Monsieur Krys?"

"You know I am."

"Tell her what you're thinking. A big part of this lifestyle is communication, voicing our wants and desires. I do believe sweet Issy would enjoy hearing your opinion on her derriere."

I cleared my throat a couple of times. I was used to joking my way through whenever I felt at all awkward, but I couldn't now. I knew a joke in this moment would destroy this beautiful creature before me. And that was the last thing I wanted.

"Baby, you have the sexiest arse I've ever seen and I'm barely holding back from finding out if it's as soft as it looks."

A dark chuckle came from Brian as Issy carefully folded the dress before she placed it on a nearby chair.

"Thank you, Monsieur."

Her face was lowered, but I caught the slight blush over her cheeks as she turned to move back to stand in front of Brian.

"You'll find out soon enough."

Ignoring the promise in Brian's words, I folded my arms across my chest once again to keep from reaching out for her as I took in her posture. She looked so sensual standing in her underwear. Her feet were shoulder width apart and her arms were behind her back. Each hand cupped the opposite elbow. Her head was lowered, facing the floor as she calmly waited.

Brian walked over to a nearby table and lifted a bundle of rope that matched Issy's g-string in color. How much planning went into these scenes? I couldn't believe they'd fluked the rope matching her underwear. I opened my mouth to ask but stopped before I said anything. Issy gracefully leaned forward and kissed the center of the coil of rope as Brian held it out. When Brian shook out the bundle, I was transfixed. The rest of the club disappeared. All I could see was that emerald rope and Issy's fair skin. Brian's movements were fast but smooth as he bound her arms together. Every knot formed part of an intricate pattern. Once he'd finished with her arms he moved to stand in front of her again.

"Where are we, pet?"

"Green, Monsieur."

Her breathy voice had my dick twitching against my leather pants. Brian glanced at me with a raised eyebrow and a smirk.

"Turn around and show Monsieur Krys how amazing you look from the front, pet."

My mouth watered when she turned. I'd seen her breasts last night, but not up close like this. They were large and soft and tipped with stiff pink nipples. What I'd give to wrap my lips around them both. Brian's hands shifted to lift the mounds, and I groaned as he released them and they fell back where they were. I licked my dry lips.

"You are stunning."

"Thank you, Monsieur."

Damn, that breathy voice of hers was going to have me coming in my pants. I ran the heel of my palm over my length through the leather. Brian grinned as he shook his head at me, and I shrugged. It was pretty obvious this little scene was arousing the hell out of me.

Brian moved in front of her and pulled a length of rope over each shoulder. He made short work of binding her breasts so they sat high and thrust out begging for some loving. He moved down her torso creating a pattern of diamonds over her flesh. Taking a deep breath, I took her in. Her face looked so serene and peaceful. I doubted she was aware of anything going on around her, other than the feel of the rope. In that moment I decided I would master shibari. I wanted to put that look on Issy's face. There was something about this woman that called to me like no other ever had ... and I was sure it wasn't simply because she was the first I'd seen tied up. Since walking in the door tonight, I'd had to turn down a couple of scantily clad submissives who offered me their services. One was particularly persistent, but she'd had that glint in her eye that said she knew who I was so I'd had no trouble turning her down. Several times. But Issy, I knew I'd never be able to turn her sweetness away.

****

Monique

I ran my tongue over my front teeth as I glared across the room. That little bitch had known Zeck was mine if he came back, and what did she do? Showed him how easy she was with anyone who could tie a knot. It was pathetic. The slutty little Australian should go back home and leave men like Zeck to be handled by a real woman. Like me.

I'd been putting up with this little hellhole for months waiting for someone powerful or famous to come through the doors. I deserved to get my payoff for all I'd suffered. Letting these so-called Doms beat on my ass night after night. A shudder ran through me. I couldn't fake it for much longer. I needed to find myself a man, someone rich that could afford to take care of me.

I was a little surprised Brian hadn't chosen a private room for this little scene of his. Zeck was obviously new to this kink crap. He was standing to the side watching Brian tie the little tart up. Sure, he was sporting an impressive erection, but come on. The man had bare tits in his face and he was only male. It didn't mean he needed this lifestyle to be happy. If I caught him soon enough, I could convince him a nice normal girl was what he really needed. I patted my hair, making sure it was all still perfectly in place. He needed someone perfectly presented that would handle being in the media. Basically, he needed me.

A growl escaped my throat when Zeck helped Brian strap the little tart down to a bench. *Oh great.* They were going to spank the little slut. I barely held in the urge to curl my lip. The silly twit looked like she actually enjoyed it. Her face was lax with bliss as Brian showed Zeck how to slap her ass. I huffed. Like any man needed instructions on how to slap a lump of flesh that big. You couldn't miss even if you closed your eyes! I'd never understood society's fascination with curvy women. I spent hours every day in the gym to keep my figure tight and trim. Unlike the fat Australian, there was no soft dimply flesh on my body.

Bile rose up my throat when Zeck pulled his palm back and landed a blow on her ass. The idiot was smiling like he'd found a case of money. I ran my palms down my dress, looking like I was simply checking everything was how it should be. When I reached my special hidden pocket, I pressed the button to activate the small camera I had carefully set up. I hoped I was close enough to get enough to work with. I tapped my finger a few times, taking more photos of Zeck beating the fat tart's ass.

I shook my head with a huff when the silly man moved to press himself against the tart's now red ass. He was pressing that impressive length of his against her. *Damn it!* It should be me he was sexing up, not her. I tapped another couple of pictures vowing to make him pay for ignoring me. When all this was over, he would come to me. He would need a nice pretty normal woman to show the world he wasn't an abusive asshole like the rest of them in here. And conveniently, I'd be there to help soothe his hurt ego and help him move on from this horrible mistake.

When Zeck helped the tart straighten from the bench, he palmed her breasts and kissed her shoulder. Like they were lovers or some shit. Gagging, I turned and strode to the change room. I'd seen all I could handle for tonight, and now I had work to do. I so loved the digital age. All I had to do was go home, upload the images and send off a few emails. I grinned. I may even be able to make some money out of the photos.

"You're calling it a night early. Everything okay?"

I turned toward Raine with as sweet a smile as I could manage. I needed to keep up the facade a little longer.

"I'm feeling a little ill, so I'm heading home. Night, Madame."

Raine didn't respond, but I could feel her gaze on me until I slipped through the door to the change room. I sighed as I leaned back against the closed door. The room was empty. After a couple deep breaths, I headed to my locker and quickly changed. I needed to get home and work out how best to use my new pretty pictures.

Chapter Two

Zeck

Propped up on one elbow I swept my gaze over the beauty lying beside me. Issy was on her side facing me and sound asleep. Her golden hair was a mess around her face, and her relaxed expression made her look so sweet and innocent. I knew better. I grinned as I remembered all we'd done over the course of the night. My little Aussie was a wild one.

Lightly with a single fingertip, I traced over a line of red that curved from her ribs to under her breast. She truly loved being bound in rope. When I'd first seen the scrapes and bruising last night I'd panicked. I hated that she'd been hurt. But she was quick to soothe my fears. Turned out, she loves the marks. Apparently they helped her remember how great she'd felt tied up. Crazy girl. Although, I was fairly certain I was as crazy as she was because when her skin had turned red beneath my palm last night I'd felt ten feet tall. I wanted to see my marks on her. I wanted to possess her.

My heart ached, and alarm bells went off in my mind. I'd never felt this sort of connection with a woman before. I'd known her for less than twenty-four hours but already she was vital to me. I needed her.

Fuck.

This was what Dillon must have felt when he first met Ashlyn. I understood now. I stroked down Issy's soft skin until my palm rested over her flat stomach. The skin was tight and smooth. What would it look like swollen with life? I shook my head. Watching Dillon and Ashlyn was getting to me. I wasn't ready to be a father. And I sure as hell wasn't going to get a woman pregnant after only knowing her for one bloody day!

Pulling my hand away I rubbed my eyes and

rolled onto my back. What was I going to do? I was falling in deep with Issy. I didn't want to send her away. But I knew I couldn't keep her. Between all the rounds of hot sex, we'd talked. I knew she had less than a month before she had to go home to Australia. Would that be enough? Could I send her off home after having her for weeks? Maybe it would be easier to send her on her way today. The way my heart was aching, I knew after that amount of time I'd be head over heels for her and would happily beg her to stay. A smile slipped over my face. No, I wouldn't be begging. I'd simply tie her up so she couldn't go.

Soft fingers slid over my chest snagging my attention.

"Morning, lover."

I shivered as her touch caused goosebumps to rise. And that voice... It got me hard every time I heard it. Not that I wasn't already hard from watching her sleep.

"Morning, beautiful. Sleep well?"

She chuckled, and the sound eased the tension from me. My worries fled as I rolled over to cover her body with mine. I loved how we fit together, her curves cushioning my hard edges.

"What's so funny?"

I took her wrists in one hand and held them over her head. She arched her spine and her eyes dilated. I nuzzled my face into her neck and nipped at her skin. She squirmed, rubbing her pelvis against mine. I shuddered when the underside of my dick slid over her slick pussy.

"Stop it. Hold still and take what I give you, *ma sourmises*."

I'd picked up a few words at the club, and I rather liked the French word for submissive. *Sourmises* had a certain ring to it. Her body stilled, except for her chest. That rose and fell as her breathing rate picked up. Her musk filled the air, and I decided I could get used to this. The control gave me a high like nothing else had since those first few concerts. But it was more than control. Issy was trusting me fully to take care of her.

Glancing around the bed, I spotted the robe-belt I'd used last night. Snatching it up, I made quick work of tying her wrists to the headboard of the bed.

"Please, Monsieur."

Kneeling between her spread legs I smiled down at her. She was so beautiful. I stroked myself as I took in all her marks and small bruises from last night.

"Don't you worry, baby. This is going to please us both."

I leaned forward and palming a breast, took her nipple into my mouth where I sucked and bit at it until she was whimpering. My dick was throbbing with each little sound she made, and I quickly gave the other side the same treatment. I wasn't going to last much longer. I needed to be inside her again.

Brian had told me that a Dom needed to learn control, but with Issy I wasn't sure I'd ever be able to hold myself back for long. I reached over to snag a condom from the bedside cupboard and rolled it over my aching length. Issy moaned as she watched me, her curvy body trembling as she tried to stay still for me. I ran my palms up her thighs, spreading her legs wider. Her waxed flesh was glossy with her arousal. I licked my lips as I lowered toward her. When I was less than an inch from where I desperately wanted to lick I stopped. Forcing myself to slow down. *Control*. I needed to control myself and the situation to bring us both higher. I knew from last night it would be worth it.

I blew gently over her, and she moaned and the muscles beneath my palms tensed. Poor girl was struggling to stay still.

I kept teasing with light touches and gentle breaths until she was begging. Looking up her body to her sweaty face I paused to take in the sight and to lick my dry lips. I'd always liked sex, but it had never given me this sort of pleasure before. The trust Issy put in me, the control she gave me was beyond exciting.

I covered her core with my mouth and thrust my tongue deep. Her fruity taste flowed over my tongue, and I swallowed her down. With a growl I pushed her thighs wider and delved deeper. I'd had my mouth on her last night, but it hadn't been enough. I was addicted. Somehow, overnight, Issy had become the center of my world. Alarm bells rang, but they were a distant thing in the back of my mind and easy to ignore. Especially when Issy bucked against my tongue and filled my mouth with her cream as my ears rang with her scream. *Oh hell yeah.* I could definitely get used to this.

I rose up over her shuddering body and entered her with one hard thrust while she was still coming down from her climax. Her pussy clenched around me, and I had to stop and take a deep breath to stop myself from coming already. She felt so bloody good, but I wasn't ready for it to be over yet. Leaning over her I took a nipple between my teeth and tugged, loving how she gasped and moaned as her flesh stretched up before I let go when she arched her spine. After suckling the sting from her, I repeated the process on the other side. As I sucked gently on her other nipple she whimpered and swiveled her hips, trying to get me to move. I growled and pulled free of her body.

"Naughty *sourmises*."

With a couple of tugs I had her hands free, then flipped her over and gave her lush ass five quick smacks. My dick twitched as her skin started to redden. With another growl I thrust back into her from behind. With a firm grip on her hips I thrust deep, loving how she whimpered at the invasion. I kept up a fast hard rhythm until my balls tightened. Releasing one hip, I slid my right hand up between her breasts to lift her back against me. I stopped thrusting a moment to turn her face to the side so I could kiss her. While our tongues dueled I started moving within her again. Pulling away from her mouth, I slid my left hand around to roll a nipple and tug on the tight peak.

She threw her head back against my shoulder and screamed as her pussy clenched tight around me and her whole body convulsed. A tingle ran down my spine, and my dick kicked and jerked within her as I orgasmed like never before. Laying my mouth on the soft skin of her throat I sucked hard. I need to mark her, for the world to see she was mine.

****

Issy

I jerked awake to pounding on the door.

"Zeck? Get your arse out here, man. We've got a shit-storm brewing, and you're in the center of it."

The arm around my middle tightened and a kiss was pressed against the back of my neck. *Hmmm, Zeck has the softest lips.* I could quite happily lie here being kissed by him forever.

His hand slid between my thighs, and I gasped and arched against him as he toyed with my clit. Then the banging started up again.

"Zeck, this is a very serious matter that needs your immediate attention. You have one minute, or I'm coming in to get you."

I echoed Zeck's groan when he pulled his talented fingers away from me.

"I'd better go deal with whatever has crawled up Phillip's arse this morning. Why don't you go have a shower? I'll be in there to help you in a few minutes."

I rolled over and frowned up at him.

"That guy sounded pretty pissed. I somehow doubt this is a quick fix situation."

He leaned in and kissed me until my mind fogged.

"Knowing you're all wet and waiting for me will have me sorting out whatever this is in seconds, baby. Phillip's our manager, and he gets his knickers in a knot regularly. Now, go on and get started."

Cupping his face, I leaned up for another kiss before with a sigh I rolled away and headed to the bathroom that was bigger than my entire apartment. *Wow.* I'd never been in a penthouse before, but I could see the appeal. Twisting the lever I started the opulent shower going before I rummaged through the basket of goodies to find some body wash and shampoo.

Half an hour later I had totally run out of things to wash. I'd even washed my hair twice before conditioning it for longer than it had ever been moisturized before. Now that my fingers had gone wrinkly I'd decided to call it quits and stop waiting for Zeck to join me.

I couldn't help but moan when I wrapped a fluffy white towel around me. These were not the scratchy threadbare things I remembered from my hotel stays. Damn, but the rich certainly knew how to holiday. I smiled and my heart skipped a beat as I ran the terrycloth over the red scrapes from last night. I'd always loved being bound in rope, but last night had been different. Zeck had turned it into so much more than simply a Dom servicing a sub.

That was what I'd realized over the course of the previous evening. All my other experiences had been with Doms who had no real feeling for me. Despite only having just met Zeck, he'd showed me that he desired me for more than my ability to say "yes, monsieur". Between our bouts of incredibly hot sex, we'd talked. I'd discovered the real man behind Right Time's resident jokester. Even if it was only to myself, I had to admit that I'd fallen half in love with him with each little piece of his soul he revealed. He was kind and thoughtful. Donating his time and money whenever he saw a need. He was also feeling guilty. He was envious of his band-mate's happiness. I'd seen the odd headline but hadn't bothered reading the articles about Dillon knocking up a woman. Apparently they were now happily married and about to have their baby. And my soft hearted Zeck was struggling to joke through his emotions.

It had shocked me at first how deep he was. I'd naively thought he was all about the fame and just a pretty face. But he was so much more than that. He'd taken to BDSM like a duck to water. He'd confessed how out of control he'd felt for so long. I'd never really considered how much of a singer's life was dictated to them by managers and schedules.

I rummaged back through the basket until I found a brush. I shook my head with a laugh. That basket had everything anyone could possibly need in the bathroom. As I combed out my very well conditioned hair I remembered why I had been drawn to BDSM. My father was a workaholic and my mother a socialite who only had kids because everyone else was doing it. I'd spent my whole life picking up after her and making sure my younger sister was okay. I'd always needed to be in control and to take charge to get things done. The idea of a man coming in and taking over, while keeping my best interests at heart, sounded pretty damn good to me. Although, I was certain I couldn't handle a man who wanted that amount of control outside the bedroom. Zeck didn't come across as someone who'd want that level of submission.

Then the first time I'd stepped into the club and seen a woman strung from the ceiling something clicked inside me. Rope was my thing. Honestly, the harder stuff like knife and flame play made me cringe.

With a sigh, I headed out the door back to the bedroom. The outer door was open an inch, and deep angry male voices floated into the room.

"I repeat, Zeck. There's photos! The press have damn photographic evidence of you beating a woman! What were you thinking? Right Time does not need another scandal."

"Jas? Back me up, man. He's obviously not going to believe me no matter how I say it, but let me try one last time. It's not what it looks like. Those photos are out of context! Dammit."

"Phillip, Zeck speaks the truth. That club is a BDSM club. The woman was there by choice and enjoyed her time with Zeck. The club also has a no camera policy. I was late here because I was attempting to call the owner about it."

I collapsed onto the bed. *Photos? Oh no.* Bile rose up my throat, and I swallowed it down. Something like that would spread worldwide in minutes. How would I ever get work when the world thought I was some kind of pain slut? Tears dripped down my cheeks as I reached for my clothes from the night before. Fortunately, I'd gotten changed into my street clothes at the club before I came back here with Zeck. I pulled my jeans on and winced when they scraped over each of my bruises. Only twenty minutes ago they'd been a sweet reminder, but now they felt dirty. I pulled my shirt over my head and reached for my bag.

Stopping mid turn I gasped when I saw my reflection in the mirror. There was a massive hickey on the side of my neck. I needed to cover up and sneak out. I didn't want to make things even harder for Zeck. He had enough to deal with already.

Looking around I saw his black hoodie tossed onto a chair. Quickly I put it on and froze for a moment. It smelled of him. I squeezed my eyes closed and took a deep breath. *Hmm.* The man smelled so damn good. I shook my head and snatched my bag up. I needed to get out of here. I'd had a night with a famous singer. It wasn't reality but a snippet out of time. I hoped back in Australia those pictures hadn't made it into the mainstream media. *Maybe if I dye my hair and wear colored contacts I could still get a job? Gah!*

I paused and peaked around the door. There was a small group of men standing around a table, but none of them were looking this way. Taking a deep breath, I put my handbag strap over my head and slipped down the hallway. With a racing heartbeat I pulled on the door and silently slipped from the apartment. The hallway outside was empty but I didn't know how long that would last, so I sprinted for the elevator and pushed the button until the thing came.

Once inside the fancy lift I leaned back against the wall and closed my eyes. What had I done? I'd had a one night stand with Zeck Evans. He'd spanked my ass, and someone had taken a photo… I pulled my phone out of my handbag and pulled up an internet search. With butterflies going crazy in my stomach, I typed in "Zeck Evans scandal". As the little circle spun on the screen, my breaths quickened until I could barely get enough air into my lungs. The elevator dinged that I'd reached the ground floor, and my phone lit up with a page of results. I stumbled and reached out for a wall when the headlines hit me. "Right Time Condones Violence Against Women." "Zeck Evans Busted Hitting Hot Blonde." "Second Scandal to Hit Right Time's World Tour."

Blinking away tears, I pulled the hood up over my head and made sure my hair was all tucked beneath the black material. Glancing out the front of the building I could see a mob of what looked like media people. Unfortunately, they were between the doors and the taxi line. *Dammit.* This was going to be the walk of shame to end them all.

"Mademoiselle? Miss?"

"Yes?"

"Would you like some assistance catching a taxi?"

My shoulders slumped in relief.

"That would be excellent. But I need to avoid the press."

The man nodded, "Of course, mademoiselle. Please, follow me."

Grateful for the help, I followed him to a side door. He quietly snuck me around to the front and into the most rear taxi.

"Good luck, mademoiselle. I do believe the press are going to be most insistent with this matter."

My stomach dropped as the taxi pulled away and headed to my small apartment. The concierge was right. I could feel it in my bones that I hadn't heard the last of the paparazzi.

****

Zeck

Scrubbing my face I paced the living area of my penthouse suite. Issy had vanished. She must have overheard us talking, or she checked her phone and saw the reports. *Dammit!* I wasn't ready to let her go. All this shit with the media would blow over. It had with Dillon and Ashlyn, so it would for us, too.

"Zeck? I have spoken with Brian. He believes he knows who would have taken the photos."

I turned to face Jas.

"That's great. But it doesn't really help. It's not like we can undo them being leaked."

"No, but the band's lawyers have begun getting the photos pulled from sites. They were illegally taken without anyone's permission. The woman responsible will be facing criminal charges, and of course a life ban from Brian's club."

"A woman did this? Submissive or Domme?"

Not that it mattered. Brian had promised a camera ban, and I'd stupidly believed him.

"A submissive. I believe you turned her down several times last night. Her name is Monique Royale. Brian is most apologetic over this. He hasn't got all the evidence he needs yet, but he is going to keep looking until he does. He's never had anyone break the no photo rule before, and he intends to make example of her so no one else get idea."

I scrubbed my palms over my face. I vaguely remembered her. She'd come on to me several times and hadn't seemed to be submissive at all. Not that I knew how a submissive woman would act.

"Brian had more to tell me."

Having spent most of the night pleasuring Issy, I was beyond tired. Wariness pulled at every muscle in my body, and I really didn't need anything else to be added to my already craptastic day.

"Spit it out, Jas."

"Issy is with him. She attempted to return home this morning, but the press were camped out at her home. She felt she had nowhere to go, so called Brian. He is with her at the club."

My head snapped up.

"Nowhere to go? She should have bloody well stayed here! Instead of sneaking off on me. Go get her, Jas. Bring my woman back here where I can keep her safe. She's too sweet to have to deal with this paparazzi shit alone."

Jas sucked in a breath and frowned at me.

"What?"

"You only just met this girl. Yet you are talking like you love her."

I rubbed my palm over the back of my neck.

"I don't know about love, but I care about her. I don't know how to explain it, man. We just … click. When we're together I feel relaxed and at peace. When she trusts me to tie her up and take her I feel more like a man than I ever have before. But it's more than simple submission. I had like, half a dozen subs try to tempt me last night, yet only Issy caught my attention. Somehow, she's become vital to me."

The big guy nodded with a bit of a smirk.

"Ashlyn will be happy to have some female company on tour. I'll head out to collect her now. Oh, and as her Dom, you need to deal with her running off. I believe a nice long spanking would set her straight."

I stood in shock as Jas left.

"He's right you know. Not sure about that spanking shit, but Ashlyn will love having another woman to talk with. Your Issy is Australian, too, right?"

I turned to face Dillon. He'd been settling Ashlyn in the second bedroom. Poor girl was about to drop that baby of hers, but Dillon refused to leave me alone to suffer through this scandal.

"It's not like the media say it is. Everything that Issy and I did last night was totally consensual, and I can assure you we both enjoyed every moment. And yeah, Issy's Australian. What can I say? I heard Aussies were the best so I had to get myself one. You know? Gotta keep up with you."

I was a little surprised my lame attempt at humor

got my best mate chuckling, but I happily joined him.

"Oh yeah, buddy. Once you try an Aussie, mate, you'll never want anything else. Trust me."

I took a deep breath, and it felt great to laugh again. The band's publicist had passed down the message that we were to respond to all questions regarding this current scandal with a "no comment". They were preparing a press release to cover the important facts, and it would also say that Issy and I wanted our privacy respected. I scoffed. *Yeah, right.* Like the media would ever respect anyone's privacy. But at least I wouldn't have to stand in front of a bunch of mics and try to defend my and Issy's choices to a bunch of strangers I really didn't give a stuff about.

"Man, you've got it bad."

I growled a little at Dillon.

"Like you don't?"

"Bro, I'm married! The whole bloody world knows I'm whipped."

I scrubbed my palms over my face again.

"I hate that the media knows about her. Last night was awesome. One of the best of my life and now instead of lying in bed with her enjoying our glow … it now feels dirty and wrong. Bloody hell, man. I just wanted to sing. I never wanted this fame shit that's taken over everything."

Dillon came over and slapped me on the back. "I know exactly how you feel, buddy. Fame is a strange beast. Like anything, there's good and bad. Don't worry too much about it. It'll blow over. Just wait. Brittney will shave her head again or Miley will flash something she shouldn't and we'll be left alone."

Laughing, I shook my head.

"Yeah, I know. It just sucks to be in the center of the storm. I'd much rather defend one of you boys than be the focus."

"I know, man. But we've all got your back. It really will blow over."

With my hands on my hips I watched my best friend return to his wife. An ache set up behind my ribs as I realized I wanted what he had. With Issy I'd started to see my future, but she'd snuck out at the first chance. Had she seen me as a notch on her bedpost? She hadn't seemed that way last night, but the evidence was glaringly obvious this afternoon.

I shook my head and scrubbed a hand through my hair. I was being ridiculous. We'd had one night, and I was going all teenage girl planning a picket fence. When Jas brought Issy here, I'd sit down with her. Maybe even include Phillip in the conversation. We'd work out how to keep her protected until this shit blew over, and then I'd walk away. It was the responsible thing to do.

It was an awesome plan. One that made total logical sense. Right up to the moment Issy walked into the room wearing my hoodie. Fuck, but she looked good in my clothes. I had several inches on her, so the thing hung down nearly to her knees. It made her look young and innocent. And mine. It definitely made her look like she was mine.

Where the hell was this possessiveness coming from? I'd never been like this with a girl before. Issy lifted a trembling hand and pushed the hood off, and my heart sank. She'd been crying. A lot. Her eyes were red rimmed and puffy. The tip of her nose was an adorable pink. Suddenly I didn't give a stuff why I was turning into a caveman. My woman was hurting. I strode straight across the room and scooped her up. Instantly she wrapped her arms around my neck and nuzzled her face into my neck. Something deep inside me eased having her pressed against me.

"It's okay, baby. I'll take care of you."

I nodded once to Jas before I retreated to my room. I'd refused to let the hotel staff in, so the bed was still rumpled from our night together. I stood her at the foot, and needing to feel her skin, I stripped off the hoodie.

"By the way, I love how you look wearing my clothes, baby."

She lowered her gaze and blushed.

"I didn't want to be recognized by the press. I was going to post it back, honest."

I put a finger beneath her chin and tilted her face up.

"Issy, baby, I don't mind you taking it. My only objection is that you snuck off without a word. I had no way of contacting you. Did last night mean anything to you at all?"

Tears welled in her eyes, and the breath in my lungs stilled when she lifted a palm to press against my cheek. Jas and Dillon were right. I'd fallen hard for this girl.

"Last night was amazing. I was looking forward to spending today with you. Then I overheard you and your manager speaking. I did a search on my phone, and the headlines turned my stomach. I felt so dirty I had to leave. I can't believe I ran like a coward, but that's what I did. I didn't mean to hurt you. I'm sorry."

I gently stroked my fingers over her face. "It kills me you've been so upset and I wasn't there to comfort you. Don't ever leave like that again. You stay and we deal with it together, okay?"

She frowned up at me. "What are you saying? What did last night mean to you?"

I smirked. "You asking a fella to talk about his feelings?"

Her eyes turned serious. "Yes, Zeck. Shit is about to get real. The media isn't going to forget about this, especially if we're together. You're going to get labeled a wife beater by the press."

Her voice cracked, and I couldn't take it. I leaned down and took her lips with mine, kissing her deep until her body melted against me.

"Sweetheart, the band's legal team and publicist are currently working on dealing with it. The lawyers are already getting the photos pulled down."

Tears leaked down her cheeks. "You know as well as I do that once those pictures are out there, there's no taking it back. Nothing can truly be deleted from the internet."

I wiped her tears gently with my thumbs. "Don't cry, baby. This will pass. All the major media outlets will pull the photo, and it hopefully won't make it to print magazines."

"But what if it does? How am I meant to find work after this?"

Cupping her face, I kissed her again. "If anyone is dumb enough to print it, we sue and then you'll have enough money you won't have to work for a while."

She leaned in, kissing me back.

"You didn't answer me. About last night."

I pulled back enough that I could focus my gaze on hers.

"Last night was special, and it wasn't only because it was the first time I got a real taste of BDSM. When Jas took me into that club for the first time I couldn't take my eyes off you. You looked so beautiful being tied up. Then, last night I got to talk with you, touch you. Baby, it was instant addiction. I need you."

The sweetest smile curved her lips, and she allowed all her weight to lean against me. A shiver ran up my spine when her breasts pressed against my chest.

"And speaking of BDSM … I do believe you've earned yourself a spanking for running off on me."

My dick twitched and lengthened when her eyes dilated and her mouth opened a little as her breathing picked up. Yeah, this Dom stuff was so my kink.

Chapter Three

Issy

As I sat watching Right Time finish their last song on stage from a corporate box, I couldn't believe how my day had progressed. I'd woken up to a hunk of a man loving on me, but then everything had quickly turned to hell with those bloody photos. I still couldn't believe the paparazzi had found my apartment so fast. Before the taxi could stop I had seen them all huddled around my building's entrance. I'd told the driver to keep going. The only place I could think to go was the club. I'd dialed Brian, and he'd already heard from Jas so knew what was going on. He'd been totally supportive of me coming to him.

He'd been waiting for me outside when the taxi pulled up. He'd paid the driver, then taken me under his arm. Holding me close he'd silently pushed past the press and gotten me safely inside. I had no romantic feelings for Brian, never had, but I liked the way he cared and protected any sub that entered his club. I could finally relax once I entered the club I'd become so familiar with.

Poor Brian. He was furious and swamped with guilt over the scandal. I assured him it wasn't his doing. He did all he could to protect those in his club. It wasn't just entertainers that sought out the privacy of Brian's club. A lot of politicians came in, too. Not to mention all the teachers or others who would lose their jobs if it got out they liked BDSM.

Brian had made me a coffee and sat down at a table and let me relax. He asked a few questions, but let me make the decision about how to handle the scandal. He'd told me that Zeck had been distraught to discover I'd slipped out on him. A smile curved my lips. If I hadn't chosen to stay with Zeck, Brian was going to give me the spanking I'd earned. Apparently putting myself in danger like that was a hard limit for all Doms.

I hadn't been able to stop thinking about the gorgeous Brit since I'd left, so it had been easy to decide to let him help me through this crap. I hadn't been sure how he'd felt about me, but I sure knew now. I shivered as I recalled how good it had felt when Zeck had stripped me down and spanked me before he tied me to the bed and made slow love to me. I closed my eyes at the memory. He'd been thorough and so gentle he'd cracked open my heart. Zeck held so much passion inside, and I still couldn't believe he trusted me enough to unleash it on me.

"What's that grin for?" Ashlyn scoffed. "Like I need to ask. You're thinking of your man aren't you?"

I chuckled. It was so nice to hang out with another Australian after so long in France. That and Ashlyn was a hard girl not to like. Even though she had to be uncomfortable in her final month of pregnancy she was still friendly and bubbly.

Curiosity had me leaning closer to her. "Those boys are something, aren't they? How'd you get caught in their web?"

"You don't know? I thought the whole world knew about it."

I shook my head on a laugh. "I've never been one to read gossip mags, and honestly I've never really listened to Right Time other than when they come on the radio."

"You know, I was the same. I was holidaying in England with my friend, Sarah. She's one of the band's back up dancers. I met Dillon through her, and it all kind of steamrolled from there."

I couldn't help but grin.

"So Dillon found himself an Aussie in England

and Zeck found one in France."

Ashlyn chuckled. "Yeah. It's a hoot isn't it? Oh, damn."

She clutched her huge belly, and I rushed to her side.

"Are you okay? What's happening?"

"Oh, it's nothing. Little bean has been doing aerobics all bloody day today. Phew."

While nannying this last year I'd been around a few heavily pregnant women, and I was pretty sure that Ashlyn wouldn't be wincing like she was from a simple kick.

"How long do the boys normally take after a show before they get up here?"

"Oh no. They don't come to us. We have to go to them. Well, sometimes one of them will dress up in a disguise and risk coming out from backstage. Zeck was the last one to try that, but the diehard fans are on to it and security had to haul his butt back to safety." She shook her head. "You have the craziest one for sure. Can't quite wrap my head around him being a Dom though."

I shrugged as a wave of unease flowed over me. I liked it better when no one knew what I preferred between the sheets.

"Every Dom is different. Some like to be in control of everything around them 24/7, but most aren't that hardcore. A lot of Doms like to control things in the bedroom because they feel out of control in their day to day life. I've only been experimenting with the lifestyle for about six months now, and Zeck's only just discovered it. It doesn't change who he is as a person, it's simply part of him. If you think about it, it makes sense. Doms like to protect and take care of those around them. Zeck's told me about a few things he's done over the

131

years that fit that theme. I'm sure you've seen that side of him since you've been with Dillon. He and Zeck are best friends, right?"

Ashlyn's forehead creased as she chewed her lower lip.

"When you put it like that, yeah. Zeck is definitely a caretaker. He's always making sure everyone has what they need. Umm, feel free to tell me to take a hike, but can I ask why you thought getting your butt smacked would be nice in the first place?"

I would have told her to take that hike if her tone hadn't been filled with honest curiosity. Still, I didn't know her well enough to reveal all my inner secrets to the woman.

"I just kinda tumbled into it I guess. The family I was working for had this maid who befriended me and invited me to join her one night. The first time I was bound in rope I knew I'd found what works for me. It's hard to explain how it feels to submit."

"You ladies ready to head out?"

I'd never been so glad to see a bodyguard. The conversation was getting too personal. Zeck had said all the right things earlier, but I still wasn't one hundred percent sure on where we were heading. While they'd been doing preshow checks and stuff I'd done some more internet searching. Seems my man was a bit of a ladies' man. So many references to Zeck and Dillon and how many women they had. Although Dillon seemed to be over it. He was all about Ashlyn now. His gaze always sought her out, and if she was in range, he had a hand on her.

With a sigh I followed Ashlyn's waddling frame from the box and headed down the hall toward the backstage door along with three bodyguards.

"Go back home, you stupid sluts!"

"You're just a perverted freak. Leave Zeck alone!"

"Right Time need to stay single!"

"How dare you take our men!"

The sneers were yelled out in French, and Ashlyn ignored them. I wasn't sure if she didn't know what they said or if she was used to it. But I wasn't. Bile rose in my throat as fans continued to yell out cruel remarks. They apparently hated everything from our hair color to our choice in footwear.

"Are they always like this?"

"Well, I don't speak French, so I'm not sure what they're saying. Although the tone kinda speaks for itself. If they're telling us to leave their men alone and go home, then yeah. There's always crazy fans."

"How do you cope with it? I don't know if I can do this."

My steps slowed, but Ashlyn linked her arm through mine and hurried me forward.

"They're not real, if you know what I mean. They have a distorted view of the men. I know even if *I* didn't have Dillon, those little psychos wouldn't have him. The boys might have been man-whores in the past, but they never went near the crazy fans. Hell, they'd likely wake up with their hair shaved off and find it selling on eBay! Just hold your head high and ignore them. You are the one Zeck wants. He's chosen you to be with, not them." Ashlyn giggled. "Just wait 'til you're pregnant. Nothing sets them off quite like seeing my baby bump. I show it off just to mess with them some times."

She stopped speaking and gripped my arm tighter.

"Little bean isn't just kicking, is it? That baby wants out. C'mon, we need to get to the men." I looked the nearest guard in the eye. "She's in labor. We have to get to Dillon fast, then get them to the hospital. Can you call an ambulance while we're on the move?"

He nodded and snatched up his radio as we sped up and finally made it through the door away from the screaming fans.

"Dillon!"

I bellowed down the hallway. Ashlyn nearly snapped my forearm when the next contraction hit. She couldn't walk for a couple minutes.

"One of you go get Dillon!"

One of the guards took off down the hall just as Dillon and the others came running toward them.

"What the hell, Issy? I think they can hear you over the other side of the building."

I smiled up at the clearly panicked men. "Well, your wife is in labor and I thought you should hurry the hell up and take my place by her side. She can have a go at breaking a few of your bones."

Dillon stumbled a little before Zeck grabbed his arm and dragged him forward.

"Has an ambulance been called?"

Zeck aimed his question at the guards.

"Yes, sir. ETA ten minutes. We need to get Mrs. Blake to the rear door where they'll meet us."

Dillon stood taller, and with a nod he wrapped an arm around Ashlyn, taking most of her weight, before he turned them to head to the location. I could see his jaw moving as he spoke to his wife. They made such a sweet couple. I sighed and leaned back when Zeck's strong arms wrapped around my middle.

"I am so glad you're here, baby. You handled that like a pro. Without you, Ashlyn probably would have had that baby on the floor in the dressing room."

I chuckled because that was highly likely. Men freaked out with childbirth. It was a fact of nature.

"Well, are we all going to follow them to the

hospital?" I wrinkled my nose. "Maybe after you lot have showers. Damn, you guys stink like a football team."

They all laughed, and Zeck turned me around then cupped my face and took possession of my mouth. Wrapping my arms around his neck, I sighed into the kiss, ignoring the smell. Damn but this man could melt me with just the touch of his lips. Within his strong embrace, all my doubts fled as I gladly fell under his spell.

****

Zeck

It was early morning before we headed for the hospital's exit. I was knackered. All I wanted to do was to take Issy to bed and sleep curled around her. Dillon and Ashlyn's daughter had made her grand entrance safely, and when I'd left the room little Grace was happily sleeping in her daddy's arms. That baby girl already had her father wrapped around her little finger, but I got the feeling that Dillon didn't mind in the least.

Tightening my hand around hers, I glanced over at Issy. What would she look like swollen with child? She'd be a great mother. All that nannying would mean she would easily handle anything their kids threw at her. *Whoa.* I mentally shook my head. It was way too soon to be planning babies with Issy. I wasn't entirely sure she wanted anything long term with me. She'd fled at the first sign of trouble the previous morning. Facing forward again, I ran my free hand through my hair. She'd chosen to run to Brian at the club rather than me, but once there she'd chosen to return to me for shelter. I was sure Brian would have taken her home to keep her safe. She'd had options but had picked me. And she hadn't tried to leave again. She could have easily left several times, but she hadn't. Thoughts of the club reminded me they were meant to be somewhere else tonight.

"What's the time?"

She flicked her wrist over to see her watch. "It's about one AM. Why's that?"

She looked up at me, and her eyes looked so tired. I really wished I could simply take her back to the hotel.

"We need to visit the club, baby. Brian wants to sit down with us to let us know what he's discovered about the photos."

She frowned, and my heart melted a little at how adorable she looked.

"I thought he told you it was Monique. Which is totally believable, in fact, it's the most plausible explanation."

That caught my attention.

"Why do you say that?"

"Monique recognized you the first time you came in. She was raving on in the change room that you would be hers if you came back in. Monique isn't liked at the club. She doesn't belong there. She plays at being submissive, but she isn't really. If anything, she looks down her nose at the lifestyle. I think she's looking for a sugar daddy or something. Unfortunately, it's all about who you know, and her sister is dating Brian's brother. Even without the photos leaking, I knew I couldn't go back anymore. She'll make my life hell. Although, I do need to clean out my locker and hand in my keycard."

I stopped walking and pulled her against my chest for a hug.

"I know I haven't known Brian long, but I can't imagine him letting this slide, and if he does I'll be setting our legal team on him to make sure Monique gets what she deserves for this stunt. I won't stand by while you get hurt. You believe me, don't you?"

She smiled up at me. "I totally believe that you'll kick arse for me, babe."

"Come, we must keep moving."

Jas called out from the doorway. He was escorting us to the club.

"Is Jas joining us?"

"Yeah, baby. Remember how I told you he's the head of our security? Well, that means he needs to hear what Brian has to say, too. And even at this hour, we can't risk going out alone without security."

She shuddered against me, and I winced. I hated that I'd brought this down on her. Unlike me, she hadn't chosen fame. She allowed me to guide her out to the car, and I sighed in relief when there were no fans or media waiting for us. Of course, we were using a small side entrance. The media were camped out at the front entrance waiting for the official announcement of the birth. Fortunately, it appeared babies trump scandals.

We quickly got into the vehicle, and with Jas driving we arrived at the club in no time. I looked around the near empty parking lot, but everything seemed quiet outside.

"I don't see anyone, Jas. Do you?"

"No, I don't either. When I spoke with Brian earlier he said he'd employed extra security. They have been making sure fans and media can't get near his place. Even with them, only a few came out to play tonight. We'll go in the back entrance to be safe. Brian's waiting for us."

Jas pulled out his phone, but Issy leaned forward and stopped him from dialing.

"I have my keycard. I can get us straight in. There's no need for us to sit out here in the car-park."

With a nod, Jas exited the car and moved around to open our door. My stomach started churning as I followed Issy and Jas across the near empty parking lot. This Monique chick sounded like trouble, the kind that wasn't going to simply vanish.

I jerked to a stop as soon as the door swung open. Brian was there as if he'd been standing there waiting for us.

"Follow me."

I frowned while I ran my gaze over him. He wasn't in club wear, but a suit. His tie was gone and the top button popped, and he'd also rolled up the sleeves. He looked like one stressed out man, nothing like the controlled, calm man I'd met the last two nights.

"Are you all right, Brian?"

I couldn't help but ask. It was ingrained in me to help those around me if I could.

"It's been a long couple of days, my friend."

He paused and opened a door into an elegant looking office, standing back to usher us through in front of him.

"Take a seat, gentlemen."

Frowning I waited for Issy to sit before I lowered myself into a seat beside her.

"What has happened, my friend?"

I was glad Jas asked the question. I didn't know Brian well enough to push him, and he was making me nervous.

"I can confirm that it was Monique that took and released those photos. However, she's disappeared." He paused to scrub his palms over his face. "I feel responsible. I should have dealt with her sooner. I knew she was causing friction here."

"Friction?"

Issy turned to me as I voiced my question.

"As I said to you earlier, she's a raving bitch. And I don't believe she even likes the lifestyle."

"You're right. She's the younger sister of my brother's partner. He'd told me she was asking about the lifestyle and her sister wanted to keep her safe, so as a favor I let her train here. It'll be the last time I allow such a thing." He sighed, and my instincts flared. "I spoke with her sister at length this morning. Monique was diagnosed recently with Narcissistic Personality Disorder. I think her sister hoped in having her trained as a submissive she'd settle down. I wished they'd told me to begin with. I'd never have let her in the door. She was constantly prowling for a Dom, clearly looking for someone rich and well known. I imagine she thought she struck the jackpot when you walked in, Zeck. Anyway, she's now missing. She hasn't returned to her apartment since last night, and she's not answering her phone. The police are looking for her also. Their cyber crime unit wants to interview her. If they can charge her they will. It's hard to get a conviction with cyber stuff, but she could end up behind bars for a couple years if they can manage it. If she's crazy enough to show up here, I'll be calling the police. Her locker hasn't been cleared out, and she obviously still has her keycard."

"Can't you get your security guys to watch for what cards get scanned? Or have her card deactivated?"

I couldn't understand the point of a security system that gave everyone individual keycards but couldn't be programmed to alert someone when a certain card was scanned.

"Sorry, Zeck. I've never intended to use the system in that way, so it's not set up for it. And without the card, I can't deactivate it. I'll be looking into changing that, but it won't help our situation now."

I sat straighter in my seat. I might be new to being a Dom, but needing to protect those around me was something I'd been doing for a long time.

"In that case, Issy won't be coming back here until Monique is caught."

A slight smile stretched his lips for a few moments.

"You're quite the natural, aren't you? I was actually going to suggest that very thing. I know Issy is due to fly home in a few weeks." He turned his attention to Issy. "I hate to suggest it, but maybe you should consider going home sooner. I fear what Monique would do to you if she found you."

Panic rose inside me, and my heart kicked up in speed. I wasn't ready to say goodbye to Issy. I wasn't sure I ever would be. I looked over to her, and the sorrow on her face kicked me in the gut.

"Come on tour with me. You'll have our security with you whenever you're out in public, so Monique won't get near you, baby."

"My visa runs out in a few weeks, Zeck. I can't stay past that date. I have to go home."

I could see in her gaze that she didn't want to go. I opened my mouth to beg, but Jas cut me off.

"Actually, Phillip and I were going to talk to you both about this. Issy, you are a nanny yes? If you had employment your visa could be extended?"

"Theoretically, yes. What are you thinking?"

A grin stretched my face while my blood heated with excitement. The solution was obvious.

"You can nanny Grace! That's perfect, Jas! The rest of the tour is going to be so busy, Ashlyn will be forced to do a lot with Grace on her own without Dillon. You could help her. You'd get paid and be able to stay with me. What do you say?"

Issy looked straight into my gaze, and my heart dropped at the seriousness I saw. Would she say no? Had I misread her feelings for me?

"Why do you want me to come with you on tour? Is it only my safety that you're worried about?"

I took a deep breath and eyed Jas and Brian.

"Don't suppose you two could step out for a minute?"

The pair snickered as they nodded and left the room. Unable to stand the distance between us, I moved to kneel in front of her.

"Baby, honestly, I'm not sure where we're going to end up, but I adore you. I love having you around, and I'm not ready to let you go. Ashlyn needing help with Grace is merely a convenient way to keep you close to me, because I can't handle you leaving me, at least not yet. I can't deny that keeping you safe is high on my list of worries, but that's because I care about you and want you safe. I'm pretty sure I'll always worry about that when it comes to you."

****

Monique

Pulling my jacket around me tighter, I stayed in the shadows at the side of the parking lot. Rage had my vision tunneled on the door of the club. The door that Zeck and his little slut had just gone through. If they hadn't had that big Russian bastard with them, I'd have jumped them and dealt with the little tart already.

It was all her fault. I couldn't go to my apartment, or my sister's place. Everyone was now on the lookout for me so they could turn me over to the police. I shook my head. What a load of bullshit. It was only a couple of photos. A grin pulled at my lips. A couple of photos that had paid very well. If only I could get to the bank to access the funds. My damn accounts had been frozen.

Straightening my shoulders, I began to creep over to the door, where I held my breath as I scanned my card. Would it work? Nothing I owned seemed to anymore. A quiet snick sounded as the lock opened. *Wow.* Guess they hadn't figured out how to deactivate my card yet.

I slipped inside and leaned against the wall for a moment. Enjoying being out of the crisp night air finally. I'd been waiting outside the rear of the hospital, away from all the media, until I heard the Russian on the phone saying he was bringing Zeck here. I'd rushed over here and managed to arrive just as they'd been entering.

What do I do now?

Change room.

It'll be warm and out of the way. I can have a hot shower and think about what to do. And you never know, my luck might change and Issy might be in there. I really, really wanted to put that bitch in her place.

****

Issy

Walking from Brian's office, my mind spun as I attempted to process what I'd just agreed to. I needed to clean out my locker. As I made my way across the main floor toward the change rooms, I looked around at all the stations. My heart ached at leaving. I'd learned so much here, discovered a whole new side of myself. This club would always be special to me. I was extremely grateful Monsieur Brian had made sure I understood I was always welcome to come back. But until Monique was found and dealt with, I was going to be lying low. I shook my head. Never in a million years did I think I'd be going on tour with a world famous band. And I was going to get paid to look after cute little Grace, too. Life was looking up.

However, I was still torn. Being with Zeck meant the media would take even more of an interest in me. Right Time's publicist had advised me to stick with "no comment" or "please respect my privacy at this time" and to ignore the whole scandal. It seemed to be working. Well, I assumed it was. The band's security was really good at their jobs and not many of the media got through. But there'd be interviews down the line. I knew it. At some point Zeck and I had to come up with something more solid that "no comment". Maybe with us together the gossip would die down about him being an abuser...

With a sigh, I pushed open the door and entered the empty room. A shiver ran up my spine at the odd silence. The club had closed early due to the lack of people and the cleaners hadn't been through yet, so there were a few items here and there that had been left out but no actual people around me. There was a strange chill to the air without all the women who normally surrounded me in this room. The skin on the back of my neck tingled, and I froze with my hand on the handle of my locker. Maybe I wasn't as alone as I'd first thought.

I began to turn around, but I didn't get far before a body hit my back and slammed me against the lockers. I gasped when a hand wrapped in my hair, and my attacker leaned their weight against me.

"You bitch! How dare you take what's mine!"

Monique. Of course. And she truly was crazy. I tried to think about what I knew about narcissists. Sadly, it wasn't much at all. I wasn't sure how long the men would chat before they came looking for me when I didn't return. Maybe I could keep her talking until they came.

"Zeck isn't a bloody toy. He's a man fully capable of independent thought. You can't just lay claim to him like he's a damn couch."

I swallowed bile down as she moved in close enough her breath heated my ear.

"I've put months into this. Pretending to like being beaten so I could land someone like him. He's the first man to come through those doors that fits what I deserve. I will not let some little Australian slut take what is rightfully mine. I've earned this, and dammit, I deserve it!"

I began trembling. Any doubt I may have held about Monique's mental health flew out the window. I was stuck alone with an unpredictable crazy woman. I took a deep breath and closed my eyes for a moment. I couldn't wait to be saved. I needed to get myself out of this. I was bigger than Monique and had more muscle, but I knew insanity could give people strength they didn't normally have.

"What? You have nothing to say to that? Of course not. You know I'm right. You're not even French. No way did that man come in here looking for anything other than a French woman. A perfect female, not some dumpy tourist."

Her insult didn't stick. I knew I had a few extra pounds, but I also knew Zeck appreciated my curves. Most men did. I knew a lot of women who were bigger that had self image issues, but not me. I was completely comfortable with my size and curves. This club had played a big part in that. Women and men of all shapes and sizes came here, and they were all beautiful in their own way. It was only people like Monique that were ugly, and that was due to her personality seeping through more than her actual looks. Monique was technically beautiful. Pole thin, with fake DD boobs. Her hair was artificially white blonde and dead straight. I wasn't sure there was anything about the woman that was as God had intended it to be. And she was the least popular sub here. I figured the Doms had all worked out she was just playing at being submissive. Only the sadists would take her on for a scene.

"Guess you thought wrong. In fact, Zeck's asked me to join him for the rest of the tour."

I allowed my inner bitch to take over. I needed her mad enough to lose her cool. This was not a time to be submissive, but a time to let all my self defense training kick in. My words had the desired effect, sending Monique into a rage. She pulled me away from the locker giving me room to move my arms and legs. Before she could slam me into it again, I raised my elbow and slammed it back into her, catching her lower ribs. She grunted and clutched her injury.

With my blood pumping fast, I spun around with my knee raised and plowed it into her cheek, knocking her over onto the ground. I had precious seconds to decide what to do with her. The last thing I needed was to get charged with assault. But I also couldn't give her a chance to run. Justice needed to be served, and maybe, if the media found out how crazy the one who sold the photos was, they wouldn't want to lose credibility by being associated with her.

I quickly ran my gaze around the room and spotted the perfect thing. As fast as I could I snatched up a pair of leather cuffs and returned to Monique. Pressing a knee between her shoulder blades I pressed her body hard against the floor. Ignoring her whimpers and screams, I quickly wrapped the cuffs around her wrists and snapped them together. Keeping my weight on her, I pulled my phone from my jeans pocket and dialed Brian. I didn't have Zeck's number. I frowned. We really needed to exchange numbers.

"Are you okay, Issy?"

"Oh, yeah, I'm great. Just had a little run in here in the ladies' locker room. Mind sending Jas down here and calling the police for me? I've got Monique a little tied up."

I couldn't help but laugh as all sorts of cursing came over the line along with the sounds of feet hitting the concrete. Men, especially Doms, always struggled when women took care of business without them. A lightness filled me as I thought about the spanking I might get from Zeck. I'd have to make sure to be extra bratty this afternoon to be certain of one. Fortunately, Zeck was too new to things to understand the concept of topping from the bottom.

Epilogue

Zeck
Three months later

Nothing could wipe the grin off my face. She'd said yes. Issy had been by my side for the rest of the tour, and in the weeks afterward she'd stayed with me at my apartment. I fell more in love with her every day, and I wanted the whole world to know about it. Sitting beside Dillon as the female interviewer nearly drooled over little Grace who was asleep in her Daddy's arms I couldn't help but look forward to the future.

It seemed every interviewer had the same damn questions lately. This woman proved my point when she asked Dillon, yet again, about the rumor of him leaving.

"Dillon, the rumors are running rampant about you leaving the group. They say you're going to become a full time dad. Are they true?"

I smirked as Dillon rolled his eyes. That man loved his little girl, but music was part of his soul. He wouldn't ever be able to give it up. I knew because I felt the same way.

"As much as I love my little saving Grace, I'll leave her mummy to be the stay at home parent for now. So to set the rumors straight, I am not now, or in the near future leaving the group. I love my wife. She is amazing and supports me in all I do. Grace is here today so my beautiful wife can catch up on some much deserved sleep. So as to another rumor I'm happy to set straight, I am happily married and more than adore my wife. I mean, look at the awesome gift she gave me. Isn't she just the most perfect baby you've ever seen?"

I chuckled as the interviewer just about melted into a puddle on her seat across from us before I leaned into Dillon.

"Good one, bro. You just made her and the rest of the female population, when they see this interview, fall even more in love with you and envy Ashlyn."

The woman must have heard me as she sat up straight and focused in on me. I swallowed nervously. *Oh crap.*

"Zeck, speaking of women. Rumor has it that you were spotted shopping at Garrard & Co. a few weeks ago. Care to comment on that?"

I relaxed back into the chair. "Of course I was spotted there. Where else would I go when I needed to buy an engagement ring?"

I covered my laugh with a cough as the interviewer tried to remain professional. After a few moments she cleared her throat and resumed.

"Have you popped the big question yet? If you have, what did Issy say?"

"Of course I have. No way would I release that info to the public before I asked her." I looked directly at the closest camera with my trademark smirk. "And naturally, she said yes. I'm irresistible." With a wink I waited for my band-mates to stop laughing before I continued. "Seriously, Issy is my other half. I didn't know I could feel like this about a woman until I met her. Issy owns my heart and soul, and I can't wait to spend the rest of our lives together."

Dillon leaned toward me. "Now who's making ovaries explode across the world?"

"Would you like to tell us how you popped the big question?"

I was so grateful the questions about my sex life had stopped. The first couple of interviews after the scandal had honed in on BDSM and domestic violence. Issy and I had followed the advice of our publicist and stuck with a "we wish to keep our private life, private". That and we kept quiet, avoiding public scenes where we'd be caught by the media. So now the hype had died down and I got to respond to questions like this one that I didn't have a problem in the world with answering.

"Well, I took her out to our favorite restaurant for dinner. Then when we got home I settled her on the couch before I grabbed my guitar. I'd written a song for the occasion so I sang it to her, then dropped to one knee and pulled out the ring."

She'd said yes, squealed like a schoolgirl, then jumped on me. But I wasn't telling that on live TV. Nor was I confessing that after I took her on the floor, I took her to bed where I bound her in rope and spent the whole night making love to her every way we could think of. But that shit was private, and always would be.

"That is so beautiful. Will the song be on the next album?"

I shook my head. "No way. That one will always be only for my Issy."

"That's a pity. Like most of your fans, I would have liked to have heard it."

"Ah well, I assure you there'll be songs about her on the next album. Just not that particular one."

Grace stirred and made a gurgling noise that drew all attention to her. Dillon rearranged his hold on her so she faced out, and naturally the cameraman zoomed in on her sweet little face.

"Zeck, you and Dillon have always been competitive in all things. Does that mean the pitter-patter of little feet for you and Issy soon?"

I threw my head back, laughing hard.

"Well, we both ended up with Australian women within the same tour. So I guess I'd better get moving to keep up with him on the baby front. Although, I will add that having a family is an important choice and not something to be taken lightly or in jest. But yeah, Issy and I would love nothing more than to give Grace a playmate."

As the interviewer moved onto Law I sat there grinning as I imagined how beautiful Issy would look with her tummy rounded out with our baby. It had become my favorite daydream. My life since joining Right Time had been a roller coaster, but now with Issy, it all seemed to be leveling out into what looked like a bright future. Life was good. I just hoped Law and Alec could find their slice of heaven, too.

The End

www.khloewren.com

DEDICATION

For Byron, who has always been a huge supporter of my work. This one's for you!

FOUR BOOK COLLECTION

LAW

Scandals, 3

Jess Buffett

Copyright © 2016

Prologue

Law
Five years earlier

Tapping the tip of my pen on the edge of the desk, I impatiently watched the hands of the classroom clock ticking over and over. Our art and design teacher droned on in the front, completely oblivious to the fact that she had lost the class's attention from the very beginning. With only a week left to not just the school year, but our very high school education, the senior class was just simply biding their time.

Behind me, Dillon drummed a beat to whatever song he currently had stuck in his head, while beside me Zeck kept leering at two giggling brunettes who seemed to be taking turns blowing him kisses and making suggestive motions. No doubt promises for that evening's activities. I had to cover my chuckle with a cough when our teacher finally zeroed in on them and drew the attention of the class.

As for me, well, I was desperate for the period to end so that I could head to the music department. I had the best news of my life to share, a meeting and possible contact with one of the largest record companies in England, and while we were meant to keep it a secret, there was one person I had to tell.

Mister "call me Byron" Patterson.

Technically our music teacher, and quite possibly the love of my life.

Now, I know that people would groan and call me pathetic if they actually heard me say that out loud, but I couldn't help how I felt. How I had felt, for some time now.

Absently I brought my hand up to fiddle with the dog tags that always hung around my neck, a nervous habit I had had since I was young and one I saw Zeck notice as he shot me a curious expression. I shook my head at him, letting him know silently that I was okay, and I was relieved when he focused back on the two girls in our class.

Dropping my hand down onto the table, I tried not to touch them again. They were the only thing I had left of my biological father, a man I had lost before I was old enough to develop proper memories of him. And it was a dead giveaway to my emotions.

When the bell rang I sprang out of my chair and grabbed my bag from the floor, racing to the classroom door. I could hear Dillon shout out something about waiting up, but I wanted a moment alone with Byron. As ridiculous as it sounded, it could very well be our last day at the school, and I just needed to know if those longing glances and subtle touches were all in my head or something more.

Knocking on the classroom door, my heart stuttered at the open and warm smile I was greeted with. "Well, if it isn't one of my favorite students. What can I do for you today, Mr. Kolera? Everything okay?"

Making my way into the classroom, I checked to

see that it was empty apart from us. "Yeah, absolutely."

Eagerness raced through me, and it must have shown because Byron looked up from the paperwork he had in front of him again, and cocked his head to the side with a curious grin. "You seem excited about something."

"Actually, that's what I wanted to talk to you about." I quickly shut the door behind me to give us more privacy and then turned back to approach his desk. Byron didn't seem bothered by any of it, and I took it as a good sign. "We have a meeting this afternoon with a big record label."

Byron's eyes widened, and the older man pushed back his chair and came to stand beside me. His face was lit up, and I nearly swallowed my tongue when large arms came to wrap around me in a hug. "What? Seriously? That's bloody amazing."

I reveled in the feeling of Byron's embrace, enjoying the feel of the other man pressed up close against me. I felt my cock thicken in response and had a moment of panic, though Byron gave no indication he noticed.

Overheated all of a sudden, I pulled back and tried to ignore the flush that crept up my pale face. "Yeah. They loved our demo, said we had the right feel they were looking for and want to meet us. Said if all goes well then we could be in the studio recording by Monday, ay."

"I can't believe it."

"Neither can we," I admitted. We were still trying to convince ourselves that it was real.

"So it all worked out with you and that new kid?" he asked, and I nodded.

While Dillon, Zeck, and I had grown up together, we had discovered Alec after our third audition rejection outside one of our favorite cafes. The kid had been busking after school for a little extra pay, and the moment we heard him, we knew we had found something special. It hadn't taken much arm twisting to convince Alec to work with us, and since then we had been inseparable.

"Alec? Yeah, he's a pretty funny guy. He blends well with us, gave us that something we were missing."

Byron nodded in understanding. "Clearly. I'm proud of you."

"Couldn't have done this without you," I told him, ignoring that fact that I must look like a beetroot right at that moment.

"Yes, you could have," Byron said with a certainty that caught my breath.

"You really don't know, do you?" I asked, bewildered at how clueless the man was to his own worth. To me and to the others. He had supported us, encouraged us, and picked us up when we were ready to give up. And he had inadvertently helped me discover a side of myself I hadn't been aware of. He awoke something in me, and he didn't even know.

"What?"

Stepping closer, I was right in his personal space, and I could see him swallow thickly as he registered the turn in conversation. "You don't see how important you are."

"Law." The sound of my name on the other man's lips made me shiver. "What—"

Pressing forward, my hands came to rest on his chest as I removed the distance between us and cut him off with a chaste kiss.

Byron seemed momentarily stunned and then he was bringing up his hands to rest them in my hips as his lips began to move against mine. Our lips parted, and I moaned when his tongue slipped between them, deepening the kiss. Elated and extremely turned on, I slid my hands into his hair, eager to feel and taste more of him.

More abruptly than it had started, everything ended and Byron pulled right back, separating us entirely. "No, Law, we shouldn't."

Taken aback by the man's sudden change, I frowned. "Why?"

Byron's expression was pained. "Because I'm your teacher."

I smirked. "Not for long."

"Doesn't matter," he insisted, leaving me more than a little confused, given that only seconds before, his tongue had been down my throat.

"Sure it does," I pressed on. "And I'm eighteen. So what's the problem?"

He crossed his arms over his chest, the move serving to create a barrier between us, and my stomach churned at the meaning. "The problem is that you're young and you have this whole journey you're about to experience … and none of this is appropriate."

"Byron, I—"

"Mr. Patterson," he said, effectively cutting me off.

I blinked in surprise. "Since when? You've always encouraged us to call you Byron."

The empty, hollow look on the normally vibrant hazel eyes gutted me. "And maybe that was a mistake."

Heart sinking, I shook my head in denial. "You don't mean that."

"Yeah, Law. I do," he said carefully, tone void of any emotion.

I swallowed down the sob that wanted to burst free. "I thought…"

Byron—no, Mr. Patterson—was shaking his head at me with a look of pity that only served to make me feel worse. "You should go, Law. You have a huge afternoon ahead that you have to plan for, and you shouldn't be wasting it here talking to me."

I nodded, too numb to say or do anything else as I turned my back on him and exited the classroom.

Dillon and Zeck caught up to me just as I reached the school gates, the eldest of us, Dillon, reaching out to stop me with a frown. "You okay, mate?"

I cleared my throat, shaking myself out of my daze. "Yeah, all good."

"You sure?" Zeck asked after studying me for a few seconds.

"Of course. Just, ya know, nervous about the meeting."

My reply was answered with identical and slightly terrifying grins.

"Nothing to be nervous about," Dillon announced with a slightly maniacal laugh. "We're gonna rock their worlds and then once those contracts are signed, we're gonna begin the ride of our lives."

"Too right!" Zeck shouted.

I focused on the energy and positivity my friends were practically vibrating with, pushing away all the negativity even if only for a little while. I was sure later on, when I was alone, I'd go back to feeling like shit again. For now though, I had bigger things to concentrate on.

Seeing Alec waiting impatiently for us on the corner up ahead with an enormous, cheesy grin, I let it all go and just embraced the moment.

"Hell yeah. Look out world, here comes Right Time!"

Chapter One

Law

"We can't go back!"

The crowd cheered, thousands of our screaming fans shouting for more as we finished off the final song for our two piece encore performance. That was it. The show was over. Hell, the tour was almost over with, just one more concert left in two weeks' time. We had gone all the way around the world and back again to finish up with two shows in London, and even though every part of my body ached, my ears rang so loudly I could barely hear my own thoughts, and I was desperate for a bottle of water, I had never felt more alive.

Well, that wasn't entirely true. I felt this way every time we performed. The rush, the adrenaline, it was damned addictive.

Being a member of the boy-band Right Time had led to some pretty crazy and amazing heights.

The boys and I ran off the side of the stage with our dancers, congratulations and applause being offered from backstage crew. Off to the side sat the area where a group of fans who had been lucky enough to either purchase or win VIP passes sat impatiently waiting for us to join them.

Fortunately, management always made sure we had a chance to clean up and compose ourselves before the meet and greet. Not that we had an issue with it, but these people went through a lot sometimes to get there, and the least we could do was not stink them out with our sweat and grime.

"What a bloody rush, ay?" My band-mate Dillon shouted as he threw an arm around my shoulder, his long dark hair only half covering the fact that he was grinning like a loon.

"Seriously ace, boys," I agreed, the excitement still pumping through me. "Still, we all need fuckin' showers, we stink."

Alec jumped me from behind, putting me in a headlock, laughing as I fake gagged. "Very true. Better hurry though, lads. Don't want to be disappointing the fans."

Making quick work of it, I showered and dressed in my room, meeting the lads out in the hall. Our bodyguard Jas stood waiting silently for us as our manager Phillip gave us the same run down he always did before these things. Smile, keep it simple, lots of hugs. This time though he tacked on, "don't answer any questions about your sex life", for good measure.

Clearly the comment was more directed at Dillon and Zeck, who had both found themselves at the center of unwanted attention lately with Dillon's girl falling pregnant, the quickie wedding, or Zeck getting caught in a European sex scandal that rivaled the controversy that was *Fifty Shades*. Still, a shiver ran up my spine, my gut coiling in panic at the thought of someone asking me that question.

I had tried so long to hide that part of me. Making sure I was seen with the right and equally famous women, spotted at the trendiest clubs with a lady on my arm, I had done it all to make sure no one discovered the truth about me.

Boy-bands were always labeled, and people always asked how many of us were gay. According to the statement initially announced by the label we had signed with … none. And it was something we were told to stick to. I didn't think any of the big honchos actually suspected, but they weren't interested in finding out either. A serious don't ask, don't tell policy reigned in the industry. And it sucked. At least for me.

Shaking myself out of those morose thoughts, because now was neither the time nor the place, I followed Phillip to the "green room" with the others close behind me.

As I stepped into the room we were met by squeals and the sounds of giggling by both men and women. I looked up and smiled brightly at the fans gathered in there as a woman in a headset, whose name I couldn't remember, began running around trying to organize the sudden chaos that had been caused by our arrival.

Behind me, Dillon snickered. Even though the man was now very much taken and in love with Ashlyn, he still enjoyed the affect we had on people.

When the headset lady—Veronica her name badge said—directed me over to a small group that consisted of one adult man with his back turned to me and three teenage girls practically vibrating, I groaned. Oh man, this was gonna be loud.

I opened my mouth to greet them, only for the man to turn around, and then it was like I lost my voice as my heart leaped into my throat.

Gaping for a moment, I eventually croaked out, "Byron?"

Fuck, that was embarrassing.

He stood at six foot one with a muscular swimmer's frame encased in tight blue jeans and a simple fitting t-shirt, and short light brown hair. Byron's hazel gaze pinned me where I stood. A little older since the last time I saw him, Byron still held his age well, looking more twenty-something than the thirty-six years that he would be now. Looking at the five o'clock shadow along his strong jawline, I had the insane urge to step forward and lick him.

The thought pulled me up short, and I blinked in

surprise.

What the fuck?

The young girl standing closest to Byron let out a strangled sound, her wide eyes darting between us. I could just imagine what was going through the young girl's head given she and her friends had our all-access backstage "super fan" passes.

"OMG. He knows your name, Uncle Byron?"

Byron flushed, glancing down at his niece before he flicked his gaze back to mine. "Ah … yeah, Emma, I do."

The girl began to ramble while her friends stared on in awe. "How? Why? When did you become so cool?"

"Hey, I've always been cool." I chuckled at Byron's offended expression, grateful that he was momentarily distracted. The man's gaze had always left me feeling open and exposed.

"Well, I mean sure, you *are* the cool Uncle Byron who bought my friends and me these really awesome tickets, but this…"

"But this is like a whole new hemisphere of awesomeness," another one of the young girls finished, almost breathless in her shock.

I had honestly never felt so self-conscious before that moment. Not because of the girls. As shallow as it sounded, I was used to the lust filled expressions on women's faces of varying age groups. Byron was another story. I wondered what he must be thinking, of me, of the situation. Even after all these years the man still had it in him to make me second guess myself. A nervous tension I felt only in his presence. It was ridiculous. *I* was ridiculous.

"Holy shit, Mr. P!"

The abrupt cursing had me turning to Dillon who, with an enormous grin, greeted our former music teacher with a solid hug, thumping the older man on the back. My band-mate was immediately followed by Zeck just as enthusiastically, all the while I stood there completely and utterly dumbfounded.

What was Byron doing there? I mean, I knew he had obviously brought his niece to our show, but Byron had to have known we'd run into each other. Had to have known what that would do to me. Or perhaps he had forgotten. Was that even possible? For me it was just like yesterday.

"Good to see ya, teach," Alec added with a small wave, having only met Byron briefly before we found our success.

"It's good to see you all, too," Byron replied, notably refusing to make eye contact with me.

Was he nervous? So, the man did remember. Or at least some version of it.

"Wait. So you really know them?" Byron's niece asked incredulously, as though she just couldn't believe it.

Byron glared at her, and I hid my smile behind a cough. "I told you I did."

Snort. "Well yeah, but I didn't think you were serious. I thought you were, ya know, trying to be all cool."

"We've established this, Em. I *am* cool."

"Extremely," Zeck agreed, clapping Byron on the back. "If it weren't for your uncle I doubt we'd be here right now."

"And what a right shame that would be, ay lads," Dillon added with a wink to the girls, who all but melted.

"Seriously?" Emma gazed at her uncle with absolute adoration. "Are they serious?"

Byron looked like he was going to disagree, and I cleared my throat, finally finding my voice.

"Definitely. Your uncle was the one who encouraged us, supported us, and when we weren't sure what decisions to make, guided us in the right direction." Byron shot a doubting look at me, obviously remembering the past as I did, but not realizing that while I may not have understood back then, I did now. "Even if we didn't know it at the time."

Something sparked in Byron's hazel eyes, and if I wasn't mistaken it looked close to relief.

"Well, I appreciate that, gents." The older man flushed a little, and for the life of me I couldn't take my eyes away from him. "You've done a hell of a job. I'm proud of you."

"And on that note, if we could hurry this up?" Phillip interrupted obnoxiously.

Part of me wanted to laugh at the man's behavior. We were used to it after all, but another part of me wanted to reach over a slap him for trying to send Byron away so soon.

However, photos, questions, and some more photos later I finally found a chance to pull Byron off to the side for a second.

The moment I laid my palm on the man's arm, I fought a shudder. Honestly, I really shouldn't have been having such a strong reaction to him. It had been years since that embarrassing classroom display, yet all of a sudden it felt like yesterday.

"Can we talk?' I asked hesitantly.

Byron nodded, allowing me to tug him over to a vacant corner. The whole time Byron kept his gaze locked onto his niece, tracking her moves and not letting her out of his sight. It was endearing. And I needed to stop thinking like that immediately.

"Everything okay?" he asked, glancing over at me.

"I could ask you the same thing," I said pointedly.

The older man winced, not even pretending to misunderstand my question. "Depends, I guess. How badly do you hate me?"

At the unsuspecting reply, I laughed. "I never hated you, Byron." He shot me a skeptical look, and I relented. "Okay, maybe I did, but that didn't last long. Not when I realized you did it for my own good."

"Oh yeah." Byron tilted his head to the side, a curious grin playing to his lips. "And how long did that take?"

"Longer than I'd care to admit," I answered with a smirk, almost immediately sobering when I could see the doubt in his eyes. "Seriously though, I get it. And thank you, for doing what I couldn't."

"I almost didn't," Byron whispered, glancing down as if ashamed, and I had to do a double take.

"What?" I asked taking a cautious step forward. Normally I didn't take such risks in public, but then nothing about my reactions to this man was ever normal. "What does that mean?"

Byron shook his head, chuckling humorlessly. "It was so hard to send you away. I knew it was the right thing to do. It didn't matter how old you were. I was your teacher. It was wrong for me to look at you that way. Telling you to go was the right thing. You couldn't turn your back on all this, I couldn't let you."

With my breath lodged in my throat, I took a step back, trying to compose myself. I had so many questions and so much I wanted to say to him, but right then was neither the time nor the place. Frustration gnawed at me. Things were never simple.

Staring off to the right my eyes caught on Ashlyn, Dillon's wife, her blonde hair falling back as she laughed at something Issy, Zeck's girl, had said. When the sound of their chatter reached the guys, both Dillon and Zeck turned in the girls' direction, their expressions of adoration and love.

A small pang hit me when I realized I wanted that. Someone to look at me like that, someone who stood off to the side of the stage for hours just waiting for me to be done. I wanted to feel what Zeck and Dillon were feeling right in that moment, and when I glanced back at Byron it hit me that maybe I could, even if it was only for a brief time.

"Are you free tomorrow night?" I asked abruptly.

My question threw him, his expression confused. "Ah, yeah. No plans."

I swallowed down my nerves and forged on. "Then grab a drink with me, yeah?"

If Byron was surprised by my request, he didn't show it. "Okay."

I tried to hide how elated I felt at his quick answer, knowing I had failed miserably when he grinned. We exchanged numbers discreetly, constantly checking the room to see that there were no eyes on us.

When Phillip called me over to speak to another group, I went reluctantly, knowing I would see Byron soon enough. As I greeted the new people, one girl around my own age telling me how much she loved my tattoos and that she knew every single one I had, I laughed.

"Oh, I doubt that." The wink I sent her had the pretty thing shaking.

"No really, I do," she insisted. "I have all your posters in my room, and on my laptop and my phone, and—"

Unable to help myself I leaned forward and whispered conspiratorially. "Yeah, but what about the ones you can't see?"

It took a moment for the girl to catch on, and then she flushed, giggling along with her friends. Honestly, she was downright adorable and had I swung that way I probably would have made some sort of move. As it was, that mere thought had me searching out for Byron again, seeing him laughing it up with Zeck on the other side of them room.

A frisson of jealousy washed through me at the sight, and I shoved the ludicrous feeling down as hard as I could. Zeck had no interest in Byron, and if the looks I was receiving were any indication, Byron held no interest in Zeck. I just had to be patient and wait to have that attention back on me.

Tomorrow, I told myself. Just have to wait until tomorrow.

****

"Where the hell are you off to?" Dillon grinned as he caught me trying to sneak out of our hotel suit the following night.

Technically it was a penthouse with five bedrooms with their own en-suites, a kitchen, plus a dining and lounge room. Which meant that I had had to make my way through the common area on my way out.

Shit!

"Ah, nowhere?"

"Bullshit." Dillon leaned against the doorway effectively cutting off my way out. "Now, tell us where ya sneakin' off to."

I sighed. "Jesus, nowhere in particular, okay? Just wanted to get out for a bit. That all right? What do you care?"

Dillon's smirked didn't fade. If anything it grew. "Well, since when are you the one who sneaks out? You never break the rules the label sets down. Guess I'm curious what it is that could have you acting this way. Or is it a who?"

"Just because every decision you make is with your prick, doesn't mean the rest of us do, Dill," Zeck said with a chuckle.

Dillon's brows rose, and I groaned at the ensuing banter that was no doubt about to break out between them. "Says the one who literally got caught with his pants down."

"My arse is fabulous. People should be grateful for the chance to see it," Zeck retorted, not the least bit embarrassed.

Dillon went to reply, and I slapped my hand across his mouth. "No. Whatever you're about to say … no. It won't end well, and it will just take longer for me to actually get out of here."

Instead of trying to speak, his green eyes sparkled with mirth as the fucker stuck his tongue out and licked my hand. I wrenched it back glaring at the prick as I shoved him to the side. Fortunately, he went easily. "That's fucking gross."

"Ha. He did that to me the other day when I was trying to get him to shut his trap." Alec chuckled from where he lounged on an armchair, fiddling with his guitar. "Hey, D. Should we let Ashlyn know about your proclivity to make out with certain body parts? I mean honestly, there is just far too much kink going on in this group."

Alec dodged the pillow Zeck aimed at his head but wasn't quick enough for the plastic bottle Dillon threw at him. "Little shit, come're and say that to me."

Dillon lunged at the youngest member of their group, a maniacal laughter springing from Alec as he launched himself out of his seat and ran for his bedroom door.

"And on that note, I'm heading out. I'll see you

all later."

I took the opening and hightailed out of there before someone else tried to stop me, grateful that Zeck had distracted Dillon long enough for me to make my escape.

I owed the lads big time.

Chapter Two

Byron

Taking a sip of the ale I had ordered, I looked towards to doorway for the third time in a matter of minutes, wondering where on earth Law could be. The younger man had said to meet him at this little hole in the wall at eight, and it was now eight-thirty with no Law in sight.

Of course the idea that I had been stood up had crossed my mind, but I quickly squashed that when I recalled how eager he had been to see me again after the concert. Sitting in the small pub in the middle of London was not my typical Sunday night, yet there hadn't been a chance in hell that I would have turned down Law's offer for drinks. I just had to be patient. Hell, I had waited that long already. What was another hour?

I hadn't seen the lads in years. Naturally I had tried to stay up to date with their success as much as possible, astutely avoiding any and all tabloid crap along the way, but I had convinced myself it was merely a passing interest in the boys I had once taught. And then I would remember that moment in the music room with Law on his final day at the high school.

God, I was a mess.

My niece had been a huge fan of the boys of Right Time since they began, and when Emma had told me about all the trouble the lads had been getting into of late, I noticed that in all the scandal, Law was never once mentioned. That sent me on a search to find out exactly what had been going on in their lives, in particular, Law's. And that's when I discovered that while there was plenty to be found on Dillon, Zeck, and Alec, there was very little on Law. Suddenly I had wanted nothing more than to see them, to see him. It was stupid and irrational, but I did it anyway.

What was it that drew me to the younger man? I had tried to place my finger on it back then and had been just as unsuccessful. Was it his fame? His talent? Was I really that shallow? I didn't think so, but I also couldn't work out what it was about Law that had me seeking him out all these years later, still fantasizing about the afternoon in the music room.

Getting my niece those tickets for her and her friends had been a strategic plan. No one would second guess a man who had so kindly taken his teenage niece to see her favorite boy-band in concert. Nor would they find it unusual for him to join her backstage, to keep an eye on her.

Once there I knew I'd see Law. What I had expected after was anyone's guess because honestly my plan hadn't gone that far. Its results, though, were more than I could have ever hoped for.

When I looked over for the fourth time, I finally sighed in relief.

Blue eyes brightened the moment they fell on me, and damned if that didn't make my heart, as well as other appendages, leap to attention. Shit, the kid had some hold on me, for sure.

At five foot ten, lean and sinewy, Law gave off an almost delicate masculinity. Peeking out from under his short sleeve shirt I could see a number a tattoos covering him all the way down to his wrist. They were scattered artistically, and if I stared even closer, which I absolutely was, I could see a hint of something at the V-neck of his top.

His platinum blond hair fell forward to curtain his eyes as he sent me a small nod, showing that when it wasn't spiked up, the locks held a little extra length at the front. As he drew closer I saw that tiny studs sat in both ears, something that had completely slipped my notice the other day.

Soft, plump lips tilted into a warm smile by the time he reached me, and I needed to remind myself how to breathe.

It was official. I was sixteen again.

"Hey," he greeted me as soon as he was in speaking range.

Fortunately, the pub wasn't too loud, just the steady stream of conversation floating while music played quietly in the background. No band stood on stage tonight, so what was usually a packed establishment only seemed to be filled with regulars.

"Hey back. Almost thought you weren't coming," I half joked.

Guilt and apology shone through his eyes as he grimaced. "I'm sorry. The lads were being dicks, and arguing, and ... well, you know how it is with a group of guys."

I nodded even if I really didn't. I had never had a large group of friends growing up. There had been a close few, and then even fewer when I came out at university. Sure, I made more after that, but most of them were like me, quiet, calm and not into a lot of attention.

The young man in front of me was none of those things. He lived and breathed a world I doubted I could ever understand or fit into.

Even now as Law slipped on to the stool beside mine, he seemed tense and alert.

"You look nervous?" I asked, watching as Law's eyes flittered around the room. It was as if the guy expected someone to jump out and mug him. "Everything okay?"

"Yeah, of course," he said unconvincingly as he fidgeted in his seat, indicating to the bartender for a drink like mine.

"Uh-uh." I watched him a little more, noticing his agitation seemed to grow not settle as time went on. "So you just normally look like a startled rabbit?"

That caught his attention as Law slowly turned to me, a small smile finally tilting the edges of his lips. "Rabbit? Really?"

"Hey, you're the one acting all weird on me."

Law's expression was one of chagrin as he accepted his drink from the bartender and took a sip. "Sorry about that. It's just, with all the pressure we've gotten from the label lately, one can never be too careful."

"Pressure?"

"Well, you know, between Dillon and his baby mum, and Zeck being caught out in an international kinky sex scandal, the record company isn't too thrilled with us right now. I think if we didn't bring in the kind of money we did they would have dropped us." Law chuckled with what I assumed was supposed to be good humor, but came out more awkward than anything. "We're expected to be a certain way. We all have our labels."

"Labels?"

Eyes lighting up with humor, Law grinned. "Yeah, you know, Dillon's the cocky ladies' man, Zeck's the kinky and mysterious one, and Alec's the baby of the group."

"What about you?" I asked, more curious than I thought I'd be.

Law snorted. "The blond one."

I blinked in surprise. "The blond one?"

"Yeah." He laughed. "Well, in truth I'm more the blond one that smiles all the time, I guess. I don't mind. I've always been something. When I was younger I was the kid with glasses. When I got older I was the kid with the weird arse name no one could pronounce. Now I'm the blond one that smiles a lot."

I wasn't sure how to respond to that. While it was amusing, I could see the obvious strain it put on him to always be on and happy. Then I recalled the part he mentioned about his name.

Przemyslaw.

Fascination had struck me when I had learned the kid's real name. "I never got to ask, where did your name come from?"

With a grimace, Law explained, "My mother's side of the family is Polish. Przemyslaw is a traditional name that is passed down from firstborn son, onwards. However my grandparents had all girls, and I had the unfortunate luck to be the first male born in my generation. When I was old enough I had it shortened. Now it's only my family that call me that, or the lads when their being arseholes and are clearly askin' for a beating."

"Wow, I honestly don't blame you. I mean, it's not a terrible name," I said, chuckling as Law rolled his eyes in disbelief. "Yeah, okay, it's not great. I know how long it took me to learn how to say it properly."

Law side-eyed me. "If I recall correctly, you butchered it just like everyone else."

I threw my head back and laughed at that. "True. I really did, didn't I?"

"Yup. Only one person outside of my family can say it without struggling."

"Oh yeah, who is that?"

"Zeck."

My eyebrows rose at that. "Zeck? He never seemed the type to concentrate long enough for something like that. The only thing I ever saw him focus on was music and girls. Not particularly in the order."

"I know, right?" Law said, and there was a pale blue lightening of amusement between his lashes. "He hasn't changed all that much, but I tell ya, sometimes the man can surprise you." Suddenly his eyes became flat and unreadable as his tone turned serious. "Still, he gets to be who he is. No regrets, no doubt."

Concern rose in me as I finally registered that the difference I saw in the younger man earlier wasn't so much confidence, a virtue Law had never struggled with, but an underlying tension as though he was always on guard.

I couldn't imagine what it would be like to live that kind of life. Always having to watch everything I said and did. I remembered the difficulties I faced before I came out, first at university and then when I became a teacher. Hiding who I was had been exhausting and time-consuming.

With that thought, my heart sank with the realization that Law was now the one hiding.

"You're not out, are you?"

As I saw him flinch, I knew the answer even before Law spoke. "Not … really."

Now it was my turn to feel uncomfortable.

"What does not really mean?"

"It means … no." Law sighed, scrubbing a hand through his hair. "I just don't think it's a good idea to let it get out, ya know? We've got enough going on, and the label doesn't want any more shit to deal with. Besides it's not really anyone's business."

"Maybe I should go," I said as I made a move to stand.

With all the grief and heartache I had faced over the years I had made a point of staying away from closeted men and straight guys looking to experiment. I had learned the hard way that nothing good ever came

175

from getting involved with someone who couldn't be honest about themselves, at least to the people they cared about most. Mainly because at the end of the day if they couldn't be open for their own sake, they sure as fuck weren't going to do it for mine.

It sucked. It was fact. It was life.

Which was why as much as I liked Law, and as much as a small part of me had always desired him even when it wasn't appropriate, I was ready to walk away.

"Wait." Law's desperate plea had me stopping before I even registered what I was doing. "Please don't go."

Sliding off of his own stool, Law made an abortive move towards me. The younger man hesitated, his hand half reaching out yet fingers curled into a fist, sweeping his gaze over the room to see if anyone was watching.

I groaned. "Law, we can't do this."

Law visibly swallowed as turned to look back at me. "Do what?"

"This," I said, waving a hand between us. "We both know why I'm here, why you invited me, but if you're still pretending you're something you're not then there isn't a point in going any further."

"Yes, there is." Law raised a hand, indicating to the others in the room. "I may have to hide from these people, but you're the one person I can be myself around, and I didn't realize how badly I wanted or needed that until I saw you again. Talking to you now, so openly, fuck, I miss that. So please, just give this a chance. I'm not making demands or ultimatums, I'm just asking you not to do the same. Can we just see what's here first before we start worrying about everything else?"

What Law was asking went against everything I had told myself I wanted. I didn't want to hide, pretend or to share in anyway. Yet even as I thought these things I felt myself cave. Who was I kidding? I would give this guy as many chances as he wanted. I would probably end up regretting most of them, but I would, because apparently I was into masochism. Who knew?

Slowly I lowered myself back onto the stool, reaching for my beer and sculling the rest of it, seeing Law doing the same.

"Does anyone else know?" When all Law did was shake his head, I sighed. "None of the guys, Dillon, Zeck, Alec? What about your family? Any friends you have outside the band?"

Law ran a hand through his already mussed up hair, shrugging as he looked anywhere but at me. "I'm not really close to many people outside of the band. Me and the lads, we spend so much of our time together, and with what we do, letting people in is hard. Sometimes you can't tell the difference between those who are genuine and those who are in it for the glory."

"Glory?" I asked innocently, even though I had only just been asking myself if that had been what I found appealing about him.

"Yeah, you know, like the fame. Being able to claim they bagged one of us. The freebies and the wild times. Hell, look at Zeck. The guy thought everything was safe and secure, but then that chick came along and caused all that shit for him."

"I had heard something, but honestly I stopped listening when I realized they were basically just invading his privacy." The fact that so many people were desperately trying to know the personal details of the boys' sex lives just astounded me. I knew I couldn't understand what their life was like, the world they lived in, but I also couldn't understand how Law went through each day not being honest with those he loved. "But seriously, not even your family?"

Law's attention was finally back on me, his piercing gaze firm and assessing as though he suddenly wondered whether I could be trusted. Which hurt more than I cared to admit. "The guys are my family. If I haven't told them, then why would I tell another soul?"

The words and Law's tone struck me silent for a moment. When I could hold it in no longer I finally said, "But you told me."

Law's gaze softened, his eyes filled with warmth and something I barely dared to consider as affection. "You're different."

"Why, because you knew I was gay?" I pushed, wanting an answer as to why he had chosen to open up to me all those years ago.

"No," he said with a smile, so gentle and sweet it made my heart skip a beat. "Because I wanted you to be."

Damn.

I had no idea what my expression must have been, but Law chuckled. "You can't honestly be surprised, can you? I all but bloody jumped you on my last day of school. I *know* you have to remember the music room ... that kiss. I do."

As that particular memory came flooding back, my cock hardened, struggling against the zipper of my jeans as those pictures morphed into future possibilities. Seeing myself reach over and grabbing hold of Law's neck and dragging him closer, the feel of those plush lips against mine as I rocked us together, grinding against him like a horny teenager who'd just discovered what his dick was for.

A throat clearing had me jerking back to the present, the smirk playing on Law's face telling me the younger man could knew exactly where my train of thought had led.

Coughing, I attempted to discreetly adjust the ever growing and increasingly uncomfortable bulge in my pants. A move that didn't go unnoticed by an extremely cocky Law.

"Got a problem there?"

"Nothing I can't handle on my own," I retorted.

Law all but openly leered. "Why would you want to though when you don't have to?"

His boldness surprised me given that only a moment ago Law had been acting all squirrelly about being caught in a man-on-man scenario. I honestly couldn't keep up.

"Law?"

"Come back with me," the younger man whispered as he daringly leaned closer. "Come back to the hotel and spend the night with me."

Now it was my turn to fidget. "That's moving a bit fast, don't you think?"

Law pulled away slightly, laughing. "Fast? I was thinking it's been a long time coming actually."

At that I stiffened, narrowing my eyes. "Is that all this is to you? A good night to fulfill some childhood fantasy?"

Losing all his assured cockiness, Law shook his head. "No, oh God, of course not. I—I just thought..."

Seeing the younger man panic at the thought of insulting me calmed me somewhat. "So this is something you want to explore? For more than just sex?"

Law flushed, darting his eyes around the room again. "Ah, yeah."

Trying not to laugh, I wasn't sure if I found Law's mixed emotions and signals adorable or just downright confusing. Either way I was willing to admit that even if only a small part of me found it adorable, then I was already sunk. The lad had me hook, line, and sinker.

Fuck, this was going to end badly.

****

Law

Waiting at the reception desk for another room key, the pounding of my pulse drowned out all the other noise in the busy hotel. All the while I could practically feel Byron's gaze on me from where he stood patiently near the lifts. Byron had taken the opportunity to duck into the small shop in the foyer to get some necessities while I found us some privacy. I knew that I needed to get another room away from the others, given what Byron and I were about to do, and was grateful that the other man hadn't question my decision.

The receptionist, Alyssa, smiled warmly as she handed me my new key. "Here we are, room five-oh-three, just below the penthouse."

"Thanks," I mumbled, giving her a brief smile before I made my way quickly over to Byron.

Wasting no time, I all but dragged Byron into the cart when the elevator opened, hearing him chuckle as he let me. Truth was, given our size and build difference, if Byron hadn't wanted me to move him then I couldn't.

Something about that passing thought shot a jolt of lust down my spine, and it was all I could do to bite my lip and not moan in the confined space. Next to me Byron snickered, and I met his gaze realizing he had been watching me the entire time. Heat infused my face, and I was eternally grateful that no one else had slipped into the elevator with us.

When the ding sounded and the doors opened, it was Byron's turn to become impatient as he wrapped a strong, firm hand around my wrist and tugged me along behind him. I had only a second of disappointment at losing the feeling of the man's touch, letting out a yelp as Byron shoved me up against the wall and crushed his lips to mine. Unthinking of the dangers of being caught, I wound my arms around Byron's neck, slipping my tongue between his lips to deepen the kiss. It was hot and dirty, and I couldn't get enough.

When Byron pulled back I made a sound of protest, blinking in surprise as he unlocked the door and pulled me inside the suite.

When the hell did he get the key off of me?

I barely had a chance to take in the small sitting room, allowing myself to be swept up in the moment as Byron took control as he stripped us of our shirts along the way.

Stumbling back onto the bed with a yelp, I groaned as Byron threw something onto the bedside table and then fell on top of me. Pinning me to the mattress, Byron ground down, rubbing our erections together. The need to feel friction consumed me as I joined him, jerking my hips up to meet his.

"Fuck, I want you," Byron muttered, continuing to thrust.

"Yes," I hissed, scoring my nails into Byron's flesh.

I could feel him shiver as they trailed down his back. Byron nipped and sucked his way down my jawline and to my neck, no doubt leaving marks as went.

When Byron stopped I opened up my eyes, which I hadn't even realized I had closed. "What's wrong?"

I followed the man's gaze to the dog tags that sat on my chest and instantly sobered.

"Whose?" he asked simply.

"My dad's," I answered, hoping that was the end of the conversation.

Byron stared at me for a moment before nodding, fortunately leaving the topic and leaning down to kiss me again. I didn't object when he reached for them and slid them off my neck, touched at the great care he took to place them on the side table.

Turning back to me, Byron's eyes heated up as he raked them down my body. "Fuck, I love your tatts."

Moaning, I arched up into him as he dragged his tongue down across my angelic tattoo, which covered most of my left pec, gasping when his teeth nipped gently. He continued tracing the rest of my ink that covered my left arm, paying special attention to the thick black band that wrapped itself all the way around my bicep, as his hand reached out blindly to find the bedside table and the bag he had discarded there.

That was a good idea. Lube and condoms. We needed those.

Above him, Byron growled in frustration when he came up empty.

"Here. It's here." I easily grabbed them as Byron began to make his way down the column of my neck, handing the lube and condom to him quickly. "Hurry."

"Bossy." He nipped my lower lip. "I'm going to take my time with you, and you're going to love it."

I moaned. "Oh God. Please, Byron."

It had been so long since I had let down my guard, allowed myself to feel something like this. Everything even remotely recent had been rushed and impersonal with a hint of fear overlying all of it. Afraid of being recognized, of being caught and outed. But this, I could have this right now, and I trusted Byron implicitly.

Tonight was for us.

Chapter Three

Byron

Hearing Law moan my name was all it took for me to lose all control, and without another thought, I stripped us of the rest of our clothing until we were both bare. Beneath me, Law strained upwards, begging as I leaned forward and latched onto one of his beaded nipples.

"Ah, yes," Law hissed.

Biting down hard, I chuckled at Law's gasp. Enjoying the sounds I elicited from Law, I worried at the two tanned discs, swapping back and forth before making my way down Law's lithe body. Parting his thighs wide I slowly licked a path up Law's now-weeping cock.

"Please."

A dark grin spread across my lips as I reveled at the sound of Law's begging. I never considered myself the kind of man who got off on hearing his lovers tortured and desperate pleas, but apparently I was. As I trailed my tongue lower, flicking it over his sac, Law jerked his hips.

"Please," he whined again.

"God, you sound so good begging," I admitted with a chuckle.

"I'll beg all you want. Just fuck me, now."

Relenting a little, I adjusted myself to be able to wrap my lips around the crown of his cock, sucking but not quite taking him in properly.

"Oh, oh yeah. God, I love that. Just … oh … yeah," Law babbled. Wetting my fingers with the lube, I pulled back from my ministrations and gradually slid two fingers in his hole. "Ah, yes … oh, God … that's it … so good!"

Adding another finger, I finally took the entire

length of Law's cock down, until the tip nudged the back of my throat. Mewling, his hands clutching the sheets, at my hair, Law was completely at my mercy. Lifting so that only the tip remained in my mouth, I sucked the head as I slid in a fourth finger. I knew it had been a while since Law had given in and allowed himself to go this far, and I wanted to make sure he was well prepared before things went any further.

It all seemed to be too much for Law however as the younger man's balls drew up at the intrusion of the fourth finger, and I found myself moaning at the taste of him as Law lost himself to the pleasure and came, coating my throat.

Releasing Law's spent cock, I rolled the younger man over onto his knees, Law happily allowing me to manhandle him into position. Reaching blindly for the lube and condom that had been dropped to the bed, I made quick work of covering and slicking myself up.

"Christ. I'm going to fuck you so hard," I told him right before I plunged my cock deep inside the temptation in front of me.

Law hissed and then shouted as he spread his legs wider, pushing his ass back onto my cock. I gripped Law's hips, pumping in and out, unable to slow down. Law seemed to be as lost as I was, meeting me with every thrust.

A grunt that sounded more pained than pleasurable shocked me out of my lusty hazy. Worried I was hurting the younger man, I slowed down. When I claimed some of my self-control back, I watched my cock slip in and out of Law's ass steadily. "So good. You feel so good. Can't get enough. Do you like how it feels, Law? Is this what you want?"

Law threw a wide-eyed look over his shoulder as he moaned, nodding and rocking back onto my cock.

"Answer me."

"Yes," he choked out. "God, yes. I love it."

"Love what?" I needed to hear Law say it. I had no idea why, but just the thought of hearing the words fall from the younger man's lips sent a jolt of lust rushing through me. Like if Law admitted out loud how this made him feel then I would own a part of him. It sounded crazy and possessive even to me, but this whole thing seemed to be. Law brought out instincts in me I never even knew I had.

Law lowered his shoulders to the bed. "I love your cock in my arse. Fucking me. Taking me. Please."

Oh shit.

Spurred on by Law's desperate words, I placed one hand flat between Law's shoulder blades and the other on the small of his back. Thrusting into Law with a little more strength than I had meant to, I watched Law slide forward. "Is this what you want, Przemyslaw?"

"Oh God. More," Law cried out, clearly reacting to the sound of his full name on my lips.

I knew he had a thing for it. The younger man's name was so difficult to pronounce, and I had spent so long teaching myself how to say it when he had been my student. At the time it had been to save us both the embarrassment of Law having to correct me, but now I saw just how much it turned Law on to hear me call him that.

I clamped a hand tight on his hip as I pistoned into Law's body. He cried out as his band of muscles began to milk my cock, his orgasm pushing me over the edge.

"Yes," I hissed, before I bit into Law's shoulder, not hard enough to break the skin but enough to leave a mark. I came hard, lights flashing behind my closed lids.

We went on and on as I ground my cock into Law

until I gradually eased back enough for me to slip out of Law's channel.

"That was … holy crap," Law panted out the words against the sheet.

Falling to the side, I cleaned up and gave us both a cursory wipe down with the sheet that had been half kicked off the bed, then curled an arm around Law's waist, tugging the younger man closer. "You can say that again," I mumbled into Law's shoulder already half asleep.

Just as I drifted off, I heard Law whisper, "Holy crap."

****

Law

The following morning I woke slowly, taking in the twinges of pain, good and bad, that I wasn't used to. It had been so long since I had been with anyone, and no one had ever taken me so completely like Byron had. A tingle crept over my skin at the memory of Byron's weight over me, the feeling of the man deep inside.

Behind me, the man in question shifted in his sleep. I rolled over to face him, taking in the smooth lines of the handsome man's features. Lifting a hand I traced across his jaw and enjoying the way his stubble pricked my fingertips.

"Morning."

"Mornin'," he mumbled, still half asleep. "Wha' time's it?"

"Just past six."

I grinned as he turned to bury his head in the pillow, making a strangled sound and scrunching up his face as though the mere thought of having to get up was abhorrent. And really it kind of was.

Byron huffed something out against the pillow, but I couldn't hear. "What was that?"

"Hafta go."

His reply left on odd feeling settling inside my chest. "Oh."

The man must have heard something in my voice because he lifted his head from where it was buried, staring straight at me. Tilting his head to the side, he examined me, and I tried hard not to squirm. "Only because I have a class to teach in about three hours and it takes that long just to get from here to home."

The uncomfortable feeling settled with Byron's words, and I nodded. "Right. I forgot it was Monday."

Byron flipped over onto his back, his arms stretching upwards as the groaned. The older man flopped back on to the bed, turning his head to the side and smiling. "Not to mention my need for a shower and a fresh change of clothes. I deal with teenagers, and they pick up on a hell of a lot of things they shouldn't."

I chuckled at that. "Ah, hormonal youth. Those were the days."

"The days?" he said incredulously. "What are you now, twenty-three? Get back to me once you've passed thirty."

"Nothing wrong with thirty-something. I've quite enjoyed it myself." The heated look he sent me had my already semi-hard cock reaching its full potential. "Don't look at me like that if you can't follow through."

Byron seemed to consider his options, slumping down in defeat. "I really do have to go."

I loved hearing how miserable he sounded at the idea.

"When will I see you again?" I asked hesitantly.

We hadn't really defined what this was, and while I had admitted to myself it could only end one way, that didn't mean I wanted things to end so soon.

Reaching out and cupping his hand behind my

head, Byron dragged me in for a mind numbingly deep kiss. "I probably won't be able to make it back here for a little while. Exams have just started for the seniors, so the next two weeks are going to be full on."

Disappointed in having to wait so long, an idea hit me. "Well, I owe my parents a visit. I was thinking of making time this week between rehearsals and the few interviews we have set up. Plus there is the time we said we'd put towards writing a few new songs..." I bit my lip, frowning as I raised myself up on an elbow and started down at the other man. "I'll make it work. I'll see the 'rents, and then I'll come see you. If that's okay?"

"It's more than okay."

After that we were both in a flurry of movement, getting dressed and out the door. Parting at the lifts, I snuck one final kiss in when I was sure the coast was clear before we went our separate ways, making plans for me to call him tonight once I was free.

It was utterly ridiculous how very much I felt like a teenager again.

Making my way back up to the penthouse, I slide the card through the automated door, wincing at the beeping it made to confirm my access. Was it always that loud?

On the home stretch, I closed the door behind me, and seeing the coast was clear, I stepped towards my bedroom.

"Late night or early morning?"

The unsuspecting question startled me, and I whipped around nearly falling arse over tit to see an extremely amused Zeck sitting on the couch.

How had I not seen him?

"Ahhh..." My mind was blank, and I struggled to come up with a believable excuse. It was too damned early for this shit.

"Wasn't supposed to be a tough one." Zeck chuckled, shaking his head. His eyes held a subtle change, almost like understanding or knowledge that had me swallowing hard. "Chill, mate. We've all had those kinds of nights. About time you did, too, but if it's got your britches in such a twist then I'll keep it between us."

I nodded gratefully, making a quick escape just as I heard a moan come from one of the other rooms. Given Dillon and his new wife Ashlyn had just welcomed baby Grace into the world, my money was on Alec. Who he had in there, I had no bloody clue, and my desire for my own privacy meant that I was happy not to find out. Regardless of how close we were, I knew better than any one of us that there was nothing wrong with having a few secrets.

All I truly wanted was to spend some time with Byron, to get to know the amazing man a little more, before things inevitably blew up in my face. Perhaps that was a negative way to look at it, and if it were just me then maybe it's a risk I would take, but I wouldn't do that to the lads.

I owed them more than that, and I knew I couldn't have it all.

Chapter Four

Byron

Two weeks had gone by since I had reconnected with Law. While I had fully intended on socializing with the others of the band as well, that had gone by the wayside since Law and I had met for drinks. Everything, and I mean absolutely everything, had been focused solely on Law.

Getting to know the real Law had been amazing, and I slowly realized that it wasn't just his sexuality that he kept hidden from the rest of the world. The normally shy man had a wicked sense of humor, loved to pull pranks on his fellow band-mates, and had a deep passion for art of any form. Even his tattoos all meant something deep and profound. Two thick black bands sat on each bicep for his grandparents that he had lost as a child. Law had said to him, it had felt as though they were the only two adults in his life who had ever shown pure love and affection for him. An angel spread across the entire expanse of his chest, a reminder that no matter how bad things could get, that if he had faith then everything would work out.

My favorite, though, had to be the four dragons circling most of his back. Law had said he had gotten them after they signed their first contract deal, and that they were a representation of the four of them. Their loyalty to each other and the fierce protectiveness that they held for one another.

I had seen him twice in person since then. One time which had been planned when Law had visited his parents on the Tuesday evening of the first week, and another which had been a pleasant surprise on Thursday afternoon in the second week just after I had gotten home from work. Finding Law Kolera waiting on my doorstep had been like a dream come true.

The rest of the time had been filled with phone calls, messages and one occasion of Skype. Which was why on Friday night I was unsurprised but happy nonetheless when my phone began to ring and I was Law's name flash across the screen.

"Hey, miss me already?" I answered happily. When all I was met with was silence, I frowned. "Law?"

I heard his breath hitch on the other end of the phone, then finally his voice. "Can I see you tonight?"

"Tonight?" Surprised at the request, I checked the time seeing it was already nine o'clock. "I wouldn't get there until midnight."

"I—I know. I just..."

As he trailed off, I became more concerned. "What happened? Is everything okay?"

A heavy sigh filtered through. "Just been a lot of crap. Had management get up in arms over some shit, and then there's the rumors. Fuck, maybe I shouldn't have asked you to come over. Might not be a good idea."

Hearing Law work himself up, I interrupted him. "Law. You aren't making any sense. What rumors? What happened?"

"I just ... I was sitting here with the lads and their girls, and ... I'd just really like to see you. Even though it's probably not a really good idea. We have a concert tomorrow night, and I have to be here first thing in the morning otherwise I'd come to you. I completely understand if—"

"I'll be there." I cut him off before he could say anything else.

"Are you sure?"

"Absolutely."

Law chuckled. "Okay. I'll get our room again."

Hanging, I stared at my phone for a good minute,

struggling not to get my hopes up. All week, through countless discussions, I had been working on getting Law to open up. Maybe this was a sign that the younger man was ready to take the next step, or at least a little nudge in that direction.

If I could get him to be open and honest about himself, then maybe we actually stood a chance. One could hope anyway. For now I would focus on the fact that when Law had needed someone, I had been the first person he had turned to. And that could be enough … for now.

****

Knocking on the door to what we now considered "our room", I patiently waited for Law to answer. I could hear him hesitate on the other side of the door and his words from earlier echoed in my mind.

Maybe I shouldn't have asked you to come over. Might not be a good idea.

My stomach clenched at the thought of being turned away, but when Law finally opened up and greeted me with a tired yet relieved smile I relaxed a little.

"Hey, I'm glad you made it," Law whispered, reaching out to pull me inside.

He had barely closed the door behind us before I stepped into his personal space, placing both of my hands on his hips. "Me too. Want to tell me what happened? You sounded pretty stressed."

With a grimace, Law pulled away nibbling on his lower lip as he moved towards the lounge and flopped down onto the cushions. I realized then just how troubled he seemed. Never had I seen the younger man such a mess. His shirt was creased, untucked and half the buttons undone, and his hair stood on end as though he had spent the better part of the night running his fingers through it constantly.

"Law?"

"There's been some issues come up."

Frowning at the vague response, I asked, "What does that mean ... issues?"

Law growled. An actual growl of frustration which momentarily stunned me. "Someone saw something. There hasn't been any confirmation. It's all talk, but..."

I watched Law pace, worried when the slightly manic look in the younger man's eyes didn't dim. Then it hit me. "You mean about us?"

When Law didn't answer me, I felt my anger boil. How was I supposed to help him if he wouldn't speak to me?

"For God's sake, would you just stop and talk to me!"

My tone had its desired effect. Law blinked up at me as though only just truly seeing that I was there. "I'm sorry."

I sighed, moving closer to him. "Don't be sorry. Just tell me what's going on. You know, this doesn't just affect you, right?"

Taking my hand in his, Law nodded. "You're right, I'm sorry. I just wasn't expecting it. Which is kind of stupid when you think about it because hasn't that been what I've been going on about since we started this? I still didn't see it coming though."

"So someone knows about us?" I hid how much relief I experienced at the idea of us being outed.

"Not us, exactly. More that there are rumors going around about one of us being spotted getting 'cozy' with another guy." Law scratched absently at his chin, but I could tell it was a sign of agitation on his part. "There's also a bunch of other stuff about drugs or something, which is bullshit, so whoever is spreading this stuff doesn't have all, if any, of the details. I know the lads, and none of them would touch that crap."

Disappointment and guilt for feeling that way hit me with his explanation.

"Earlier on the phone you mentioned your management. What did they have to say about it?" I asked, draping an arm across the back of the lounge and enjoying the feel of him as Law didn't even hesitate to move closer to me.

"The usual," he said with a shrug. "They don't want to know if it's true or not, just keep our noses clean. And if there is any chance of it surfacing, squash it now."

The agonizing pain that shot through me took me by surprise. I hadn't expected such a violent reaction from the idea that Law would call it quits between us.

"Is that why you called me here?" I asked, unable to look him in the eye.

Law bolted up in his seat, jaw clenching. "No. Just … no, Byron. Do you really think I would do that?"

Instead of answering, because honestly a part of me didn't know, I raised my hand to trace a finger across his furrowed brow. "What do you want me to do? How can I make you feel better?"

Because that was really all I wanted to do. Make him feel better, safer … loved? The thought slammed into me, almost leaving me breathless. *Oh shit!*

For the first time since I had arrived Law gave me a genuine and effortless smile. "As corny as it sounds … can you just hold me?"

"Always," I whispered without hesitation.

No matter how much I tried to convince myself that I was in control, that I knew what I was doing, I was sinking fast. Somehow I had managed to push Law away all those years ago, but for the life of me I couldn't find the strength now. I didn't want to. And when I got to hold him like this, I didn't even want to no matter the outcome. Right in that moment with stark clarity a thought hit me—this was going to end up hurting.

****

Waking up to the gentle glow of the morning sun filtering through the large window the next morning, I buried my head into the soft curls of blond hair that belonged to the man wrapped up in my arms. I found there was something incredibly intimate about holding Law like that. As if Law trusted me by turning his bare back to me in the dark.

When I had arrived the night before, Law hadn't been seeking anything but simple contact and affection. A thrill had shot through me when I had realized he hadn't called me for sex, just companionship. The rumors and his managements response had led him to seek out comfort … from me. It was like Law had acknowledged that what we had growing between us was more than physical. It was a hell of a feeling.

"Morning," I whispered when Law shifted and his breathing changed to let me know he was awake.

"Morning," Law muttered, still half asleep.

"You okay?" I asked, still concerned by how off he had seemed before I arrived. "Last night, you seemed … upset. Just want to make sure you're feeling better."

"Yeah. I just needed…"

I waited for Law to finish the sentence, never more aware of how important one word could be, never more understanding of the difference between *this* and *you*.

Law didn't continue, his breathing evening out slowly as his hand reached up to rest over mine on his chest, crossed over his sternum like a shield.

"Sometimes it feels like I'm inside myself, trying to escape me, y'know?" he said, voice unusually quiet, weak like I had never heard before. I nodded silently, waiting for Law to continue. "And I don't know why, but you're ... see, Dillon, Zeck, Alec, they help. They get some of it, but they're not—not ... you."

My fingers curled, pressing into Law's chest like I wanted to reach in and grab his heart, hold it, protect it. I held him steady, exhaling softly against the nape of his neck where his hair was getting a little too long, curling against the skin. So white and perfect.

"Sometimes, I just need you, here."

It was almost like a confession, and with it, Law's body went lax and pliant against mine. I pressed a leg between Law's, letting my head fall forward against a cool, pallid shoulder.

"Okay," I said, pressing a kiss there without another word.

Law let out a little chuckle.

"Did you just kiss my shoulder?" he whispered. I lifted my head to look at Law.

"Yeah. Problem with that?" I asked, knowing there really wasn't.

After a second, Law lifted his hand to his neck, touching two long fingers to the pale stretch of his jugular. He pushed his head back.

"Why not here?"

My pulse skipped a little as I lowered my head and placed my lips against the curve of Law's neck, open mouthed and a little wet just below his fingers. Law exhaled slowly, moving his fingers up further, to the tender soft skin just below the cut of his jaw, between his ear and his throat. So vulnerable.

"And here?"

I trailed the path Law's fingers had taken, and Law moved his hand away so I could press a sucking kiss to the softness, tongue sweeping out over the salty skin.

Law murmured quietly in approval, the palm of his hand reaching up to cup the back of my head, spreading through my short hair.

Pulling away with a wet noise, Law turned his head and had barely breathed out the word, *here*, before I was kissing him, Law's lips were a little cold from the early morning breeze coming through the window, but his mouth hot and wet and sweet. Law groaned, nudging his hips back into mine as I pushed myself up on one elbow and wrapped my other arm around Law's waist and rutted forward against, loving the feel of him flush against me.

"God, Byron, please," Law whispered breathlessly, taking my hand and guiding it down over his flat stomach and to his hard cock. Law closed his eyes and moaned as I got a hand around him, dry as fuck at first but quickly wet from the pre-cum Law leaked.

"Oh fuck," he breathed, grinding back against me as best as he could, fucking into my fist simultaneously. "C'mon, Byron, need you."

Law blindly reached out to grab my hip and tug it forward, both of us groaning at the new skin-to-skin contact. Law tried to wrap his long fingers around the girth of my erection, making a noise of loss when I slapped his hand away and pushed his legs together, my cock slipping in between.

"Lube, lube," Law panted, reaching out for the bedside table and returning with a little bottle, slicking the space between his thighs that I was slowly fucking into.

"Fuck, Law," I groaned as I continued to jerk him off, every so often feeling the head of my cock nudge against his balls, feeling Law shudder and moan in return.

We aren't kissing any more. Why aren't we kissing?

"Przemyslaw," I whispered in his ear, earning

myself a whimper before Law turned his head back, capturing my mouth as best as he could, keening into the kiss and digging his fingers into my thigh.

"Fuck, I'm, oh God, By—"

"C'mon, that's it, sweetheart. Come for me," I murmured a little desperately, almost like I wanted Law's orgasm more than my own. And maybe I did. Law released an absolutely wrecked cry as he came into my fist, stomach and thighs taut as his back arched. Cursing, I thrust three more times before I was coming, too, panting against Law's jaw.

Pressing my face into Law's shoulder blade, I tried to catch his breath, enjoying the way Law was practically vibrating next in front of me.

"Fuck, that was perfect," Law whispered, a little hoarse, but ultimately gratified. I hummed in agreement, kissing the skin beneath his mouth, most of the right side of his face and shoulder. I noticed his normally pale skin was pink with stubble burn, and there was a dark messy bruise I had left behind just below his jaw, stark and purple against porcelain white.

Fuck, that was hot.

"Shower?" I asked, after a moment, knowing that if we didn't clean up soon things were going to only get worse.

"Also perfect," Law replied, sitting up.

We cleaned up as quickly as was possible when a loud noise from outside the bedroom door altered to someone else's presence in the suite. Law froze immediately, panicked eyes widening when the familiar sounds of his band-mates filtered through the door.

"Oh Law. Hunny bunny. Whatcha up to in there?" Zeck called out with a cackle.

A loud thump banged against the door, and then Dillon's voice could be heard. "Got some little chicky in there with you, mate? It hurts our feelings that you haven't introduced us."

Law covered his face with his hands as though that would somehow make them disappear.

"Law—" I started only for the younger man to cut me off with a hiss. Frowning, I tilted my head to the side, silently questioning him.

Law approached me slowly, leaning into whisper. "Just stay here okay. I'll get rid of them."

I nodded, taking a seat on the bed and watched him tug on a pair of pants before slipping out the door and closing it firmly behind him.

"What the fuck are you guys doing here?" I heard him ask, his tone harsh and accusing.

Silence met him for a moment. Then Dillon spoke up. "Sheesh. What crawled up your arse? We came to see what the hell was going on. You've been skipping out a lot lately, and then we found out that you had another room here in the hotel. So call us curious, we came to check it out."

"Curiosity killed the cat," Law muttered.

Curiosity indeed, I found myself stepping closer to the door, pressing my ear up against the dark mahogany, in hopes of hearing more.

"Seriously though, what's up?" That had to be Alec, the one voice I wasn't completely familiar with.

"Nothing. Just, can you guys go?"

"What, leave before you introduce us to the beauty that has finally captured your attention? I think not," Dillon answered, and I could practically hear his grin. "Unless … ya know, she's not the easy on the eyes, in which case it's all good. Looks aren't everything you know. It's what's on the inside that counts."

Someone snorted.

"I'll be sure to tell Ashlyn you said that, mate,"

Zeck added with a chuckle. "Listen, maybe we should go, give them their privacy."

"H-how do you even know I have someone here?"

Even I rolled my eyes at Law's stupid question. God, the man could be an idiot.

"Ah, you mean apart from the fact that you're covered in hickeys the size of Europe and you're acting like the guard dog to the motherfucking queen's bedroom?" Dillon replied incredulously. "Back me up, Zeck."

"Oh hell no. I've know you two long enough to know that *back me up, Zeck*, is two seconds away from *shut the hell up, Zeck, who asked you?*"

A bubble of laughter burst through my lips at that, and I didn't have enough time to cover my mouth to muffle the sound. *Shit.*

"Ah, Law?"

Law sighed loud enough that I could hear him through the door. "Okay, yes, someone is in there. Yes, I have been spending time with them. I'd like to spend more time with them. The last two weeks have been amazing, and I would appreciate it if you guys didn't fuck this up for me. Happy?"

My heart skipped a beat at Law's words. The man sounded so honest and open that for the first time I seriously believed Law might be ready. I tried not to get my hopes up, but Law had never come so close to telling the others the truth before. Maybe this was it?

"Extremely." There was no doubt in my mind that Dillon was leering. "So, can we meet her?"

I waited for Law to speak up and correct Dillon, to tell him there was no *her*. I should have seen it coming, though.

Law laughed. "Nah, not yet. She's super shy, and things are only just starting to get serious. You know what girls are like. Have to get the feelings talk out of the way first."

His response was met with laughter even as I felt like I had just been hit in the gut with a cricket bat.

"Law." Zeck's tone held a wealth of censor that would have surprised me more had I not felt so completely torn apart.

Having heard enough I pulled myself away from the door and threw the rest of my clothes on. I couldn't believe how stupid I had been. Christ, what had I honestly expected? Too much clearly.

I paced the room for a second before thinking, *fuck it*, and stormed to the door. I knew the moment I opened it and stepped out that Law's whole world would quite possibly come crashing down, but given the aching pain currently coursing through me at that moment, I didn't care.

Grabbing the rest of my belongings I reached for the handle, turning it and tugging it opened. The group had still been talking, but the moment the others saw me, silence fell, awkward and uncomfortable.

In front of me Law's shoulders tensed, and I braced myself.

Well, here goes everything.

****

Law

Turning around I was momentarily stunned to see a completely dressed Byron standing in the doorway of the bedroom. He stared at me, apprehension clouding his handsome features, and my stomach churned.

He had heard.

"Byron."

"Holy shit," sounded behind me, but I ignored it, focused on the man before me.

"Byron, is everything okay?" I asked tentatively,

unsure if I really wanted him to answer given his expression.

"No. No, it isn't." Sadness dimmed his usually bright blue eyes. Shaking his head, Byron moved to stand in front of me. The stiffness in his shoulders belied the calm tone in which he spoke. "I'm sorry, Law. I thought I could do this, but it was a mistake."

His words slammed into me with such force I almost stumbled. This couldn't be happening.

"What? Why? Byron, jus—" Aware that I was all out begging in front of my band-mates, I paused, which just served to aggravate Byron more.

"I can't pretend, Law," Byron said, cutting me off and raising his voice slightly at the end. "This isn't me. I'm not this person. Lying, hiding. I've done that. I fought so hard to not have to be that person, and here I am jumping right back into that closet with you? I can't. I won't."

I fought for control, so many words and accusations wanting bubbling inside me. Byron had known what he was getting into. I had not hidden the fact that I wasn't out, wasn't ready to be. I had never lied to him. And now he had just outed me to the entire group.

"Are you serious right now?" I asked, somewhat bewildered and extremely pissed off.

"If you want to be with me, Law, then no hiding, no lying."

I couldn't believe what I was hearing.

"So this is an ultimatum then. Come out to the world, or we're done? Is that it?"

"Oh, for Christ's sake, Law. You make it sound like a death sentence."

"For me it may as well be."

"Don't be so bloody dramatic."

Oh, if he wanted dramatic, I'd fucking give it to

him.

"Dramatic? This is my career, my life. Everything I've worked so hard for, and you're asking me to throw it all away after a couple of weeks together. Which one of us exactly is being dramatic here?"

Byron sighed irritably. "It won't end your career, Law."

"You don't know that," I all but shouted.

How could he not see the damage this could cause? And it wasn't just me I had to think about. The scandal my coming out might cause could ruin the guys as well, that's if they even wanted to speak to me after this. And that thought killed me. They weren't just my band-mates or my friends. They were my family.

Even as I explained all of this to Byron, it was obvious he either didn't understand, or didn't want to. And I wasn't sure which hurt more.

"Maybe you're right," I whispered, my voice cracking slightly. "Maybe this just isn't going to work."

I saw the moment all the fight left Byron, and my heart ached at the utter defeat we both exuded.

"Then I guess there is nothing else to say."

I knew that was a lie. We both did. There was plenty that should be said, so much that needed to be, but neither one of us were going to be the one to break this awkward and heartbreakingly painful standoff we were in.

I watched in silence as Byron moved passed me and to the door. I couldn't even bring myself to turn around as I heard the main door open and close, like a final nail in the coffin of what might have been the best thing I could have ever had.

Part of me was screaming to race after him, tell him how sorry I was, that I would do anything to make this thing between us work. All the while the more cynical, more rational part of myself was demanding I not be an idiot, that I was already lying if I truly thought I'd be willing to do anything. Wasn't that the whole point of what had just happened? I wasn't prepared to give it my all, to sacrifice everything.

I honestly didn't know who was right and who was wrong between us. I just knew how utterly miserable I now felt. And I wasn't sure if it was worth it.

"Holy shit," Dillon whispered again, and it was all I could do not to crumble right in front of them.

"Yeah," I responded, tone void of any and all emotion. I still couldn't force myself to turn around and face them, but that didn't matter when all three of them came to me.

The first touch of a gentle and reassuring hand shocked me, and I turned to look at Dillon, concern marring his friend's features. "I want to ask you if you're okay, but I know that's stupid right now. So … do you need anything?"

I blinked at him. "What?"

"Do you need anything?" Dillon repeated himself, shooting a look at Zeck. "You think he's in shock? Is that a thing that can happen when you jump out of the closet?"

Zeck snorted. "I think it was more the tumbling out forcibly and having his heart ripped open that's left him this way."

"You with us, mate?" Alec asked tentatively.

My gaze darted back and forth among the three of them, leaving me shaking my head. "You're not … mad? Disgusted? Something?"

"Seriously?" Dillon seemed outraged and extremely pissed at the question. "You think any of us would give a fuck? What kind of friends do you take us for?"

"Dillon," Alec began, but the man cut him off, and I didn't try to stop.

"No, fuck that shit." Dillon glared at me, and I could read the hurt behind his mask of fury. "I'm not a bad person. I'm not. Why would you think, for even a second, I could ever turn my back on you?"

I gaped at him. "Is that what you think? That I think that badly of you?"

"Well, don't you?" he snapped at me.

I shook my head. "God no. It wasn't about any of you, it was about me. I … I didn't … you have to believe that."

Panic whirled inside me as I pleaded for them to understand. Dillon seemed to understand this, and most of the fight left him.

"Please don't hate me?" I whispered, knowing I couldn't handle that on top of everything else.

"Hate you? We don't hate you, you moron. Worried 'bout ya, sure, but none of that other shit," Dillon replied. "Did you really think we'd be anything but supportive? I mean, fuck, it's a shock, but…"

Zeck stepped closer and laid a hand on my other shoulder supportively. "We're good, Law. More worried about you right now."

"Why don't you seem so surprised?" Dillon abruptly asked Zeck. "You're not, are you?"

Shaking his head, Zeck frowned, his long hair falling into his face. "Not really, but that's not what is important right now."

"He's right," Alec interjected. "Come on. Why don't we all take a seat and you can explain things to us. Properly, from the beginning."

"The beginning?" I laughed, sounding a little hysterical. "We'll be here all day."

Dillon frowned as he led me to the couch and sat

down next to me on it. "How long has this been going on?"

"You mean Byron, or the whole gay thing?"

"Both," Dillon replied simply.

"That's the thing. Knowing I'm gay and being crazy about Byron has pretty much been as long as each other."

"Come again?" This time Zeck actually did seem surprised.

I sighed, staring at all of them. I felt lighter than I had in a long time in the face of their unflinching acceptance, but the thought of Byron marred any positivity. With a steady breath, I steeled myself and nodded.

"All right, lads. You want it from the beginning, then let me tell you a story about what happened on our last day of high school."

And that was how I revealed everything.

Chapter Five

Law

"I really don't think it's working, ay?" Alec said, his strumming of his guitar coming to an abrupt stop.

"Try a different chord," Zeck offered with a shrug.

"It's not the music, it's the bloody lyrics," I snapped, chucking my pen and paper to the ground. All the lines I had written on it were worthless anyway. We had been spending days in and out of the studio coming up with new tracks. A few had been pretty decent, but for the most part they had all felt like they were lacking something to me.

"Got something to offer then?" Dillon asked, his eyebrow quirking up in question at my behavior.

I gritted my teeth. "Not like I'm not trying."

Dillon glanced at the others then back at me, just irritating me more. "What gives with you lately?"

I glared at him. "Don't know what you mean."

"Mate, you've been pissy for a few weeks now. I thought all was good, ya know. You had seemed a little happier at least. Then all of a sudden you're going off your trolley and no one is safe."

Rolling my eyes, I flipped him off. "Oh belt up. I haven't been that bad."

"Yeah, you have," Alec said, interrupting us.

Staring at them, I eventually looked over at Zeck, who hadn't said anything yet. "Do you agree?"

Zeck shrugged but otherwise didn't answer.

Miserable, annoyed, and completely uninterested in getting into another tiff with the boys, I stood up and left the room we had all gathered in to get some work done. Walking the halls of the studio, I found an empty room off to the left and ducked inside, sinking down onto the couch and letting my head fall into my hands.

"You gotta stop, mate."

My head shot up, and I sent a confused look at Zeck, who had slipped into the room without me realizing. In his hand I noticed he carried a bag of chips. "What?"

Zeck made his way over to me, dropping down onto the couch in a lazy sprawl. "I said you gotta stop."

"And I said … what?" a bit back with frustration, snatching the bag of chips out of his hand and eating some, pulling a face at the salt and vinegar taste. "And who the bloody hell did you filch these from? They're disgusting."

"Then don't eat them," Zeck snapped, taking them back from me. "And don't ignore what I said."

I knew what he meant even if I didn't want to acknowledge the truth. I had let the others think that I was okay, that I didn't spend every waking moment thinking about Byron. About Byron and that guy. But that was the thing about Zeck. He was loud and proud, and the joker of the group, but at times there was this intense silence about him. He saw more than he let on, and he cared more than he implied.

The others didn't always notice, and maybe it was only because I spent so much time hiding myself, that I saw it, too.

"You have to stop pretending you're okay." When I went to deny anything, he cut me off with a wave of his hand. "Shit, Law. We're past denials. You can't say it out loud to me or the rest of the lads then fine, but I can see it eating you up inside. I've seen it since that morning Byron left. I saw it get worse a few weeks ago after we made the trip to see our parents back home."

I bit my lip, groaning at how transparent I had been. "I saw Byron at the cafe I went to before meeting up with you lot again. And he wasn't alone."

Zeck had the decency to wince. "Ah, man, I'm sorry. Really. Doesn't mean you can keep going the way you're going though. I get it, okay. I get being so used to hiding a part of yourself, even when you don't have to anymore. The anger that comes with it. I also know what it's like to not have what you want, and the frustration you feel for it."

Zeck gave me a moment to let that all sink in, and I knew he was right. He understood what it was like to want and not have. Knew what it meant to have a part of yourself that was private, secret. He also knew what it was like to have that side of him exposed, and somehow, Zeck had come out on top.

Could it really be that easy?

As if reading the question in my eyes, Zeck nodded. "It's no walk in the park, and there are days you want to curl in a ball and stay safely tucked away in your bed. I'm not gonna sugarcoat this for ya."

"So how do you get through it?"

At that, the man smiled. "You ask yourself if it's worth it. And as long as you can always answer yes, then you make it through."

Biting down hard on my lip, I considered his words. Was it worth it? Was Byron worth it?

I knew the answer already. Yes. Always.

"I have to go," I said abruptly, standing a reaching for my things.

Zeck chuckle. "Thought ya might say that."

I checked the clock and saw it was only midday. By the time I reached Yorkshire, Byron would be close to finishing up classes for the day. If I managed it right, I might even catch him in the music room. A grin tugged at the corner of my mouth. Wouldn't that just be the most appropriate place to beg him for another chance?

Stopping just before I opened the door, I turned to my friend. "Thanks, Zeck. I know it's not easy tamping down your sarcasm, but when you do, you're pretty damn hardcore, mate."

With a glare, Zeck flipped him off. "Beat it, Przemyslaw. Before I announce a press conference for the sole purpose of revealing your real name."

"Bitch."

"Jerk."

****

Byron

As I finished writing the weekend's homework assignment on the board I heard the whispering of my senior class pick up. Frowning, I turned, my gaze catching on a figure standing just outside my classroom door.

Law.

The younger man waved to me, and I stood there, too stunned to respond. What was he doing there? I hadn't seen or heard from him in almost three months.

I watched as Law opened the door to his classroom, his eyes never leaving mine as the whispers turned into all out shrieks from the girls in the front row.

"Hey," he said softly.

"Hey," I choked out, looking between him and my class. "What are you doing here?"

"Came to see you," Law answered simply, like it was something so natural.

A chorus of *oh my God* and *holy shit* echoed in the room, and I had to agree.

Law came to stand beside me, turning a cocky grin on the class.

"Hey, I'm Law." The kids all laughed at his simple introduction. There wasn't a chance in hell that any of them *didn't* know who he was. "So you all have this guy as your teacher, huh?"

My students all answered in varying degrees.

Nodding, Law smirked at me. "Well, you're all really lucky. This man is the best. Seriously. You'd be crazy not to listen to him. He'll never steer you wrong. Be grateful to have him in your lives."

The bell ringing interrupted anything else Law had planned to add, and I watch in stunned silence as my class slowly filtered out of the room, most of them taking a moment to speak to Law. For his part, Law took it all in stride, even when a few of the females of the group let their hands wander.

When we were alone, I opened my mouth to say something, but nothing came out.

"Was that okay?"

I frowned at the question. "What?"

"Interrupting your class." Law let out an uneasy chuckle, his hand coming up to rub the back of his neck. "I didn't think classes were still going, as otherwise I would have waited outside, and then they saw me, so I…"

He trailed off with a shrug.

"Yeah. It was okay. It will keep them interested in my lessons at least."

Law nodded, shuffling a foot and remaining quiet.

The awkward silence drove me insane. "What are you doing here, Law?"

"Came to see you."

I rolled my eyes. "Obviously, but why? It's not like we left things on a good note, and I haven't seen you since."

If I hadn't been paying close enough attention, I would have missed Law slightly flinch. "I saw you."

I squinted at him. "When?"

The flush that crept up his cheeks was endearing,

and I had to momentarily close my eyes and compose myself. Now wasn't the time to crumple into a complete mess. I had already done that and had spent the last few months picking myself back up again.

"About four weeks ago. You were in that café on the corner of Wellington and York Street. You were with a guy, tall, brunet. Seemed like the two of you were on a date." The whole time Law explained he focused his eyes on the back of the classroom, not once glancing at me. There was a faint tremor in his voice as though some emotion had touched him.

I frowned, trying to remember and smiling when I recalled exactly who I was with. "That was no date."

"You sure?" Law asked hesitantly, tilting his head to look at me.

"Seriously?" I outright laughed at that, but when I spoke again, my voice was tender, almost a murmur. "I'm sure. I think my sister might take issue with it if it were. Seeing as how it was her husband I was with."

The heavy lashes that shadowed his cheeks flew up. "Your brother-in-law?"

"Yup. Emma's dad."

"Oh."

"Yeah, oh."

I saw him struggle with his uncertainty, and I wanted nothing more than to reassure him. Was that what he wanted from me? Reassurance? Was Law jealous? Could he forgive me enough to be?

It had taken a good while, but I had acknowledge, at least to myself, that I had overreacted. I had expected so much, so quickly from the younger man who lived his entire life in the limelight. I had briefly forgotten how difficult that must have been, and I had forced my own feelings and fears on to him.

By the time I had come to terms with this,

however, it had been too long, and Law had shown no interest in reaching out. Not that I blamed him. I had seriously fucked up. No one had the right to forcibly out a gay man, least of all another gay man.

How did I say that to Law though, after what I had done?

"I'm sorry," I blurted out, just as Law did the same.

We both looked startled, a small grin creeping onto his face as Law snorted. "What are you sorry for? I'm the one who acted like an arse, denied who I was to the point of hurting you, and then had the nerve to get jealous over your brother-in-law. Fuck, I've been acting like a miserable jerk to everyone since I saw the two of you. I think the lads were ready to throw me over a bloody rail."

"So you were jealous?" I failed at hiding my happiness at his admission.

Rolling his eyes, he sighed. "Just a little."

In that moment there were no shadows across my heart. "I probably sound really shallow, but I kind of like the idea of you being jealous. Even if it's just a little."

Law's expression was full of strength, shining with steadfast and serene peace all of a sudden. "I've missed you, and I've wanted to talk to you so badly, but I convinced myself that staying away from you was for the best. I couldn't give you what you wanted, what you clearly need, and it wasn't fair for me to let you think I could. All this time away from you though has been complete and utter torture. Staying away from you, not being open and honest, it's not worth how much this hurts any more. And I don't know if you could ever forgive me, but I had to find out."

Every word he said chipped away more and more at walls until I felt them crumbling down around me.

"There's a lot of pressure to be you, isn't there?"

His brows drew together in an agonized expression. "You think?"

"I just mean, you seem to handle it all so effortlessly on the surface, but behind the scenes…"

"That's the thing, no one stops to really see. They all think they know. You know, I have fifty percent of the people out there saying that there's no way I'm not a closet coke addict or something. That I must be hiding some seriously kinky love life to not be flaunting it all around the place. The other fifty percent want to congratulate me for being such an outstanding role model. They say I have morals and virtue in a corrupt industry. They don't know that I hide my love life because I'm scared that everyone who claims to love me would actually hate me if they found out I were gay. That I'd rather die than touch drugs because my mother's a drug addict. That I spent the first part of my childhood in perpetual fear. While the rest of the kids were terrified of the dark outside their home, I was paralyzed by the monsters that lived inside mine."

A tumble of confused thoughts and feelings assailed me. "But I met your mother when you were in school. She never—"

"She's not my mum. Not biologically. Miranda is my foster mum, my last foster mum that is. I had a few."

"I never knew."

"Of course you didn't. No one did." Law pressed both his hands over his eyes, as if they burned with weariness. "That's the way I prefer it. I spent years bouncing around from one foster family to another after my dad died fighting overseas. Mum couldn't handle it or something, and numbing her feelings was easier than facing them and being there for her own bloody kid. And really no one is more surprised than I am that that hasn't come to light yet. I guess, everyone is so focused on what I do now that none of them have stopped to ask who I was before. Small blessings right?"

I edged closer to him, raising a hand to cup the side of his face. I smiled in wonder when he didn't flinch and attempt to draw back in any way. There was no quick looks to the door to check for people, and Law's eyes never left me. Leaning in, I pressed my lips to his, caressing his mouth more than kissing it. "There really is a lot I don't know about you, isn't there?"

"People think that if they read enough tabloids that they can get a general picture. They have no clue."

I kept my hand where it was, even though I pulled back a little. "It's my turn to be sorry."

"For what?"

"You've dealt with so much shit and you just keep going, but no one stops to ask if you're okay, do they?" Law tried to say something, but I stopped him by slipping my hand to his mouth, my fingers covering his lips in hopes that he would just listen. "And here I was solely focused on what I want or what I think I need, and once again you're letting someone get their own way. The consequences to you be damned."

"Byron, no, I—" The muffled words were silenced when I pressed my hand firmer to his lips.

"You have sacrificed enough, Law. I've had it so damn easy. Maybe it's time I work for something, huh?" I removed my hand, using it to push back some of his wayward hair that had fallen forward. "Maybe I take the time needed to prove this, what we have, is worth the risk before I demand you take that risk."

Law started at me for a moment, and something intense flared through our entrancement. There was an invitation to the smoldering depths of his blue eyes as a smile tipped the corners of his mouth, a depth to it that had seemed to be missing for too long. "Maybe you could just shut the hell up and kiss me?"

"Now that, that I think I can do."

Epilogue

Law
Two years later

Sitting in a comfortable high back lounge chair, I smiled cordially as our interviewer, Georgina, asked us another question left by a fan on her show's website. We had agreed to answer a number of small and mostly innocently requests by fans, and for the most part it was pretty entertaining. Especially when they skirted topics that left both Zeck and Dillon more than a little embarrassed. Alec and I seemed to be coming out pretty unscathed.

The label had set up a number of these types of interviews leading up to our next world tour, the first one we had been on since our group had been rocked by one scandal after another. It had been a rough two years, but the results were definitely worth it.

"So, our next question left by a fan is for you, Dillon," Georgina stated with a sly grin.

Dillon moaned and covered his face with his hands dramatically. "Oh man, can one of the others take a turn?"

"Nope, afraid not," she said sweetly, though we could all tell she was taking great pleasure in watching the normally cocky man squirm. "It seems that with Issy's pregnancy and news of her carrying twins has spread, rumors of baby number two are in the wind for you, and this fan wants to know if that's true. Is little Grace going to be a big sister any time soon?"

I chuckled when Dillon sighed, looking relieved and even a little giddy as he responded. "That would be a yes."

The audience erupted into a mixture of applause,

217

whistles and a few misplaced but expected boos.

Georgina's face lit up. "How wonderful for you. I know a few more hearts break each time one of you boys settles down, but you must be so excited."

Dillon nodded, but it was Zeck who answered, and by the wink he sent me, I knew he was about to give me the opening I had been waiting for. "Yeah, it's going to be amazing. Five babies in the group by Christmas. We can't wait."

Our host froze, her eyes widening when she looked at Dillon again. "Well that doesn't add up. Are you saying Ashlyn is having twins as well?"

"Nope." Dillon shook his head emphatically. "I doubt I'd ever have sex again if I did that to her."

The crowd laughed and cheered at his response, and I hid my amusement behind my hand when Georgina's eyes latched back onto Zeck. "Zeck, something you want to tell us?"

Zeck raised a brow at the woman, shooting her an incredulous look. "You kidding? If Issy were having triplets I'd be celibate right alongside Dillon for the rest of my life. I mean, clearly we wanted to catch up with Dillon and Ashlynn, but not pass them. Damn."

Georgina peered at Alec and me, as if trying to size up which one of us was more likely to have knocked a chick up. "Law, Alec? Something either of you want to share?"

I could see the strain in Alec's expression at her question. Jo had decided to focus on finishing university and becoming a doctor, and Alec was supporting her one hundred percent of the way, which I respected deeply. They were sick and tired of the expectation and pressure they were getting to get married and have kids, and I knew I had to say something.

It is time, I thought.

"It's me," I announced, almost laughing when the entire studio went quiet. I sat there patiently waiting for it to all sink in, absently twisting my wedding band that I hadn't removed for the interview, which no one had seemed to notice.

Wait until they find out I'm married ... to a man, I thought with a great deal of amusement.

I had to give Georgina some credit when she recovered a lot quicker than I thought she would. "Ah, I have to admit, I'm a bit surprised. Law, have you been holding out on us?"

Zeck snorted. "You have no idea."

I nudged the wanker in the ribs, as I smiled at Georgina. "You could say that. I have a daughter."

"A daughter?" Georgina asked bewildered.

"Yes. My husband and I started the process for adoption a little over a year ago, and just last week everything was finalized and we were able to bring our baby girl home."

"Husband?" This time as Georgina asked the question she looked a little dazed.

"Yes, my husband," I answered holding up my left hand and indicating the wedding ring sitting there.

Over the last few months the lads and I had decided how we were going to handle my coming out. After a year together Byron and I had tied the knot in a private ceremony that we had kept under the radar. At the time we had considered making the announcement then, but when talks of adoption began surfacing we had agreed to wait. Not because we were afraid, no, I hadn't been afraid of how much I loved Byron for a long time, but because we were concerned the public scrutiny could adversely affect our chances.

With another full year under our belt, a solid marriage, and our baby girl, Madeline, safe at home, we were ready for the world to know. Dillon, Zeck, and Alec supported us as we had known they would, as did the record label, surprisingly enough.

"Sorry, can we just cover that again?" Georgina requested, staring out at the audience and then back at me.

I chuckled, leaning forward and resting my elbows on my thighs. "Let me break it down. Two years ago I reconnected with someone I cared deeply for. His name is Byron. Those feelings grew, and a year later we got married. We chose to keep it to ourselves partly to make sure nothing interfered with our plans to adopt, and partly because it was no one's business but ours. We now have a beautiful baby girl named Madeline who you will all get to see pictures of in the next issue of *Who Magazine*, and ah, yeah … that about sums it up. Did I miss anything, lads?"

I turned to the others, seeing matching sets of amused grins.

"You forgot the part about that time when you—"

I slapped my hand across Zeck's mouth to stop him and glared. "I really didn't forget that part."

Behind my hand Zeck grinned and licked me, making me draw back and wipe my palm across his pants.

"Bloody disgusting."

Everyone, including the audience, laughed at our antics.

"Well, you certainly have kept a lid on things," Georgina finally said, trying to get the ball rolling again but still focused on my reveal.

"That's true, but now I'm a parent, and I'm more concerned with what kind of a role model I am for my child. I'm not exactly doing a very good job if I can't be honest about who I am. I'm proud of who I am, I'm proud of my husband. He's been a support of mine, of ours, from the very beginning. I tried doing this without him, and I never want to do that again. This is who I am, this is who we are."

"I have to ask, what made you decide to come out now?"

I grinned winking at the others as I answered. "I guess it was just the right time."

The End

www.jessbuffett.wordpress.com

FOUR BOOK COLLECTION

DEDICATION

To the beautiful authors of the Scandals series—you ladies rock. Thank you for letting me be a part of this great new series.

FOUR BOOK COLLECTION

ALEC

Scandals, 4

Tamsin Baker

Copyright © 2016

Chapter One

Alec

"This sucks."

I chugged back a cold beer, the hops sloshing around my mouth and sliding down my parched throat. Summer in London was certainly not the warmest climate on the planet, but this beer was the hair of the dog, and my thirst was nowhere near quenched.

"You're complaining about having time off to drink? You're kidding me?" Law took a sip of his own drink and tapped his fingers on the round table in front of us.

It was easy for Law to be relaxed and happy. At least he was getting laid on a regular basis.

"Why the hell do we need time off? Just 'cuz you guys are breeding and falling in love like it's a catching disease, does not mean the band needs to take a break. We were traveling so well and the concerts were selling out. Why stop?"

I was a member of Right Time, which was being described by the paparazzi as the "hottest boy-band in the world at the moment". It was all pretty full on. I was also the last member to join, which made me feel, on more than one occasion, like a spare tire. All the other guys had been friends since high school and were close because of that bond. I guess I shouldn't really complain though. When Right Time hit the big time, I'd counted my lucky stars to have found them when I did. It had been like jumping onto a blazing comet just as it began to burn, a tail of fire trailing behind us.

It had been an amazing few years, concerts, women dropping at our feet, and more money than I knew what to do with. But all the guys were falling like dead flies. Dillon had knocked up Ashlyn, and they now had a cute little daughter. Chuckling, I shook my head. Zeck had met Issy in a BDSM club, tied her up and brought her home to keep.

Law, the only one who'd actually turned up today for a drink, had hooked up with their old music teacher Byron, but he hadn't come out publicly yet. Not that I thought it was a big deal, but according to our publicity team, the rest of the world seemed to think it was. I didn't care who the man was screwing,

"Because we need a break, Alec. No offense, but I'm exhausted." Law's eyes slid away for a moment. "Plus, Byron wants to go to the Greek Isles for a couple of weeks."

A snarl rose in my throat, and I smothered it by taking another long swallow of my beer. I kept drinking until I'd finished then banged the empty bottle/glass down onto the wooden table, wincing a little at the noise. I hated being jealous of Law and the other guys. It was an ugly emotion that made my skin prickle and my belly heat with anger and rolling sickness.

I may be the youngest of the band, but I was man enough to admit my failings. I was as surprised as anyone when I became envious of my mates getting hitched. I'd never wanted a long term relationship before, but I found myself sick of the chicks that wanted me for money or fame. I kind of liked the idea of having the honest closeness the other guys had achieved with their partners.

My friends deserved their happiness and their relationships did not reflect on my own sorry state, but even with all the rational reasons rattling around in my head telling me it shouldn't matter … I could still spit.

"When do you leave?"

Law's gaze met mine again. "Next week probably." He shrugged, and I let out the breath I'd been holding.

An idea occurred to me that I hadn't considered before they condemned us to leave without any notice. "Maybe I should do the same thing. Get away somewhere and find some beautiful women to have some fun with."

Surely there would be some decent women on holidays over there that wouldn't be like the dumb, shallow types I kept running into here?

Law's face lit up with his grin. "Everywhere in the Northern Hemisphere is pretty awesome this time of year, and you've never had any trouble with the women no matter where you are."

I lifted my hand and called the bartender. He nodded and began pouring another beer, placing it on a tray and waiting for a waitress to bring it to me.

"Nah, why would I? It's not like they're the most complicated things on the planet to work out how to handle."

I smirked as Law choked on his drink and began coughing and wiping at his mouth until he finally turned and stared at me, his eyes incredulous.

"What?" I asked.

"You're unbelievable."

I shrugged as my eyes slid down the back of a

woman in a tight black skirt and white shirt as she picked up my drink and turned around with the tray on her well balanced hand.

Wow.

Law said something to me, but I couldn't quite make out the words. "Huh?"

I couldn't drag my gaze away from her. She moved so gracefully and her face was perfect. There was no artifice to her. Her skin was flawless, her face heart-shaped, and she had high cheekbones and bright blue eyes. I'd never seen such a naturally beautiful woman before.

"Here you are, sir."

She bent forward, flashing an awesome amount of cleavage and a killer smile as she straightened up once again.

Say thank you, you idiot!

"Ah. Thank you."

Pull yourself together!

"Can I get you anything, sir?" She turned to Law, and I sat up straighter in my chair. My body was throbbing, and I wasn't ignoring it tonight. This chick was hot, and I wanted her. Despite my craving for someone special, I had to survive between now and then.

Law shook his head. "No thanks."

"I could do with something else, baby. What time do you finish work?"

She turned to me and the smile didn't waver, but for some reason the heat in her eyes dimmed.

"My shift ends at four AM, sir."

I leaned back against the leather booth and lifted my arm to lie across the back. "I'll speak to the boss and get you out early. Come out with me for a late dinner and a drink."

She inclined her head and gripped the tray tight.

"Thank you for the offer, but I'd prefer to stay and work."

She turned and disappeared into the crowd, leaving me staring after her tiny waist and swinging hips.

"That's a first."

I finally managed to drag my gaze back to Law's smug face. "What is?"

"A woman knocking you back, didn't think I'd live to see the day."

I laughed off the implied insult although a weird coldness sat in my gut. "She's just playing hard to get, which I don't mind one bit. Makes it sweeter when they finally fall at my feet."

"Or on their knees?"

I let my grin and wink at Law speak for me. I was tall and kept myself pretty fit. Well … I worked out seven days a week actually. My body alone was usually enough for me to have a new chick whenever the need arose. But since adding the fame of Right Time to my list of charms, I hadn't been knocked back in a very long time.

"I'm going to stick around for a bit. What about you?"

Law tossed back the rest of his glass and winced. "Home time for me, it's getting late."

"Bit early to turn in, isn't it?"

I shook hands with my friend and stood up as Law pushed himself to his feet. "It's almost midnight, my friend."

I shook my head. Once upon a time I wouldn't have even left the house to go out yet. "The night is still in its infancy, you old codger."

Law chuckled and leaned forward. I pulled him into a short hug, patting him on the back for a moment before letting go.

I winked at him again, and he smiled, then turned and left.

I clapped my hands together and headed for the bar. I wasn't sure what it was going to take to get the brunette waitress with the blue eyes in my bed, but I wanted her.

"Oh my God, you're Alec from Right Time!" A trio of blonde women at the bar literally bounced up and down beside me. I grinned at them and looked around. This was a private bar in a very expensive hotel, so what were a gaggle of groupies doing in here?

I plastered a smile on my face, aware of the bad publicity that came out of these sorts of moments. Last thing Right Time needed was another scandal. Huh, maybe that's why we were on holidays. Phillip needed a break after all the scandals we'd had.

"How are you girls doing tonight?"

They squealed and carried on, and I chatted with them for a moment while my eyes scanned the crowd for the woman I actually wanted.

"Are these girls bothering you at all, Alec?" The owner, Paul, stepped up next to me and whispered into my ear.

I shrugged. "They're harmless."

"They're friends of a new member." I could hear the strain in Paul's voice and patted him on the shoulder.

"No need to worry, Paul, but you could do me a favor … let me know where the brunette waitress is?"

Paul lifted his chin and looked straight at me, his eyes harder than I'd ever seen them. "Joanne is new. She's a student at Cambridge."

I swallowed the lump in my throat, a rather foreign feeling swamping my usual confidence like a tidal wave surrounding a drowning town. Hot and dumb I'd done a hundred times before. Stunning and smart would be a very new and welcome experience.

"Any tips?"

Paul grimaced. "Don't tell her who you are."

I stilled for a minute and then laughter bubbled up and burst out of me. "Thanks, mate."

Paul had the good manners to flush with heat and look away for a moment. "She's a pretty straight girl and shy, too. If you want to have a chance with her, pointing out your star status won't help."

I clapped the owner on the back and thanked him, my heart rate picking up as I spotted Joanne serving a corner table before she moved back around the bar.

I walked over to her, running through every lame or brilliant pick up line I'd ever used. None sounded any good.

Her eyes lifted and met mine, the blue as brilliant as the Mediterranean waters Law was planning to visit next week.

"I … ah … your eyes are beautiful."

She smiled at me with genuine interest this time, and it was as stunning as I had feared it would be. Heat flowed straight to my groin. Her soft pink lips were curved up, her clear skin pinking with pleasure and her eyes sparkled at me.

Damn.

"Five points for honesty."

I ran a hand over my head, the prickly stubble of my very short hair cut bristling beneath my palm.

"Yeah, well … I didn't think a pick up line was going to get me a good response."

She chuckled softly this time, picking up a tea towel and polishing a wine glass.

"And another five points for a show of intelligence. You're just full of surprises, aren't you, Alec?"

"You know who I am?"

She rolled her eyes at me, and I sat down on the

stool, relaxing my shoulders and trying to not look as big as I actually was. Most women loved my huge shoulders, but I had a feeling Joanne was not going to have big muscles on the top of her priority list.

"Sorry, of course you do. Didn't mean to infer you were stupid, I suppose I hoped you might treat me like a normal person for once."

Her face softened again as she swapped glasses and kept buffing. "Fair enough. Are you having a rest from all those world tours at the moment?"

I couldn't help noticing the slight tone of disdain as she spoke about the world travel. *Jealous Joanne?*

"Yeah, since all the other guys have settled down, they all want time off. I'm trying to work out what to do with my time. You don't happen to want to come on a holiday to France next week with me, do you?"

She ignored my offer and frowned. "Oh that's right, you're the only single one left aren't you?"

I shook my head. People weren't meant to know about Law yet.

"No, Law's pretty single still."

She stared at me with wide eyes. "Really? I'd heard he was keeping it pretty quiet, but he was paired up, too."

"Ah, no."

I looked away, finding it hard to lie to this woman who seemed so relaxed, so confident.

"What's wrong, Alec? Feeling a bit left out are you? Not sure I'm the girl for you, but there's lots around that would be ecstatic to jump on the Right Time circus."

I grimaced and looked away, my chest aching from the well aimed shot.

What the hell are you doing trying to pick up a chick like this? You're an idiot.

I began to pull out my phone to call my driver to

pick me up. This night had started out shit and had not improved. May as well give up the ghost before I put a knife through my eye.

"Well, it was nice to meet you."

I wandered away and headed for the door, swiping open my phone and putting it to my ear.

"Hey, Tony, can you pick me up out the front of The King's Bar ASAP?"

"No problem, Alec, however I'm just dropping Law at Byron's. I'll be about thirty minutes to get back."

I didn't really want to wait that long, but I wasn't catching a cab home.

"Sure, Tony. Thanks."

"See you then."

I hung up, and small hands grabbed at my arm. "Going home already, Alec? Oh no! Please stay and have a drink with us."

I had thirty minutes to kill. Why not?

I lifted my arms and pulled a tiny blonde against me.

See, women still like you! Stop being a dick.

"What would you like?"

"A coffee daiquiri, please."

"Me too, please!"

I nodded at the bartender and ordered myself a double whisky.

The drinks were laid down, and one of the women turned me towards her, tugging on my neck to bring my lips down to her.

I let her do it. Why stop her? Her cold, sticky lips touched mine as a flash went beside my head.

I groaned and pulled away. *Opportunistic bitch.*

I grabbed my whisky and threw it back, the taste a little odd as it slid down my throat. Probably the mixture of good whisky and bad woman. Always a shitty combination.

"Another, please."

My drink was refilled, and I threw that back too. May as well make what remained of the night as good as possible.

"I so loved you at your last concert! I couldn't believe how hot you all looked up on stage with the lights…"

Blah blah blah.

Her words were circling around me with all their high pitched intensity, and my head began to spin.

Whoa. I did not expect that to hit me so quickly. Must be getting old.

"Come home with us. You know you want to."

I batted away the three leeches clinging to my coat and checking I still had my phone and wallet, made my way for the door.

I heard my name being called behind me, but the whirling in my head and the flashing lights going off around me were making me nauseous.

I pushed through the front door and tripped and fell, more camera flashes surrounding me as the concrete hit my knee caps and pain flared as skin scraped from my hands.

"Come on, baby. Kiss me."

Those women were draping themselves all over me and flashing photos, pulling me to stand again. The world swung before my eyes.

Fuck off!

I growled and pushed them away. I needed to get up. I had to get home.

Fingernails dug into my arms, and cold air breathed over my skin as someone tore the shirt from my chest.

Vomit rushed up, and I swung my hands wide,

connecting with flesh I heard a scream, but didn't know who it came from. My vision was completely shot.

Bile and hot alcohol spewed from my lips and I rolled to the ground again.

Pain exploded in my head, and I let the darkness swirling at the outside of my mind enclose me completely.

Chapter Two

Joanne

I rearranged the jacket beneath Alec's head and checked his breathing once more.

Where were they?

Sirens began to ring in the distance, getting louder and louder as they made their way to us.

Thank God for that.

"Keep those people back." I motioned to one of the security guards as more women stuck their phones around and flashed a photo of Alec lying half naked on the concrete in his own vomit.

I shook my head and glanced down at the comatose man at my feet. "This is so going to be all over the papers in the morning."

I groaned as the sirens rang loud in my ears and the ambulance pulled to a stop on the sidewalk.

They turned off the shrieking, and I sighed with relief.

Thank you.

Two men popped out of the back doors when they opened and pushed a stretcher over to us.

One of them dropped down and started checking Alec's vital signs as the other man spoke to me. "Did you see what happened to him?"

I nodded and wrapped my arms around myself.

I had, unfortunately.

"I saw a woman in the bar slip something in his drink and about ten minutes later he charged out here and was sick. I couldn't follow him fast enough to see everything that happened, but his pulse is fast and thready."

"Let's get him to the hospital."

I stood next to them as they rolled Alec's big body

onto the stretcher and began tying him down and covering him with blankets. I asked the guys, "Will you get his blood work done and check for possible drugs? Or do you think he'll need his stomach pumped?"

The paramedics looked at me with a puzzled expression. "Have you been through this before?"

I shook my head, my teeth chattering together since I hadn't gone in to get my jumper. "No, I'm pre-med at Cambridge."

They pushed Alec towards the ambulance and began rolling him up the ramp. "The police will need a statement on what went on tonight. Do you want to come with us now? Or make your own way there later? "

I wasn't sticking around here for more photos and paparazzi. The hospital would be safer.

"I'll come with you now."

I followed them and jumped into the back of the van. I slid onto the perch and put a hand out to rest on Alec's arm. I felt so bloody guilty at the moment. I thought I'd seen the girls slip something in his drink, but had been across the room at the time and hadn't really been sure. I hadn't wanted to accuse someone of something they didn't do, so I'd dismissed the thought as my eyes playing tricks on me. When he'd started whirling and carrying on like a drunken sailor, I knew I'd made a mistake.

A big mistake.

He hadn't had that much to drink. A couple of beers and two whisky shots for a guy that big was nothing. Well, certainly not enough to have him slurring and bumping into things like he'd drunk the whole bottle, so I'd run after them to help him. Those girls did not have good intentions for the Right Time star, and I wasn't letting them get away with it on my watch.

When I'd gotten outside the poor guy was on the

ground, sick and passed out, and one of the chicks was screaming that he'd hit her. Another had his ripped shirt in her grip.

That was going to cause an absolute shit-storm of bad publicity.

"Is he going to be ok, do you think?"

The paramedics were attaching an oxygen mask and a heart monitor to him. What the hell had those two girls slipped him?

"His blood pressure is really low, and his pulse is ninety-two. Looks like Rohypnol, but we should know more once we're at the hospital and run some tests."

I sent up a prayer and squeezed his arm tighter.

A bloody roofie! Since when did men get date rape drugged?

Only an hour ago I'd been forcing myself not to swoon at Alec's feet. He was the only member of Right Time that I found attractive, but I knew better than to fall for a playboy's charm. Now he was unconscious in an ambulance and the paramedics were talking numbers that I knew full well spelled trouble.

I shook off the thought and closed my eyes. *Almost there.*

The next hour was a blur of questions, doctors, and stress. My head ached, my feet throbbed, and I could barely keep my eyes open despite the adrenaline pumping through my system which was making my heart race.

"Excuse me, are you the woman who brought Alec Masterson in?"

I turned away from the vending machine I'd been staring at to see an older man in a suit staring at me. It was two o'clock in the morning. Who wore a suit at this time at night?

"Yes, that's me." My voice sounded a bit weird, but I wasn't surprised.

He reached out a hand, and I shook it on autopilot as another bigger man stepped up behind him. A bodyguard by the looks of him.

"I'm Phillip, Right Time's manager. Could you tell me exactly what happened tonight?"

I rubbed a hand over my face and let the moan of exasperation escape me. "I've told that story twenty times already tonight."

Every doctor, nurse, or policeman I spoke with wanted to know everything I did. I knew nothing but what I thought I'd seen, and even those memories were starting to blur with fatigue.

Phillip's hand took my elbow and guided me over to a chair. I let him direct me because I was just too tired to argue. I couldn't feel my legs properly anymore.

"I can imagine, but I really want to be able to minimize the effect this is going to have on Alec's reputation, so if you could tell me everything you remember, I would be so appreciative."

I took a long breath and then let it out again. "There were three girls hitting on Alec at the bar, and while one of them pulled him over to kiss him, the other touched his drink. When I saw it, I wondered if she may have slipped something in, but I was on the opposite side of the room so I told myself I was being paranoid. But within a couple of minutes he was swaying and jerking around. He made his way outside with the three girls grabbing at him and taking lots of photos."

The bodyguard type standing over us said something in a foreign language under his breath that sounded a lot like a curse.

"I followed them outside as fast as I could to try to help him, but I missed a minute or so, so when I got there he was vomiting on the ground and one of the blonde chicks was saying he hit her. Another was holding his ripped shirt. I'm not sure exactly what happened, but I don't think he would have meant any of what he was doing. He could barely stand, let alone coordinate his arms."

A muscle in Phillip's jaw tightened and flickered, anger flashing through his dark eyes.

"That's not good at all. I suppose lots of photos were taken?"

I nodded and leaned back in the uncomfortable plastic hospital chairs. "Yes, most definitely. I called for the security guards, made them hold people back and waited for the ambulance. I didn't want to move him, but that unfortunately meant that people milled around taking photos of him lying on the ground, passed out in his own vomit. Joy of the digital age, they're no doubt trending on social media by now."

Phillip looked directly at me. "Do you have any photos?"

I straightened up and glared at him. "Are you bloody kidding me? I don't even have my jumper, let alone my phone! I've spent the whole night looking after your playboy charge, not that I expect a thank you! But you could at least not insult me."

I kept glaring at him until he finally chuckled. "I am so glad Alec had you on his side tonight. Please go home and get some rest. Our head of security, Jas, will take you."

That sounded like a bloody fantastic idea.

I pushed myself to my feet and nodded, even though my head felt like it was barely connected to my shoulders. "That sounds great, but my bag is at the bar still. It has my house keys and phone."

"That will be no problem. Jas can take you wherever you need to go. Here's my card. Please call me anytime if you think of anything else."

I began shuffling my feet towards the exit, the call of my bed and sleep like a siren in the night. I turned back around and called to Phillip again. "Will you let me know how Alec pulls up? I think they pumped his stomach in the end, so hopefully the drug gets out of his system quickly."

Phillip cocked his head at me and then nodded. "I will. How can I reach you?"

He pulled out a smart phone, and I recited my number to him. My eyes were getting really heavy.

"Jas, take her home before she falls down."

I let the big guy usher me into a waiting black car and got driven to the bar for my things, and then home to my tiny apartment. If it hadn't been such a stressful night, I might have enjoyed being chauffeured around. But as it was, I barely got out my thank you as I pulled myself up the steps, let myself into my building and fell into my apartment.

****

Alec

Oh fuck, my head hurts. And oh God, what is with my throat? It feels like they stuck a hot poker down my neck.

I reached up a hand to my head in an attempt to stop the anvil going bang, bang, bang against my skull.

"Rough night?" Phillip's sarcastic tone made my headache worse.

A groan left my lips as I opened my eyes. "Yeah, much rougher than it was meant to be. What time is it?'

"It's one PM. You've been out of it for twelve hours, which is about what the doctors predicted, which is a good sign."

I sat up straighter in bed, my bladder busting. "I've gotta piss. Do you know when I can go home?"

Phillip moved out of the way, and I swung my

legs off the bed and stood up. "Fuck…" Lights flashed before my eyes, and I fell back onto the mattress and grabbed for the sheets, trying to anchor myself. "What the hell did those girls slip me?"

"A roofie … you've really done a good job of landing yourself in the shit this time, Alec."

I rolled my eyes and pulled myself up off the bed. Be damned if I was using a pan or whatever they called that thing they stick up your dick. I weaved a little, but made it to the bathroom and lifted my damn ugly hospital gown to piss.

I returned to where Phillip stood holding out his phone.

"What's up?"

"Check it out, Alec."

I grabbed Phillip's phone and stared at the screen. What was the big deal?

"Oh … holy shit!"

Picture after picture of my disgusting self, assaulted my eyes. "How the hell did these pictures even get online? Of course, those bloody girls."

I fell onto the rock hard hospital bed, my mind whirling with the implications of what those headlines would mean for me, and the band.

"They're calling me a druggy, a drunk, and…" I scrolled through the top ten stories on Google. A gasp ripped its way through my vocal chords. "A woman beater?"

I stared at Phillip, my sluggish brain struggling to process all this new information. "I've never hit a woman in my life! I'd never do that! I mean … look at me." I indicated all the muscles I'd accumulated since that fateful night I'd been beaten up on a train and I'd been unable to protect either myself or my girlfriend at the time. "I've worked my ass off to become a protector. I'd never…"

Hurt anyone. Especially not a woman.

"I know, Alec. I know." Phillip heaved a huge sigh and took his phone back.

Phillip knew my back story and had had me investigated to confirm it when I'd first joined the band.

Knock. Knock. Knock.

"Am I interrupting?" A sweet, hesitant voice entered the room, and I jumped.

"Joanne?"

I grabbed the white cotton blanket and threw it over my lap as the gorgeous brunette that shafted me last night stepped into the room.

"Jas brought me back to see you. How are you?"

"Huh? Why would you know Jas? Did I miss something?"

A small smile lifted Joanne's lips, and Phillip pulled a chair out for her next to the bed.

"What did I miss? The last thing I remember was you turning me down."

Joanne looked away, pink slashing across her high cheekbones.

I looked back at Phillip and raised my eyebrows. Was someone going to explain what was going on?

Phillip cleared his throat. "You won't remember this of course, but Joanne was the one that found you outside in your own vomit, protected you while she waited for the ambulance, then came to the hospital with you and waited until we got here. She probably saved your life last night."

I couldn't believe it.

I stared at the girl, who was now looking down into her lap at her fingernails.

"You helped me?" No one had ever really helped me like that before. "Why?"

Her head snapped up, and her blue eyes flashed fire at me.

"Because you needed help, that's why. What else?"

I was suspicious of her motives. Why would she help me? What did she get out of it?

I turned on Phillip. "What have you cooked up, Phillip? I feel like I'm in the middle of a bad joke."

Joanne jumped to her feet and glared at me. "What's wrong with you? We're trying to help you out of this situation you got yourself into, and you're being totally ungrateful."

"Well, why are you here?"

"Because they asked me, and I…" her eyes slid away, "feel a bit responsible for last night. I saw those girls do something weird, but wasn't quick enough to realize what exactly until it was too late."

I knew it.

"So you let me get drugged and now you feel guilty? I knew there was something behind all this."

I stood up and swallowed hard, nausea rising and falling in my belly like mercury in a thermometer on a hot day.

"I'm going home. I'll figure this all out myself. Are there some clothes around here?"

I couldn't trust anyone to help me. I had to look after myself. I'd learnt that in high school when some guys had beaten me up on the train. I'd been looking after myself ever since.

I began looking around for my clothes and groaned at the sweat breaking out all over my body, heat flowing through me like molten lava.

"Alec Masterson." A male voice entered our private room just as the stars in the darkness began to twinkle and the night clouded in.

Chapter Three

Joanne

"Catch him, catch him!" I screamed at the men in the room as I dove towards Alec, grabbing his arm and holding on tight as he keeled over.

He was bloody huge, and way too heavy for me to hold up.

The doctor and Phillip helped me, and we turned Alec around so he could lie back down on the bed and rest. Fortunately, the stupid lump came to pretty quickly.

"Whoa, what happened?"

I placed my hand on his chest and pressed down, glaring at him like I would a five year old.

"You passed out. Again. Would you stop being such a stubborn arse and just rest?"

I tried to ignore the heat of his chest beneath my palm and the deep desire settling in my gut. Fuck, he was hot, too hot. His brown eyes were prettier than any man's I'd ever seen, and the look of vulnerability I could see in them now I was so close made me want to melt into a puddle of goo on the floor.

"Ok." He quieted down, and I went to step away but he grabbed for my waist and held tight.

He didn't say anything, but he obviously got the point and stayed put, turning towards the men who had come to help.

I perched my butt on the bed and moved further into Alec's grip. It was a little strange, but it also felt right, like I should be there with him, which was stupid. I barely knew the guy.

"What's the deal, doc? Can I go home soon?"

My stomach was wiggling and my breath was hitching in my throat.

"Alec, you were given a pretty nasty version of

what most people call a roofie. With good hydration and rest, you'll be feeling better in about seven days."

He groaned loudly behind me. "I'm not staying in here for a week."

Phillip stepped up next to the doctor. "It may not be a bad idea, Alec. It would keep you safe and out of reach at least. The paparazzi are already swarming your house, your band-mates, and the major hotels in the city."

Whoa, already? Those poor boys! Last thing they needed to happen on their down time is having the bloody media camped on their doorsteps.

"I do not want to stay in here for a week. I'll find somewhere to crash where they won't find me."

"Like where?"

Phillip looked directly at me, and I swallowed hard. "What?"

"No one knows you've helped us."

True, but...

"Umm, my place is pretty tiny, but he could probably crash there for a week. I'll be at school or work most of the time anyway."

My heart leapt in my chest as Alec's hand squeezed my hip.

"You don't have to do that, Joanne. I can find somewhere else."

His tone was annoying me now. I groaned and twisted to glare once again at the man in bed. "It's Jo, ok? No one calls me Joanne, and I hate it when they do."

He grinned at me just like he had that first time in the bar last night. All sparkly eyes and white shiny teeth.

I looked away because my nipples were aching and my clit throbbed.

God, I want him so bad.

"Ah ... I think I better head home for a bit. You have my address, Phillip." I pushed away from the bed and headed towards the exit, my palms sweaty and my chest aching.

A squeal rose from my belly and escaped as I pushed through the steel door and rushed out the front of the private hospital.

Flashes exploded in my face and I covered my eyes, and just as quick as they'd come, they'd gone.

"Bugger."

I made my way to my car and got out my phone, typing in a quick message to Phillip to tell him the journalists were out the front of the hospital. They hadn't been there when I arrived only twenty minutes ago. Shit, they were fast.

I turned the car on and squeaked again as I drove out of the car park. The hottest member of the biggest boy-band in the world was coming to stay at my tiny apartment.

"Holy-moly…"

It was too surreal to be true, but then again, who would have ever thought Law could be gay and Dillon would marry a woman he got pregnant while on tour? These boys had proven to the world how different they were, and I knew I'd regret not seeing where this adventure led.

****

Alec

Sneaking out of the hospital had not been easy, but we'd found an emergency exit and gunned it to the parking lot. Jas had been waiting with a car, and we'd gotten away pretty smoothly.

"I just hope no one finds me at Jo's place."

"We'll move you if they do."

I pushed myself back in the seat. My body was still weak and I ached all over, but I could finally breathe now that I was out of the hospital. There was something vaguely creepy about a hospital room—even in the absurdly expensive one I'd been staying in.

"I don't mean for me. I've been dealing with this shit for ages now. Jo hasn't asked for it and doesn't deserve it."

Jas snorted from the front seat.

"What are you laughin' at?"

Jas, our Russian head of security, outright laughed this time. "You gone into love tornado now. One married, one engaged, one came out, your turn now. You plan to have baby first like Dillon?"

My jaw clamped down, and I snorted out my nose. If we'd been in a cartoon, hot steam would have blown out my ears.

"Back off, Jas. You're out of line."

That brought a laugh from both of the men in the front seat, and I crossed my arms over my chest. "I barely know the girl. Don't stir up shit you don't know about."

The men chuckled some more, but they fortunately didn't say anything else.

The car slowed, pulling up outside a huge apartment building that was crumbling at the edges.

Oh crap.

"Not what you were expecting?"

Not one tiny bit. Shit. I didn't even stay in places like this when I was a broke muso.

I didn't answer them out loud though, just opened the door and pulled out my bag. Law had brought some clothes in for me at the hospital, but I had no idea what was in the bag or if I would wear them.

If things develop with Jo, maybe I won't need them at all.

I frowned at my own thought. I was totally confused by that chick. She hadn't wanted me when I talked to her last night at the bar, yet she'd helped me when no one else did. Had she not stepped up, anything could have happened to me. Now I was staying at her place.

Why? Because she felt guilty for not stopping those blondes from drugging me? Or because she actually liked me?

No one had ever helped me for no reason, so naturally, I was suspicious. But also I was grateful for the help.

The doctor had said Rohypnol could kill. I was bloody lucky.

I shivered and pulled the duffel bag over my shoulder. Too many foreign emotions had my still tender stomach churning.

Jo opened the front door in a white tank and old jeans, her long brown hair down around her shoulders.

Fuck, she's beautiful.

I signaled goodbye to Jas and Phillip and headed for the front door.

"You made it."

She gave me a gentle smile, and I returned it, unable to make a joke while she looked so sweetly perfect.

"Yeah, thanks. You sure about this? You know if the papers find out I'm here they'll be swarming you like a beehive."

She shrugged her shoulders and waved to the men behind me. "No one will find you here, and I kinda feel like I owe you."

The hairs on the back of my neck prickled up.

"Ah, so it is just 'cuz you feel guilty. Cool." I pushed through the front door, brushing past her and looked around for the lift.

She pointed to the stairwell. "Third floor."

I nodded and stormed up the stairs. If that's the

way she wanted it, then so be it. I knew I shouldn't be feeling shitty at her, but something inside me wanted her to want me to stay with her for more than altruistic reasons.

Dammit. I like her.

My legs burned, and the air I was sucking in was aggravating my sore throat. I tried to hide the fact I was panting.

"This way."

My eyes ran down the back of Jo's body as she brushed past me to push open the front door to her apartment. She had a great arse, round and perky, and long legs that would feel amazing around my hips.

I walked into the smallest apartment I'd ever seen.

"It's tiny, I know. You can take my bed, and I'll sleep on the couch."

"I can't take your bed."

My eyes roamed over the well kept, homey room. The kitchen was quite new, and the floors looked recently done. The room in which I stood was the kitchen, dining room, and lounge all in one, and there was obviously a bedroom and bathroom somewhere else. The furniture was careworn, and on one wall rested an antique book case full of books.

I'd been expecting dirty student digs, and I was completely wrong. Her home was lovely.

"You have to. You're like, a foot taller than me and you'll never fit on the couch. It's totally fine. Whenever my family visit they stay in my bed and I sleep on the couch—it's quite comfortable."

She picked up my bag where I'd dropped it on the floor and took the three steps to a door, opened it, and disappeared.

I walked around the living room for a moment, suddenly feeling a little claustrophobic. I didn't know how to cope with this. My bathroom was bigger than this whole living room.

Suck it up, princess. It's only for a few days.

I took a deep breath and followed after Jo. The warmth and intimacy of the small bedroom hit me instantly.

"Thank you for this. I really do appreciate you hiding me while this blows over."

She played with the light sheer curtains for a moment, then sat down on the—*shudder*—double bed, facing me.

"I read over some stuff this morning. I can't believe what they're saying about you."

I moved around the other side and sat down on the bed, too, trying to not get too close to her, but at the same time, aching to reach out and kiss her.

"Our publicity team wants me to just ignore it and say no comment, but I'm dying to set the record straight. Especially about me hitting a woman—that really got my goat. I don't care about the drugs and alcohol stuff."

"I know you didn't hit her, although to be honest, she's lucky she didn't get a swat from me when I found you. Stupid bitches."

The vehemence in her voice surprised me.

"Thanks."

She reached over and put a hand on mine, her fingers soft and warm, making my skin tingle and my breath catch.

"I'll leave you to settle in. I was just about to put some lasagna in the oven. Do you want some?"

On cue my stomach grumbled, and I stood up, covering the offending organ with my hand. "Yeah, that'd be great. I'm not sure how much I'll be able to eat though. My gut still isn't right after them pumping it."

Her eyes shifted over my chest. "You don't have a

no carbs rule or anything like that?"

I laughed at her. "I eat everything I can find. I work out so that I can eat pizza every day if I want to."

She smiled, her eyes lighting up. "Awesome, was a bit worried you'd be super strict or like … on some weird diet."

I laughed, images of my hoovering everything in sight since I turned sixteen flooding my brain. "I just need lots of it. I'll get some food delivered here tomorrow or I can give you money for groceries if you want. Otherwise I'll just eat you out of house and home."

She glanced down, her embarrassment obvious. Money seemed to be a bit of a problem. "Whatever you want is totally fine by me. See you soon."

She closed the door, and I allowed myself to look around her room.

There were no fancy clothes draped over hangers, no massive pile of makeup in front of an equally abhorrent mirror. It didn't even have a dressing table. There was a bed, a small cupboard, and a desk full of books.

I stepped up to a framed photo on the wall, a montage of school and family photos by the looks of it.

It was tacky but totally authentic and perfect.

I sighed and ran a hand over my skull trim.

I didn't think I had a single non professional photo up in my apartment, and they were all of me and the band.

How vain could I be?

I needed a shower.

I stripped off my t-shirt that still stank like the hospital and pulled off my jeans.

The door swung open.

"I, ah…" Jo stood gaping in the doorway.

I froze.

Jo's eyes roamed up and down my body, and I let her look. I was no Einstein, that was for sure. If I had anything to work with to get a woman like Jo, it was my body. If Jo liked it, she could look as much as she wanted.

The silence stretched on, and neither of us moved. I had to say something, but what? The wrong thing would make this week unbearable for both of us.

"I was just going to have a shower, you know. Wash off all the hospital smell."

I smiled at her, and she flew into action, flapping her hands about.

"Oh, yeah, of course. Sorry! That door over there, towels are under the sink." She pointed to a door next to what must be her wardrobe and closed the bedroom door as quickly as she'd opened it.

A grin spread along my face, and I glanced down at my rising cock. She was hot, even when she was surprised.

I stepped into the shower and enjoyed the zings of lust running through my blood, pushing the last of the drug out of my system and making the adrenaline in my body pump with each thump of my heart.

Now that's what I'm talking about!

Chapter Four

Joanne

Oh my God. Oh my God. Oh. My. God!

He has the most beautiful body I have ever seen! I've never even seen a man in real life who has a body like that! Such huge shoulders, muscled abs and his ... oh, shit.

When his dick, which was already long and kind of hot, had started to get hard and rise up from simply looking at me, all of my common sense had drained away. My body was still throbbing. I ached between my thighs, and other than taking myself into a room by myself for ten minutes, I didn't know how to make it stop.

A vision of Alec's body surfaced as the solution, and I huffed out a giggle. Yes, that man was sure to cure the ache my long starved body was feeling.

I checked the lasagna in the oven, and the cheese was going brown and the pasta edges were curling up crispy. It wouldn't be long now. I chopped up a salad and set the small table in the corner of the room.

Fifteen minutes later he surfaced, smelling of my body wash, dressed in a black tank and tight jeans.

I smiled at the way he hunched his shoulders. Why did he look so uncomfortable?

"These aren't my clothes. Law brought them into the hospital for me, and they're a bit small."

I grinned at him this time. "You look great, don't worry about it. It's only me."

He straightened to his full height, which was at least six foot three against my five foot six, and his shoulders seemed to fill half the room. "Just you I want to look good for."

Then you need to be naked because the clothes

don't do you justice.

I cleared my throat and fluttered my hands at him. "Sit. You want a glass of wine or something?" I turned away to hide my burning cheeks.

Having this man in my house all week was going to be a major problem for my self-imposed male ban. I'd been concentrating on study and work so hard lately I hadn't wanted the interference.

"Water please. After last night I don't think my poor liver will cope with wine for a long while."

I poured two glasses of water and rolled my eyes at myself. "Sorry, that was a pretty stupid question. You were drugged twenty-four hours ago. You look so well I keep forgetting."

And I prided myself on being a smart woman. *Pre-med my butt!*

"No stress. Any other night I would have loved a glass of red to go with my lasagna. Smells incredible by the way."

I placed the salad bowl on the table and took the lasagna out of the oven, quickly serving two portions onto plates and carrying them across to my guest.

"Thanks so much."

He took his plate with hungry eyes and a massive grin on his face. He was so much more real and down to earth than I'd expected.

We tucked in to the creamy sauce, well seasoned meat, and mouth watering cheese. Browned on the top and crispy around the edges, just the way I liked it.

"Yum." I patted my tummy and reached for the salad.

"There's not any more is there?" Alec looked around the corner of the kitchen towards the oven.

I nodded, took his plate and filled it up with the other half. One lasagna would usually last me four meals.

If this was how he was going to eat every day I was definitely going to need to accept the offered money for groceries.

"Here you go."

I watched in awe as he downed the rest of the pasta. *Incredible.*

He groaned as he finished and swallowed the whole glass of water like a pelican. Just opened his mouth, threw it in, and it disappeared.

"That was so good, and I so needed that after all that crappy hospital food. Thank you!"

He beamed at me, and something shifted in his expression. I saw a whole new person emerging who was relaxed, happy and young. Not the smarmy rock star I'd met the other night. That man was fortunately gone.

I took the dishes away and called over my shoulder. "What do you want to do tonight? I usually just watch a movie, study, or get an early night. After the day we've both had, sleep is probably in order."

"I agree, but I'm not quite tired enough to go to bed. A movie would be great."

I nodded and reached for the packets of popcorn in the cupboard. Each minute with this man was a surprise, and I was enjoying the twists and turns more than I'd enjoyed anything in my life so far.

****

Alec

I arranged myself on the couch, sliding down the soft cushions and dropping my head onto the back rest. "This couch is super comfy. I can see why you could sleep here so easily."

Jo put a bag of popcorn in to the microwave and pushed the button.

"Yeah, I know. It was my parents' couch actually. When I moved to London I took a few of their household possessions, and they replaced it all with new stuff."

I chuckled. "Why didn't they just buy you all new stuff?"

She turned and stared at me like I had two heads, her eyes wide and her pretty mouth slightly open.

"Ah, because they've worked their whole lives so that they can now afford new furniture. Second hand suits me just fine. I'm starting out and am more than happy to earn my own way."

She lifted her chin as she spoke with pride, and something hit me right in the solar plexus. Wow, a chick who wasn't obsessed with money and status. Who knew they existed?

"Sorry, didn't mean to imply anything about you or your parents."

Yeah, you idiot. Not everyone had money falling from the sky.

She turned away to take the popcorn out of the microwave and served it up in a bowl. "Yeah, well. They paid for my education and got me to Cambridge. They've done more than enough for me."

I took the bowl of popcorn from her and mentally kicked myself for being insulting. I'd obviously been out of the real world for far too long.

"So, you're going to be a doctor huh?"

She looked at me, her face startled. "How did you know that?"

I grinned. "Phillip."

"Oh."

She chewed on some buttery popcorn, the smell wafting up my nostrils and making my mouth water.

I put my hand into the bowl and stuffed some into my mouth.

"Yeah, hopefully. What do you want to watch?"

"Anything." I yawned and blinked a few times. "I

might not make it through a full movie after that awesome meal."

She nodded and selected a comedy I'd seen before. "This ok?"

"Yeah, perfect."

I nestled into the couch, enjoying the quiet and how comfortable I was with Jo. I wasn't feeling like I needed to speak, goof around, or fill the silence. It was odd. But good.

We settled into the movie, commenting on the douche of a hero and the pretty heroine.

I must have fallen asleep because I was watching the movie one minute and the next, Jo was shaking me awake and the lights had all been turned off.

"Alec, wake up and go to bed. You need to get a good night's sleep."

I grumbled and groaned at her but managed to pull my exhausted body off the couch and took the two steps to her bedroom. I was swaying a lot, and she stayed by my side, hovering like a mother watching her child.

I collapsed on the bed still wearing my clothes.

"I'm all good now, thanks."

"All right."

She disappeared, and I groaned again as I pulled myself up to sitting and tugged off my tank and jeans, crawling under the thin covers in my cotton boxers. I usually slept naked, but something told me I should keep that one thin layer on.

I rolled onto my side and ignored the aching loneliness of the bed. The floral scent coming off the pillow was making me want to call out for Jo.

I grunted and shook my head. *No. Stop.* I really needed to just get some sleep.

"Can I get you anything before I go to sleep?"

Her voice was so sweet, and my defenses were all

gone.

"Yeah, you could climb into bed and keep me company."

There was a stretched out silence. "That's probably not the best choice tonight, Alec."

I groaned and flipped back the covers. "I just mean to stop me being alone. I've had so much crap pumped through my system today I don't think I'd be able to perform, even if you wanted me to."

I'd got hard before when she'd looked at me, so I probably could if I had to, but the need to sleep was so much more pressing.

Another long silence stretched and I clenched my teeth together, but I waited.

"You just want to cuddle?"

I would have rolled my eyes if they weren't already shut.

"I get lonely, and yes, a warm body next to me would feel like heaven after the day I've had."

"Just any warm body huh?"

I would have balked at the words if the tones hadn't been teasing. Jo moved around the bed and slid in, turning away from me so that I could spoon against her back.

I grabbed her small waist and pulled her into me. She squeaked like a little mouse but didn't move as I settled behind her.

God, she feels good.

I inhaled the soft fruitiness of her shampoo and sighed as the tendrils of sleep began to pull at me.

"No, Jo. Not just any warm body, I like the fact that it's yours."

Chapter Five

Alec

I awoke slowly and stretched my arms out, and my palms landed on cold sheets. *Hmmm, not how I'd expected to greet the day.* Where was she?

I groaned and arched my back, testing out the muscles that had ached last night. *God, my body feels better!*

Opening my eyes, I searched around the room for a clock.

Ten AM.

Bloody hell! No wonder I feel so rested.

Jo's soft, warm body had certainly done the trick last night. I'd slept so solidly and with no nightmares, I could barely believe the difference. I never admitted it to anyone, but I'd struggled with proper sleep ever since being attacked as a teenager. I was strong and fast now, but the memories of being jumped from behind and not being able to defend myself still haunted me.

I pulled back the covers and got to my wobbly feet, sleep and lethargy still making strength impossible, but life was good.

I grabbed my phone on the way to the shower and saw several missed calls from Phillip and the boys.

"Argh. I'll deal with you guys when I'm awake."

A note was taped to the mirror in the bathroom.

Alec, I've gone to University for the day.

Back at 6 PM.

Help yourself to the fridge, but you may need to order some more stuff in as well.

Jo xoxo

Wow. Xoxo huh?

I laughed to myself and turned on the water, marveling at how light and euphoric I felt. Here I was in the smallest bathroom ever, with a girl I barely knew, and I couldn't wipe the smile off my face. I stepped into a tiny cubicle with lots of hot water and sighed as any lingering stress leached out of my system.

Once I was dry and wearing the one comfortable pair of pants Law had packed for me, I grabbed a bowl of cereal and sat down on the couch with my phone.

"Hey, Phillip. What's up?"

"Have you checked the news this morning?"

I rolled my eyes at his terse tone and crunched down on my cereal. "Course not, I just got up. What's happening now?"

"Photos of you are all over the papers again this morning. This time they're more graphic and horrible. You vomiting, passing out in the street. Photos of the woman you hit with a black eye. It's pretty bad, Alec."

My stomach rolled, and I dropped my spoon into the bowl, splashing milk in my lap.

"I didn't frickin' hit her! The only way it could have happened was if I clipped her as I fell. What are we going to do about this, Phillip?"

"I think the best thing we can do is refrain from commenting … but…"

I sat up straight on the couch, putting my cereal on the coffee table and narrowing my eyes at the wall.

"But what? This could turn into a criminal charge, Phillip. We can't just do nothing!"

Those stupid bitches had deliberately drugged me, for God knows what reason, but it wasn't for my benefit. And now they were getting paid for photos of me doing things I would never have done if I wasn't under the influence of that bloody roofie!

"I agree. I think we have to put out an official statement in regards to the drugs that were slipped into your drink, including the fact the hospital found evidence of it and focus on you trying to recover from the effects of such a breach of your privacy and personal safety."

"That's a better plan, Phillip. I don't like the idea of being labeled anything so horrendous as a girl basher."

We talked for a bit longer and finally worked out a strategy that unfortunately had the best chance of success if it included Jo, since she was the best witness of the night. I didn't really want to include her, but if she could tell her side of the story it really would be the best way of fixing things.

The rest of the day went by pretty fast. I had some of my favorite foods delivered to the apartment and ordered takeout for dinner. I spoke to some of the other guys who were all rapt to hear I was safe and well, and staying with the chick who'd saved me from being trodden on in the streets.

"Yeah, yeah. Say hi to Issy for me." I hung up on Zeck, who was being far too mushy for me. Bloody boys had gone from normal skirt chasing band members to pussy-whipped "we're now on holiday" pansies.

I tried to scowl, but I had to laugh in the end. Never in my wildest dreams had I thought that this was where we would end up.

We?

I groaned and rolled my eyes. When had I decided I was in the same boat as all of them?

I lay down on the couch that smelled vaguely of Jo's shampoo and drifted off into sleep.

****

Joanne

What a horrendously huge waste of a day. I'd had two anatomy classes, human biology, and surgical theory, and all I'd done during those classes was Google information on Alec and fantasize about his beautiful body.

I growled at myself as I opened my front door. So much for being an intelligent woman. At the moment, my hormones were leading me around and not my brain.

I stepped inside with a few groceries to the sight of Alec fast asleep on the couch, my small kitchen benches now covered with bags of food and takeout.

He ordered food in. Awesome.

I crept in on tiptoes, trying not to wake him, but Alec groaned and began stretching like a cat when I got about halfway across the room.

"Welcome back, beautiful."

My stomach dropped. Didn't he sound like a practiced man-whore today?

"It's Jo, in case you'd forgotten who you were staying with." My tone was icy, but I couldn't help it. When he'd needed help, he'd come to me, not any of the hundreds of women who'd professed to have slept with him—if the internet was anything to go by.

A slow, rumbling chuckle surfaced from the couch, and I hurried over to the kitchen, unpacking what I'd brought home and noticing how full the fridge now was, too.

Camembert and salami. Yum.

"I know who you are, Jo. You don't need to get so huffy."

Huffy? Ha!

"Well I'm glad you've remembered my name, but obviously you didn't know where you were before. How many women have you greeted with that phrase anyway?"

Watch it, Joanne! You sound like a jealous, lovesick idiot.

He laughed a little louder.

"None. You're more beautiful than any woman I've ever seen. You deserve the title."

263

I snorted at him, not believing for a moment I was the only one he'd used that line on. "I am not beautiful."

He was lying, he had to be. But the heat in my cheeks belied my interest. It would be so nice if someone actually thought I was beautiful.

"I'm not fighting you on this, sorry, 'cuz you're just plain wrong. I just about swallowed my tongue when I saw you at the bar the other night. You aren't hot, gorgeous, or cute."

I swallowed hard as tears prickled my eyes. I kept my back to him and pretended to be perusing the food in my fridge. "I know."

"You are more than that. You're beautiful, stunning, angelic. You are someone I could look at for the rest of my life and not ever get bored."

I whirled around and stared at him open mouthed. *Pardon me?*

"I ah…" He glanced away, red slashing across his cheeks. He'd obviously said far more than he'd intended. The silence stretched, and I tried to divert the conversation for both our sakes.

"Did you order something for dinner, or do you want me to cook up something?"

He lifted his arm. "Those blue bags have pretty awesome gourmet pizzas in them. They were delivered about an hour ago so they may need ten minutes in the oven though."

I turned on the oven and put the two pizzas in, a weird giggle floating around my throat at how surreal this night was already. "They look great."

And they did. Covered in a variety of meat, cheeses, and a few veggies, they were mouth-wateringly yummy to look at.

"They're from my favorite pizza place in Covent Garden. They deliver for some select people."

"Well, I suppose there has to be some perks to being all rich and famous." I stuck out my tongue to him, and he laughed, grinning at me with his super white teeth.

"Yeah, there does. You want a drink? I had heaps of different mineral waters and stuff brought over in case you wanted some?"

"Thanks."

I pulled open the fridge and got us some drinks. He'd been pretty thoughtful actually. I was surprised.

Fifteen minutes later we were sitting down in front of the TV with our very expensive tasting pizzas and lemon drinks.

"Did you have a good day?"

He nodded, swallowing his sixth piece of pizza. Where did he put it all?

"Yeah, it was ok. It's a bit hard not being able to go out to the gym, or see one of the guys. But I feel so much better after sleeping all last night and today. That drug is finally working its way out of my system. Should be good as new soon."

I looked down at my food, my stomach turning when I realized that in a day or two, I probably wouldn't see Alec again. I had my life to get back to and all of my goals to achieve of course. I wouldn't be bored. I had a bright future ahead. Graduating from university, then I'd get a good internship and make my parents proud.

I shook my head to clear the fuzziness and had some lemonade. Why was my bright future suddenly leaving a sour taste in my mouth after the excitement of the last day or two?

"Cool. I'm glad you're feeling better."

He ran a hand over my thigh, the heat and suddenness of his movement making me jump. Once the initial shock passed, I couldn't help but press a little closer to him.

"You going to miss me?"

I shrugged and concentrated on the movie. I had no idea what was going to happen with Alec.

Time to change the subject. I wasn't a good liar, so I didn't even try to bluff my way out of it. "Do you have plans for tomorrow?"

He twisted around and slid his hands around to my waist and pulled hard.

I dropped my plate and stared at him. "What are you doing?"

Unable to resist how his palms felt on me, I allowed him to guide my movements and I soon found myself straddling his lap. Facing him, my heart began beating hard against my ribs.

"You *are* going to miss me."

Of course I am.

My belly quivered in my body as he cupped my face and pulled it towards him. *He's going to kiss me! Oh. My. God.* I held my breath as he moved closer, and I let my eyes drift shut. A moan left my mouth as his lips touched mine, the gentle passion new and perfect to me.

He groaned in a really male, primitive way as I opened my mouth to him and he slipped his tongue in to taste me.

I pressed closer, my aching body rubbing against the hardness growing in his jeans.

God, that feels so good!

His fingers grabbed my t-shirt and lifted. *Yes! That's what I want!* His palms against my skin. We broke lip contact so that he could pull my top off, and I opened my eyes for a brief moment, his lust filled face beautiful to me.

I reached for his black t-shirt, pulling it off him and running my hands over his tight muscles and hot skin.

Wow ... so beautiful.

He kissed me again, deep and long while his hands moved around my back and unclipped my bra.

The swollen weight of my breasts was released, and my lacy bra went flying across the room. I groaned as his fingers found my tight nipples, rolling them between his fingertips.

I broke off our kiss, throwing my head back on a gasp and arched my back. Alec took advantage of my new position and suckled one nipple and then the other.

"Fuck, you're so beautiful," he said against my skin as he continued to swap from one to another.

All conscious thought slipped away. I was swimming in a hot pool of sensation, trails of fire cascading over my shoulders, my neck, my back.

Even though my eyes were closed I could feel wetness beneath the lids. He made me feel beautiful; he made me feel loved. I didn't know how he did it, and I didn't care, because this was the most perfect moment of my life so far.

Hs grabbed hold of my hips, shifted his weight to the edge of the couch before he stood up, holding me and lifting me as though I weighed nothing at all.

I held on tight to his neck, squealing as he walked with me to the bedroom. "I'm too heavy for you!"

"Never." His voice had changed into a deep bass, his brown eyes now flickering with fire as he stared at me.

I slid my hands up to his head, grabbing hold of his face and pressing my lips against his.

He turned and sat down on the bed, rolling us until I was beneath him.

He pushed up onto his hands and stared down at me. "You sure you want this?"

I nodded, swallowing the panic down as he

looked at me. "Only if you do."

"Of course I do."

I laughed, a happy bubble filling up my belly and giving my body a giddy feeling. "Come here then."

Chapter Six

Joanne

I pulled Alec's head down, locking our lips together as we fought to undress each other further. My skirt and his pants went flying, underwear, socks and shoes all descending into a big pile on the floor until we were both panting and as naked as the day we were born.

He settled between my thighs, his lips tracing a path of fire all the way down to my pussy. When he finally found my throbbing clit I could have wept. It had been so long since anyone except me had touched there.

He stroked it with his tongue, and I cried out as pleasure pulsed through me. I couldn't believe he was doing this for me, wanting *me* to feel this good rather than just taking as everyone else always had. "Alec, that feels … amazing!"

I grabbed at his head, moaning and thrashing as he worked my clit until I lost control. Feral, wanton noises left my throat that he encouraged with his own moans and harder tongue-lashings.

He slid two long fingers into me, and my body exploded in a ray of stars and moans. I shuddered and clung to him as he licked me one more time and then slid up my body until we were lip to lip, pelvis to pelvis once again.

He kissed me long and deep, and I wrapped my legs around his strong waist, arching up to him with need. I was aching so badly, and my body was screaming for him to slide deep inside me.

"I'll just be a second."

He rolled to the side and grabbed for his bag, searching through it frantically. He put it down and turned to me. "Dammit. I don't have any protection, do you?"

I bit my lip and sat up. *Oh shit.* "If I do, they'd be pretty old."

I slid off the bed and stepped into the bathroom. I pulled out my bottom drawer, the cool air in the room chilling my hot body. What a horrible way to ruin a beautiful night.

It was so great he was being the responsible one. I hadn't thought of it, but this was just so cold.

I pulled out an unopened box and stepped back into the room. "Not sure if these are expired but…"

I threw him the box and sat down on the bed. "Well, that wrecked the mood, didn't it?"

He stared at the box and opened it, drawing out a string of silver aluminum squares and laying them on the pillow next to him.

"Yeah, kind of, but I would have found it a bigger turn-off if you'd just whipped one out from your pocket like you do this every day."

I crossed my arms over my naked breasts and huffed at him. "I was a bit surprised *you* weren't prepared. Don't you have women in your bed every night?"

He shrugged and glanced away, and my belly tightened. Now *I* was the one ruining the moment. He'd tried to defuse the situation with humor and a compliment, and I'd just made it worse.

"Sorry, I just don't do this very often, sorry … again."

He patted the bed and smiled at me with that smile I adored. Gentle. Sweet. And with a fire building in his gaze again. Maybe it wasn't too late to save this night?

"Lie down for me?"

I nodded and crawled over to the spot he indicated, lying on my back and smiling up at him.

He stood up, and my eyes were drawn to where he began to stroke himself with two hands, curling and pulling until he began to harden and thicken once again.

I licked my lips. I so wanted to taste that. Him.

"May I suck you?" His eyes went wide, and I bit my lip. "Um, only if you want me to, that is."

He groaned and rolled his eyes with a *wow* look on his face. "Absolutely."

He knelt on the bed and swung his leg over my shoulder.

I gaped up at him. He was literally straddling my face.

He grabbed hold of the bed head and stared down. "Is this ok, Jo?"

I nodded and swallowed down the fear that rose. A small part of me had always wanted a big male to dominate me, make me feel things I'd never felt before.

But this was very confronting. It was either step up and try something I'd never done before, or back off and never know how good it could have been.

I took a deep breath and stared at his face for one more moment. Alec was offering me an incredible night out of time, and I needed to stop overthinking it, and simply jump on board and enjoy the ride.

I wrapped my hand around his hot, thick shaft and drew him towards my mouth.

I opened and moaned as his silky flesh passed my lips, his dick already starting to thicken and grow as I licked, sucked, and curled my tongue around him.

He gasped above me, rocking his hips, thrusting his cock in and out of my mouth.

How hot is this!

I moved my hands around to his thighs and then his tight ass, pulling him deeper as he tried to move away. I wanted him closer, making those sexy noises that hit me right in the belly. Those moans that told me I was doing a good job.

"Fuck, you're amazing at that. It feels … argh…"

He pulled out of my mouth and moved down the bed, grabbing a condom and sheathing himself with finesse as he went.

He lay down beside me, his fingers moving between my thighs as his lips captured mine again.

I grabbed hold of his shoulders, kissing him deeply as his fingers slid into me, my body still so sensitive and wet for him that my pussy opened easily.

A moan moved through my throat and I arched and gasped as he slid a second finger inside me.

"Please, I need you."

I flushed with heat, up my chest and onto my face. I couldn't believe I'd just said that, but as he rolled on top of me and growled into my neck with passion I was so proud I'd found the courage to voice my needs.

He reached down and moved his cock to the entrance of my body.

I stilled and waited for him to thrust in.

He pushed up on his arms and stared down at me, a beautiful smile spreading across his face as he kissed me softly on the lips and surged forward.

I cried out as he forged into my body. It had been so long, and it was so perfect. An orgasm rippled through me and I buried my head into his neck, gasping and crying out as the tremors rippled through me.

Alec kissed my neck, my hair, thrusting in and out of me, harder and harder while I moaned and dug my nails into his shoulders. Tingles were running down my legs, and my belly tightened with desire.

Alec kept moving until I was screaming out with each slap of our flesh meeting.

Alec's back was sweaty beneath my hands, and I

couldn't get close enough to him.

He moved forwards, kissing me harder, biting my lips and licking the inside of my mouth. He reached beneath me, tilting my hips and causing fireworks to go off in my head.

"I'm coming again! Don't stop please, Alec, don't stop!"

He pounded me harder, groaning and gasping until I screamed out his name, the tightness in my pelvis exploding and pulsing as my orgasm ripped through me again harder this time.

Alec cried out as though his soul was being ripped from his body, the call of satisfaction echoing around the room and making tears swell and tingle in my eyes.

Alec withdrew slowly, kissing me gently on my lips, the tip of my nose and the center of my forehead.

I hiccupped as the emotion clogged my throat and the tears slipped down the sides of my face.

I hoped he didn't see them, and considering it was dark, he probably wouldn't.

"I'll be back in a minute, my beautiful girl."

He slipped from the bed and made his way into the bathroom.

I took a few deep breaths to calm myself, wiping my eyes while my body continued to sing with pleasure and tingle from head to toe.

I stretched my arms over my head and smiled up at Alec as he climbed back into bed.

"You ok, Jo?"

I grinned up at him and nodded. "Yeah, of course."

I rolled away from him and nestled my butt back into his groin.

He made a low contented noise and wrapped an arm around me, pulling me close.

"Thank you for an amazing night." My voice was small in the room, but his response was perfect.

"Oh beautiful girl, tonight was a once in a lifetime experience. Thank *you*."

I closed my eyes and let the darkness enfold me, a slight tremor of fear rippling through me as I realized this one moment in time made me feel more loved than I ever had in my life, and I couldn't keep the one who'd given it to me.

Chapter Seven

Alec

"I have to go…" Her voice whispered into my ear the very words I did not want to hear.

"No!" I rolled and grabbed her, pulling her now clothed body onto the bed with me.

Jo giggled and nuzzled into me a moment before slowly pushing on my chest again. "I have an exam later this afternoon, and I need to study beforehand. I'm sorry."

She bit her lip in the most endearing way, and my heart folded like a pack of cards. "Fine, but when you get home tonight I'll be keeping you in bed until tomorrow."

She blushed and looked away, the move so innocent and charming that I laughed. "I seriously cannot get enough of you."

I swooped up for one more kiss, tasting her sweetness, before I released her.

Her cheeks were rosy, and she looked so young dressed in an oversized jumper and jeans.

"God, you're adorable."

She gave me a little smile and turned towards the door. I watched her go, and my body stirred to life at the sight of her legs. They had felt so perfect when they were wrapped around me last night.

"Thank you again. For … you know."

I climbed out of bed and walked with her to the door, loving the way her eyes goggled out of her head and perved on my groin as I walked.

She reached for the door and began opening it, a cacophony of sounds, screams and lights flashing hitting us like a tornado.

"Shit!" I slammed shut the door with my hand, clicking the deadlock in place. My eyes slid closed, and I rested my forehead against the door. "Oh … shit."

"Oh my God! Did you just see that? Alec! What are we going to do? My parents! My friends! What are they going to think about me…"

I turned towards the high pitched shrieking in the room, my heart sinking. The first thing she could think about was what people were going to think about her?

You're kidding me?

"What? Am I such a bad catch everyone will think you're crazy for hooking up with me?"

I took the few steps towards the bedroom and began yanking on clothes. I felt way too vulnerable having this conversation naked, and I needed to get out of here as soon as possible now my hideout was blown.

"That's not what I meant, Alec."

I twisted back around, glaring at Jo as heat raced up my neck. "What did you mean then? And how did they even find me? Who did you tell?"

"Me? I'm not the one ordering takeout and letting people see you. I hadn't told anyone! Everyone I know would be shocked to know I let *any* man sleep in my bed, let alone a playboy singer like you!"

Ouch, those arrows she slung are far too accurate.

"What are you? Some virgin that never looked once at a guy?"

She glanced away and moved over to the sink, shuffling things around nervously.

"No, but it's been a long time since I was with anyone."

"Good, then they won't find anything on you."

"Of course not!"

"Good!"

I grabbed my bag and stuffed the few clothes I had into it. The room still smelled of sex, and my stomach was rolling with unease and anger. I didn't want to go face the music out there, but it looked like it was going to be friendlier than what I was dealing with in here. "I'll go. You have your exam and your bright future to protect. I'd hate to taint that."

She gasped, and the pain in her eyes and in the noise she made hit me right in the chest. I stopped for a moment and looked straight at her. "Sorry ... that was uncalled for."

She nodded and crossed her arms.

I cleared my throat. "Thanks for all your help, but I better go sort all this stuff out."

Part of my brain was telling me to call Jas, or Phillip, wait for the cavalry. But I couldn't stay this close to Jo when she was so mad at me, and there was no back entrance anyway. I had to go out that front door at some stage, and if that meant jumping into the lion's mouth sooner rather than later, then I would.

"Ok." Her voice was as quiet as a mouse in the tiny apartment, and my heart was racing in my chest as I prepared myself to walk out into that hallway. I hated this part.

I walked over to the front door, pulled on my shoes, took a deep breath and opened the door.

Questions were screamed at me, photos were snapped, but I focused on my mission. I pulled shut the door to Jo's apartment and held tight to my bag.

"No comment," was all I muttered as I forced my way through the bevy of people in the hallway, down the stairs and all the way to the street.

I loved the band, the money and fame, but this part was fricking annoying.

I pulled the hoodie up over my head and marched down to the street, a bitter taste in my mouth fouling up what had to be one of the best nights of my life.

****

Joanne

They followed me to university that day, despite the fact Alec had left. I'd hoped that they would leave me alone, but the story was obviously still juicy, Alec's scandalous behavior from the two nights previous was too much to ignore.

I managed to study a little and sit my exam, but I had no idea how I went or if I even passed. My mind was far too full of the consequences of my actions. I'd let my hormones override any morals I'd thought I'd had, and I'd slept with a famous boy-band star. Not only did Alec have a reputation for one night stands, I barely knew him. What did that make me?

I swallowed hard, tears clogging my throat. Would my parents be furious?

I shuddered at the thought as I entered my apartment and began making dinner. How would I explain it to my mum? That Alec was actually a good guy, that I enjoyed his company. That's why I'd slept with him, not because he was cute and convenient.

I blinked away the tears that kept blurring my vision. The beautiful memories of last night were fading fast, and I wasn't sure if I was relieved or devastated by that fact.

My phone rang, and I looked at the screen. A growl arose as I picked up the phone and answered with a scowl on my face.

"Argh, what do you want from me now?"

I couldn't stop the words as they poured out of my mouth. Helping Phillip and Alec had got me into this mess.

"I think you need to look at channel four. Right now."

I put a hand on my hip and glared at the black

screen TV. My world had been turned upside down since I let these men into my life. Why should I do as I was told once again?

Another trick, Mr. Manager? "And why would I do that, Phillip? Do you and your boys want to ruin my life more than you already have?"

"Joanne, no one's ruined your life. Just turn the TV on and watch. Alec might surprise you."

I rolled my eyes and exhaled all the air I'd built up, anger still rolling through me despite the fact I knew he had a point. When had I become such a drama queen? "Fine … and thanks."

I hung up on the meddling manager and switched on the TV, flopping down in the couch and groaning as memories assailed me. My belly clenched tight as Alec's scent clouded around me. It was only last night he'd been here, holding me, laughing with me.

I ran a hand down my face and gripped the back of my neck. It was just an ad for face cream with some supermodel on it. Why had Phillip gone to the trouble of calling me to watch this?

The ad changed, and it was a news show.

A woman spoke directly into the camera. "Tonight we have an exclusive interview with the man at the center of Right Time's latest scandal, the effervescent Alec Masterson. Alec, thank you for appearing on the show."

The camera swung around, and my gorgeous man was sitting there, looking every bit as beautiful as I remembered him. He wore a white shirt that accentuated his muscled shoulders, and skinny jeans. He was dressed to impress, and I couldn't pull my eyes away from the screen.

My heart thumped in my chest as I imagined all the reasons he could be on the show tonight. His smile was making my legs shivery.

"Thank you, Carolyn, I appreciate you letting me come onto your show tonight to speak to you."

He looked relaxed, happy. Not at all how I felt at the moment.

"Thank *you*, Alec. Right Time's legal team has been very vigilant in keeping a no comment rule so far, and I myself was very surprised to hear from you. Why break your silence now?"

"Simple really, Carolyn. I need to set a few things straight, and I'm not one to sit back and let the people I care about get hurt because of me if I can help it."

I swallowed hard as hot tears prickled in my eyes.

"Firstly, I need to set the record straight in regards to three nights ago. Something terrible happened that night, and it is my public duty to report to the people of England the truth. My whisky was spiked at a bar I was having a drink at, a roofie according to the blood tests the doctors in the emergency room did for me that night. An almost lethal dose."

Carolyn did a dramatic gasp. "That is a horrible thing to have happen to you. Why would anyone do such a thing to you of all people?"

"I have no idea, but the photos that have been flashed all over the media for the last two days have to be put into context. I had been badly poisoned, and if it hadn't been for the quick thinking and actions of one of the bar's staff, I could have been in serious cardiac distress before anyone stopped taking photos to help me."

A single tear leaked out of each of my eyes, and I swiped them away, not wanting them to interfere with my vision. It *had* been pretty bad that night. I'd been so worried, and felt so guilty for my unwilling part in his drugging.

"That bar staff member, Joanne? Is that the woman you were photographed with early today?"

The Carolyn woman's face disappeared, and photos flashed up on the screen of me and Alec in my apartment, his naked body blurred out, my shocked face there for all the world to see.

I let my eyes close as my heart sank. My parents, everyone who knew me, would potentially hire me, be treated by me, would remember those photographs.

"Yes, Jo is the woman who helped me get to the hospital after I was drugged and then took me into her home to give me a few days to recover away from the prying eyes of the world."

"That was very kind of her."

"It was, and I'd like to send out a message to her tonight if that's possible."

Carolyn practically slid off her chair as she smiled at Alec. "Of course."

I scowled at the blonde puddle of goo. She was getting the scoop of the century. At the very least she could try to look professional.

Alec regained my attention as he sat up straighter in the leather chair they'd put him and spoke directly to me.

"Jo, I hope you're watching tonight. If you aren't I hope someone tells you to watch the YouTube replay tomorrow."

A strange gargly giggle burst from my throat, and I fell to my knees on the carpet, my eyes glued to the black box containing the man of my dreams.

"I am so sorry about how I acted this morning. I should have stayed by your side and protected you from all the shit I'm sure you had to deal with today." He shrugged his shoulders, his lopsided smile so endearing I couldn't help but wrap my arms around myself. What sort of man did this? Took all the blame for something that was not his fault. He was a much better person than I was. I'd still been so angry with him and the situation, and here he was, accepting the blame for not only the paparazzi's behavior but his own. It took a strong man to do that.

"This life I lead is like a three ring circus sometimes, but I want you to be a part of it. You're the kindest, most beautiful woman I've ever met. Will you forgive me? And let me be a part of your life again?"

There was silence on the TV as everyone held their breath.

I reached out a hand and touched his face.

"Oh Alec."

The tears truly began to run down my cheeks now as I hiccupped and gasped. I had to make it up to him. I had to get to him, tonight, now. Where was my phone? I had to call Phillip back.

His face disappeared as Carolyn's face reappeared. "We'll be right back, hopefully with the conclusion to this unlikely romance."

I turned off the TV and got to my feet, my phone beginning to ring once again.

My mum.

I picked up the phone, my pulse skipping a beat, my stomach in knots. Even if I could deal with the rest of the world thinking badly of me—this woman, I couldn't.

"Hi, Mum. Did you see the channel seven news?"

"Yes, I did. Whatever did you do to that boy?"

I burst out with a gasp. "What do you mean, Mum?"

"Oh I don't mean like that. You've only known him a few days by the looks of things, and yet he's proclaiming his feelings for you on national television. *When* did this happen? *How* did this happen?"

"You're not upset with me?"

"Upset with you? Why would I be upset with

you?"

I squeezed my eyes shut and hung my head as I clung to the phone. "Because I slept with a boy in a boy-band … because I look like a tart in every newspaper in the world!"

There was silence on the end of the line, and my stomach squeezed so tight I thought it would explode inside my belly at any moment. "Oh sweetheart, if I'd had the chance to sleep with Jon Bon Jovi at your age I would have jumped at the chance."

"Mum!"

She laughed softly, and the tension drained out of me so fast I had to sit down on the couch once again.

"Jo, I raised a good girl, with a beautiful heart and a bright future, I know that. But it's up to you who you spend that life with, and if this boy is going to get on TV and tell the world how wonderful my girl is, then he has my seal of approval. Even if he does look like some sort of wrestler."

I giggled with relief and lay down on the floor, my hand to my head. "Mum, thank you so much! You have no idea how much I've been afraid of what you would think of me."

"I was young once, too, Jo. I'd say you made a good choice there anyway. He's smitten."

I nodded even though she couldn't see it. "Yeah, I think so."

"You better get going then."

"You're right." I pushed myself up off the floor and headed to my bedroom. I had to get changed and get to Alec somehow. "Love you, Mum. Better go."

"Bye, darling."

****

Alec

"Do you think she saw it?" I asked Law as we sat

down to dinner at his favorite restaurant, a little Italian place in the village. It was small but offered great food and the privacy we all craved. Phillip and Byron finished up our small party.

"Yeah, I'm sure she did." Phillip told me while signaling to the waitress to come serve us.

I went to grab the menu, then stopped. Why did Phillip sound so sure?

"What makes you so sure?"

Phillip looked straight at me. "Because I called her and told her to watch."

"What?" I stared at Phillip, but my manager just shrugged and went about ordering food for everyone. We ate here often and we all liked to share anyway, so I didn't care what he ordered.

I turned to Law. "He doesn't stop when it comes to our business lives, does he?"

"Nope."

"Speaking of which…" Phillip interrupted, "Our lawyers have tracked down the names of the women who drugged you that night using the photos they posted online, and all three have been issued arrest warrants. They should be picked up and charged either tonight or tomorrow. The police acted pretty swiftly, which was lucky."

Yeah, for them. I grinned with thanks and nodded at Phillip. The law team Phillip had around him was a force to be reckoned with. I wouldn't have liked to see what they did to the local law enforcement if they hadn't followed what the lawyers wanted.

"Thanks for that, Phillip."

"No problem. Those girls deserve to be prosecuted. They could have killed you."

I glanced away, a tightness across my chest bringing with it an even greater fondness for our manager.

Law elbowed me in the side, and I looked up to see my friend grinning at me and sliding his eyes sideways.

I followed his gaze and saw Jo standing in the foyer of the restaurant, the maître d' barring entrance to someone who obviously couldn't lie quickly enough to get into the restaurant without a reservation.

Heat spread through my chest as she waved and tilted her head towards the man blocking her way.

I stood up and walked over to where they stood, my heart pumping faster with each step that I took. God, she was beautiful. Her skin was positively glowing, and her smile hit me right in the belly.

"Thanks, but she's with me."

I held out my hand, and Jo took it. Tingles of awareness moved over my skin as I pulled her close to me.

"Is there somewhere we could sit to have a quick chat?"

The maître d' politely indicated a booth to the side. "If you'd like."

I pulled Jo into the booth, keeping her hands in mine and staring into her blue eyes. I wasn't sure what she was going to say, and my erratic pulse told me that I cared about the outcome of tonight.

I swallowed hard, trying my best to not look as awkward as I felt.

"How did you know where I was?"

"Phillip sent me a message after the news aired and told me where you'd be."

I grinned and rolled my eyes. "I think I need to give that guy a raise."

She rubbed her small soft hands over mine. "I'm sure you all look after him pretty well."

I laughed, the move freeing up some of the tension in my tight muscles. She was right. Considering all four of us gave Phillip a percentage of our money, yeah, he was doing pretty well.

I took a deep breath, ready to apologize again, and this time in person. "I'm so sorry for leaving you this morning with all that mess. Part of me thought they'd all follow me, but if I'd been smart and stopped for a second and actually thought about it, I would have known they'd want an exclusive from you."

And although I hadn't thought of it at the time, it just occurred to me that she could have sold her story for a pretty penny. As a cash-strapped student who'd been shafted by a boy-band upstart, you'd think she would have taken the opportunity to blab.

I lifted her hands to my lips, kissing them softly. *Obviously not.*

She shrugged. "You don't need to apologize again. That's what *I'm* here to do. This morning was not your fault. I knew the risks when I asked you to stay at the apartment. It was just a little unexpected, that's all. I didn't cope with it, and that's on me, Alec. I'm sorry."

I looked away from her beautiful face for a moment to think about what else I needed to say. "Are you still regretting last night?"

She slid closer, her thigh pressing up against mine. "Absolutely not, and I'm sorry if I gave you the impression that I did. I was just worried about how people would see me. I'm a bit old fashioned like that. I'm sorry."

I kind of liked that about her, even if it had felt like she'd cut my balls off this morning.

"You know, people are always going to say things about us, about you. You can't please everyone, and unfortunately, it's all kind of part of my deal. I don't worry too much about how other people see me, except those I love. Everyone else can go jump."

She looked down, blinking fast as moisture slid across her cheeks.

When she lifted her head again the tightness in her face made my chest ache. "You're right, Alec, and I'm sorry. I shouldn't have worried so much about how everyone else saw me, especially not stupid reporters that don't know me, nor do they care how they hurt me. I am sorry, Alec. I'll try not to let it happen again."

That's more like it, sweetheart.

"You're beautiful, Jo. I've never known anyone like you, and if you think you can handle my world, I want to spend a lot more time with you if you'd allow it."

"So would I, but ... I have to tell you..."

Her face looked so worried my belly fell through my body, making me feel sick.

I swallowed hard. "Tell me what?"

She glanced away, red cheeked as she bit her lip. "You're going to think I'm stupid."

"I guarantee you, I won't, Miss *I'm going to be a doctor.*"

She giggled and looked up, her blue eyes alive and bright and oh so happy I just wanted to kiss her again.

"I've had a few boyfriends before, and they were all serious, long term things."

"Yeah..." I wasn't sure I liked where this was going. She didn't want to know about my past relationships, did she?

Hope to hell she doesn't!

"And no one has ever made me feel more ... loved ... than you did the other night. I know it's too early, and we barely know each other ... but this feels so right. I don't mean to scare you, but there it is."

A chuckle rose, and I laughed out loud. "That's what you were worried about? Telling me you loved what we did last night?"

Women!

I shook my head and reached out for her, cupping her perfect face in my hands and drawing her close. She tilted her head up, and her lips touched mine in such a way that I moaned, molten sensation melting through me.

She grabbed my shirt with her fingers and held on tight.

We kissed and kissed, until my jeans were becoming uncomfortable and her breathing was sounding like she'd been for a run.

"Home? Or dinner?"

She looked at me for a moment, her eyes slowly clearing as she registered my question. "Umm, have you eaten yet?"

I shook my head, not that it mattered.

She nodded once. "We better eat then. I don't want you getting sick again on my account."

"Wow, you're not going to actually look after me are you? You'll spoil me for all those grasping bitches that keep falling at my feet."

My tone was joking as I slid out of the booth, but she gave me a glare and bumped me hard with her hip. "You better believe it, and those women are just going to have to get used the fact that you're taken. At least for a while."

I slung an arm over her shoulders and directed her back to where Phillip, Law, and Byron still sat waiting for our meal to arrive.

"Hopefully for longer than a while," I whispered into her ear as we slid into our chairs and I made the introductions.

"Jo, you know Phillip, and this is Law and

Bryon."

She gave them all big smiles and settled against me. I lifted my arm and dragged her close, her presence as soothing as it was arousing.

"So, did you decide what you're going to do with your time off?" Law asked me.

I gave the guys a big smile and squeezed the girl beside me that had come to mean too much to me.

"I think you were right, Law. A holiday is definitely in order, especially if Jo will come with me. When do you get time off from university?"

She looked up at me with bright, wide eyes. "Ah, I finish exams in a couple of weeks, but I really can't afford a holiday at the moment."

I kissed her soft lips gently, loving the flavor and their pillow-like texture beneath mine.

"Don't be silly. After you saved me from dying in the street the other night, and then took me in to save me from the media while I regained my strength, it's the least I can do."

"But Alec…"

I kissed her quickly again. "Jo, I'm serious, that cocktail those girls gave me was pretty lethal. If you hadn't kept me safe, called an ambulance, God knows where I'd be. I owe you, more than I can ever repay."

She blushed and pressed closer, sighing as our food arrived.

The men started serving themselves, and I leaned close once again to whisper into her ear.

"I hope you're going to let me thank you for as long as it takes."

"What if it takes forever?"

A grin spread across my face so big I was worried I might strain a muscle.

"I fully intend to make sure it does."

She laid a hand on my thigh, and we began to converse with the others once again. I'd finally found a woman with a heart like no other, who slotted into my world like she'd always been there, and I wasn't letting her go.

Epilogue

Alec

Two years later

Excitement flickered around the room like a jumping livewire. After Phillip had announced our return to the world stage the reporters hadn't stopped murmuring and our interviewer, Georgina was beaming.

My heart was beating a little faster, too, if I was honest. Another world tour had finally been organized, and I was so ready for it.

We'd agreed to answer a few personal questions sent in by viewers, and I was pretty happy not to be in the hot seat. Zeck and pretty boy Dillon copped most of the questions, and as Law leaned back in his high back chair, we shared a grin.

"So, our next question left by a fan is for you, Dillon."

I chuckled as Dillon moaned and buried his head in his hands. "Oh man, can one of the others take a turn?"

"Nope, afraid not. It seems that with Issy's pregnancy and news of her carrying twins has spread, rumors of baby number two are in the wind for you, and this fan wants to know if that's true. Is little Grace going to be a big sister any time soon?"

I heard Law chuckle this time and looked over at Dillon. *Time to spill the beans, mate.*

"That would be a yes."

The audience went wild, and Georgina's face lit up. "How wonderful for you. I know a few more hearts break each time one of you boys settles down, but you must be so excited."

Zeck spoke up this time. "Yeah, it's going to be

amazing. Five babies in the group by Christmas. We can't wait."

Georgina's eyes were wide, and I locked my hands over my chest. It wasn't me, so they better not look this way. Jo and I were bloody brilliant, but nowhere near babies.

"Well that doesn't add up. Are you saying Ashlyn is having twins as well?"

"Nope," Dillon said. "I doubt I'd ever have sex again if I did that to her."

Everyone whooped and laughed, and Georgina's eyes locked in on poor Zeck again. "Zeck, something you want to tell us?"

Zeck shot her an amused look. "You kidding? If Issy were having triplets I'd be celibate right alongside Dillon for the rest of my life. I mean, clearly we wanted to catch up with Dillon and Ashlyn, but not pass them. Damn."

Georgina finally turned to Law and me as though she'd finally remembered we were there. "Law, Alec? Something either of you want to share?"

I shook my head and looked away for a moment. Sure, I wanted kids someday, but my beautiful woman was smart and going places. She had a great internship and was on her way to being an amazing doctor. I wasn't going to slow her down.

"It's me," Law announced, and I relaxed back into the chair.

Georgina stared at Law with the look of someone who knew that Law and his partner having a baby was kind of an impossibility.

Bubbles of laughed tickled my throat. That would kinda be funny actually. I wonder who would rather be the pregnant one. Law or good ol' Byron?

"Ah, I have to admit, I'm a bit surprised. Law,

have you been holding out on us?"

Zeck snorted. "You have no idea."

"You could say that. I have a daughter."

"A daughter?" Georgina asked bewildered.

"Yes. My husband and I started the process for adoption a little over a year ago, and just last week everything was finalized and we were able to bring our baby girl home."

"Husband?" Georgina's voice squeaked, and I covered my laugh with my hand. What was the big deal? You'd think this chick was twelve with all the shocked expressions dancing over her face.

"Yes, my husband," Law repeated, lifting up his hand and displaying the cool piece of metal lying there.

"Sorry, can we just cover that again?" Georgina blinked at us.

Law leaned forward as though he were speaking to a young child. "Let me break it down. Two years ago I reconnected with someone I cared deeply for. His name is Byron. Those feelings grew, and a year later we got married. We chose to keep it to ourselves partly to make sure nothing interfered with our plans to adopt, and partly because it was no one's business but ours. We now have a beautiful baby girl named Madeline, who you will all get to see pictures of in the next issue of *Who Magazine*, and ah, yeah … that about sums it up. Did I miss anything, lads?"

I grinned at my mate, proud of his coming out. It was about bloody time really.

"You forgot the part about that time when you—"

Law slapped his hand across Zeck's mouth before he finished that sentence. "I really didn't forget that part."

"Bloody disgusting."

Everyone, including the audience, laughed at the group's antics, and pride swelled in my chest. I loved being a part of this world and the people in it.

"Well, you certainly have kept a lid on things," Georgina finally said.

"That's true, but now I'm a parent, and I'm more concerned with what kind of a role model I am for my child. I'm not exactly doing a very good job if I can't be honest about who I am. I'm proud of who I am, I'm proud of my husband. He's been a support of mine, of ours, from the very beginning. I tried doing this without him, and I never want to do that again. This is who I am, this is who we are."

"I have to ask, what made you decide to come out now?"

I grinned winking at the others as I answered. "I guess it was just the right time."

I pushed at Law's shoulder as the other three chuckled. "That was bloody cheesy, mate."

Georgina turned her beady eyes on me, and I regretted speaking instantly. I'd *almost* got away with it!

"Alec! We have time for just one more question, and I'm sure we can find one in this pile for you."

I grinned at the woman before us and shrugged my shoulders. "I don't mind if you don't mind if you don't. These guys are much more interesting than me."

She pulled a flash card up and grinned triumphantly.

Damn.

"Firstly, I'd just like to say how much I admire the work you're doing with outreach drug programs in the city."

Well, this was a safe topic.

I glanced at the guys for permission. After all, this wasn't just my stage. But all three grinned and leaned back in their chairs, opening up the floor for me.

"I have actually. After my unexpected experience

with Rohypnol, I've been working with some people to better educate young people in England about the dangers, symptoms, and side-effects of date rape drugs. They can be fatal, and noticing the effects and acting fast is the key."

I'd really enjoyed the work I'd done so far, and using my fame to forward a really good cause and education program made everything feel even better.

"Alec, one final question for the night from our viewers. Are you still seeing Jo, the waitress that saved you that night? How is it going, and are we set to hear in wedding bells or babies in the near future?"

I looked over at Phillip. "Phillip, that's at least three questions. Do you think I should answer when she said just one?"

A general laugh went up again, and I turned back to the woman and crossed my arms over my chest.

"Yes we're still together, and no, no wedding bells or babies as yet. Jo's still on her road to being a brilliant surgeon, and I'm supporting her in that one hundred percent."

"So it's going well?" the woman repeated again.

I looked at Georgina and sighed, a beautiful myriad of emotions and pictures flickering through my mind. Jo was beyond spectacular. She was a delight, my best friend and my savior. Every day she told me she loved me, and every day I fell a little more in love with her.

"Jo is an angel, my light. She loves me, and I love her. Simple as that."

The interviewer gave me a last, lingering smile and turned back to her camera to end off the interview. I sat back, enjoying the spotlight being taken off me once again.

Life was good, better than good. I had a beautiful

girl at my side, great mates, and the world at our feet. Nothing could be better than this.

The End

www.tamsinbakererotic.com

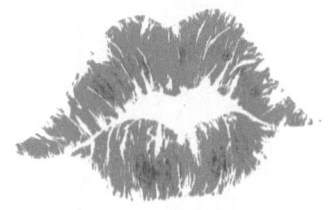

EVERNIGHT PUBLISHING ®

www.evernightpublishing.com